Kitten Heels

Maureen Cullen

Ringwood Publishing

Glasgow

Ringwood Publishing
0/1 314 Meadowside Quay Walk, Glasgow G11 6AY

www.ringwoodpublishing.com
mail@ringwoodpublishing.com

ISBN 978-1-917011-01-3

British Library Cataloguing-in-Publication Data
A catalogue record for this book is available from the
British Library

Printed and bound in the UK
by Lonsdale Direct Solutions

For Frank

Chapter 1

Cabinet Bed

October 1962

I came home from school after a day full of grief. A day I'd failed a maths test, a day I sunk under the disappointment heavy on Mrs Richard's shoulders as she passed me my jotter wi '*40%*' circled in red. It was a day that reached into the future and destined me to work forever in the bra factory, and there was my mum in the lobby, in apron and rollers, eyes bulging under her jars of glasses, a big smile splitting her chops. Martin was asleep in her arms, one wrinkled bare foot escaping the shawl like a rabbit's paw.

'A surprise fer ye, Hen,' Mum said. 'Wait tae ye see it.'

Our mum was the most crabbit woman in the town; she rarely chanced a smile, was slap-happy most of the time, and now this grin was stretched across her face. She pushed open the bedroom door wi her hip and there was a single bed.

'A diva-an,' she said.

I stared at the velvet headboard and pink candlewick cover, and panic set in.

Where was my cabinet bed? My special bed, my private place. My cabinet bed that folded away in the morning and folded out at night. My bed wi a secret drawer on top, the whole length, three inches deep. My bed where I kept my books safe. My grand bed wi whorls in the wood and flowers carved along the doors, wi its own lightbulb that worked by pulling a string. My cabinet bed where I holed up for a modicum of privacy, only last night living Sidney Carton's agonies, '*It is a far, far better thing that I do'*, courtesy of Havoc's lending library, five more adventures lying flat in the compartment ower my head. Where the hell was it?

'Ye willnae find any woodworm in this.' Mum waltzed in and sat on this atrocity wi the bairn in her arms, his shawl opening, a brown half-ring staining the rim of his rubber pants. Wee Rosie scampered past me and clambered on beside them, her chestnut bunches swaying. Mum began bouncing, a manic smile on her face, and not for the first time I wondered if she'd suffered a head injury, a trauma that was sparking in her head, making her take leave of her senses. I clapped my eyes on Martin's rubbers. Nothing leaked, thank God. Morag kept her distance at the kitchen door, still in uniform, carrot ponytail pinned in her navy blue ribbon, tie askew, one white knee-sock sunk to her ankle, eyes fixed on something mysterious ower my head, like she knew advanced events. Sometimes I thought she'd been born an auld grannie, and couldnae just be nine.

I began to seethe. How come I never got a say, never got a choice? Like the time Mum got on the back shift at the factory. Ask me first if I'd watch the weans? Naw. Every night she was out, I had to give them their tea, wash their faces, and put them down. Nights I couldnae get out to my pals' houses. Nights I couldnae get on wi my homework. Then there was the 'surprise' for my birthday. I was expecting the surprise to be those shiny patent boots in the shoe shop window I'd been hinting at for weeks, but no, it was a bloody gas fire. 'Tae keep ye nice and warm,' she said. But when I stood next to it, she took to nagging. 'Watch they tartan legs, ye'll never get a man wi tartan legs.' Didnae know why I'd ever want one. She hadnae got one, had she? My dad had gone off wi

2

some bit of stuff. My dad: philanderer, liar, and cheat.

Well, I supposed Mum did have a lot on her plate.

My seething evaporated and I swallowed the venom clogging my throat.

'Mum,' I said, 'What have you done? Where's it gone? Where's my library books?'

She rolled her eyes. 'Bugger, they must be in the lid. Ye better run doon tae the chapel, Hen. The Saint Vincent de Paul fella might still be there.'

Morag stomped down the lobby, retrieved my school bag and presented it to me. Wi a wan smile, I scraped past her legs and emptied the bag out on the dresser, hearing that stuck-up librarian say, 'Kathleen Gallagher, you'll not be getting another book out for the rest of your stupid life.' The fines for they books would cripple me, and I could get banned from the library and never pass any of they new O-Grades. But I'd rather die than tell her the Saint Vincent de Paul fellas took the books away wi my woodworm bed.

I squeezed out, freeing my ponytail from its tight ribbon as I passed the hall mirror. What a relief. I pulled the tangled curls apart wi one hand, hoping that wasnae a spot appearing on my chin. A commotion rose up from the bedroom. Martin's pooh had finally leaked and the girls were screaming blue murder.

'It's up his back, Mum... Mum...'

I scrunched my nose, sped downstairs and hurried down the street wondering what woodworms looked like. They must've been razor sharp to drill through mahogany. When I was sure no one could see me, I broke into a run, hardly pausing as I passed Grannie Meikle's flat at the edge of the scheme, and then past darkening fields that whiffed of soil and cabbage leaf. I slowed as I took the path through Havoc Common, between lines of trees, their leaves burnished gold in the lamp light. It was the time of year when dusk came down early and lights pinged on, but folk still went about

3

their business, the shops still open, and on a dry evening there was a buzz about the town before closing time. Normally, I'd be happy to linger, not often having the chance to be free of the madhouse, but now I was too fretful to waste time. I hurried along Bowhill Road, under the station bridge, mindful of the warbling of pigeons in the rafters and their splats, and past the Church Street shops, slowing in front of Saint Aloysius' red brick bulk.

Going around the back of the chapel was a risky business. The priests' house faced the church hall entrance and I was in danger of meeting Father Murphy on one of his prowls.

The Devil in his black eyes pierced you to the spot as if he knew every sin you'd ever committed. Bad enough you had to go to the confessional wi him on the other side of the grille, not seeing those eyes, just imagining what they could do. Sure, there was never a queue for Father Murphy, but auld Monsignor aye had a snake of sinners waiting for him. Course he was deaf as a post, so that helped. Murphy was known to get stroppy wi the queue and barge out of his cell into the aisle, like the Black Death itself, and pick some poor soul at random. Och, you might wheedle, 'But it's not my turn, Father.' No good, he'd got you.

I crept along the hedge, peeking through twisted branches to make sure he wasnae walking in the gardens or praying, fag in fingers, at the life-size Jesus statue under the oak tree. It might've been October, but he'd be warmed by the light of his vocation. He'd a nose on him too, wouldnae let you pass without sniffing out where you were going. He aye took the line that folk were up to no good. I supposed that was his job; listening to sin after sin would make you suspicious awright. And he hated women wi a vengeance. I'd watched him at chapel and saw him look down his nose as if in pain whenever a woman approached, whereas any man could insert himself into the rarefied air around his holiness wi impunity. It made my flesh crawl. It was a man's world, that was for sure. It certainly wasnae a thirteen-year-old girl's.

4

Now, my heart thumping, I was sure Murphy wasnae around. The only sound was the cackle of a seagull beyond the church, in the direction of the Clyde. I sprinted from the hedge to the hall door. A white van was parked outside, its lights shining, and a fella was just about to shut up the doors at the back. I rushed forward, my heart thudding two, four, six …

'Hey, Mister, is my cabinet bed still in there?'

He looked half asleep, his head heavy. 'Whit's a cabinet bed?' he said, blinking.

'Just like a big cupboard.' I dropped my schoolbag and made the shape of a rectangle in the air.

'Och aye, that. Ah didnae cotton on that wis a bed.'

'My library books are inside.'

'Awright. Ah'll have a look.'

Animated now, he jumped up on the tail, the van tilting and squeaking, switched on a light and clambered into what looked like Aladdin's cave.

'There … there.' I pointed.

'Whit?'

'On top, a secret compartment.'

'Yer joking, Hen.'

'Naw, lift it up.'

He gingerly lifted the lid and, as it opened, his face lit up wi delight, as if he'd discovered the Ark of the Covenant. Our eyes locked. Here was a total stranger, a glaikit one at that, who understood my deepest desires, where my fool of a mother had no idea of the damage she'd done to my existence. I doubt she cared at all. He extracted six books, one at a time, laying them in a bundle on a three-and-a-half-legged chair next to my cabinet. My eyes welled up.

'Where's it going?' I sniffed.

'Kindling, Hen.'

I drew in a sharp breath. My magic bed, my den, the only possession I had in life, reduced to sticks for the fire.

Chapter 2

Pest Control

Furniture had been cleared out of Mum's bedroom and stacked at the back of the living room two days ago by Uncles Joe and Jack in-between sups of McEwan's. I swore that Jack's hand was welded to a can.

Mum's bed frame was against the wall, her chest of drawers in front, wardrobe at the back of the couch, and the mattress stood on its side, ready to be dragged out at bedtime. Bags of clothes littered the lobby beside Martin's high pram, and vases and ornaments doubled up wi the usual paraphernalia on the windowsills, fireplace and cabinet. Mum's row of pottery country cottages had been pushed together higgledy-piggledy and looked more like a tumbledown terrace, one lawn disappearing under the next, than a row of detached buildings wi spacious gardens. The place was a sight, but it was only until the woodworm had been exterminated. Mum was doing extra shifts at the factory now it was school break and we were home alone wi the grave instruction not to open her bedroom door. She'd showed us why last evening, after the council men had finished work.

'Stand there, girls, behind me.' She reached for the doorknob, mouth pursed, her auburn hair in big pastel rollers, and opened the door into the room. It arced open stiffly, making her extend the arm. 'Kathleen, huv a look.'

I peered down through the gap. A sneeze threatened, the room smelled sour, a mixture of damp and sawdust. The floor was gone. There was a drop of about a foot onto boards cut wi joists that ran the full length. 'Jings, is that McCann's ceiling?'

'Aye,' she said. 'Morag, c'mere.'

Morag inched forward, shimmied under Mum's arm and knelt down. 'Oh wow.'

She slanted her curly head upwards towards me, mouth open, as if she'd won the coupon. I gave her a warning look; she clamped her lips, but her eyes still sparkled.

'Rosie, come here too.'

Our Rosie aye had a question mark on her face, her world was just a big puzzle, and now she hung back, her lower lip quivering, thumb loose in her mouth.

'It's awright, Hen,' I said. 'I'll hold you.'

I lifted her onto my hip and clutched her tight around the middle as she veered forward into the void. When she started to wail, I eased her back to her feet on safe ground.

'Whit is it?' she muttered, before sticking her wet thumb back in her gob.

'It's the floor's gone, silly.' Morag was upright now, hands on hips.

'How?'

'You mean why, Rosie,' I said.

'Uh-huh.'

'Cause the woodworms have eaten the floor,' Morag offered.

'Aye, that's aboot it.' Mum closed the door fast. She bent backwards, balancing Martin on her chest wi one hand and reached into her pinny pocket extracting a piece of cardboard and a tack. 'Pin it tae the door, Kathleen.' She'd written in bright red pen, *DO NOT ENTER.* I pinned it up.

'Right, nae trouble noo, hear me?' She glared at Morag, but the message was meant for me. My mum had ten hands, all of them itching to slap skin, mostly mine. At thirteen, I was the most blameworthy, as I *should know better.* I did

7

know better than our Morag, who knew nothing, and was aye in bother in the house and at school. Sure, at school, she had to contend wi, 'How are ye no like your big sister, Kathleen? Her wi the head on her shoulders.' Though these days, I wasnae sure my teachers would recognise that sensible, clever student as my marks kept on sliding downwards.

This morning, because it was a school holiday, Mum had gone to work at eight. Now, at ten, the day was cold but dry and sunny, and I was fixing to put Martin in the pram for a walk to the swinging park wi the other two. I was a bit harassed as he was only twelve weeks auld, and I had to work out what he needed; milk, nappy, cuddle, nothing at all. Into the bargain, the pram had to be eased down the stairs first, then I'd climb back up, lift him down and into it, because he was too wee to be strapped in and bumped down in a oney.

The doorbell rang and Morag scooted down to answer. Heavy feet stomped up the stairs, but it was most likely a relative so I didnae bother to rise. I was too busy teasing Martin's bunched fists through the sleeves of his jumper. A loud crash and a howl startled me. Rosie's eyes bulged, and Martin whimpered. I clutched him close to my chest and stumbled out, Rosie clinging to my skirt. Mum's bedroom door was wide open, dust-speckled sunlight streaming into the lobby. Morag balanced on the brim, a hand on each jamb, peeking in wi her tongue hanging out. Curses and shouts came from the room, a man's voice, one I didnae recognise. Despite the 'bloody hells' and the 'buggers', the voice was posh.

Morag twisted round, stepped back, met the question in my eyes and did her *it wisnae me* shrug. I peered into the room, careful of the drop. Between two of the struts running from the window to the door hung a portly man in a dark suit and a blue tie, stuck by the belly in the hole he had made when his feet shot through. He was the spit of Hardy from

Laurel and Hardy, whom we saw on wet Sunday afternoons round at Auntie Patsy's. But this fella wasnae silent; he screamed and flailed about, thumping the joists. Finally, he twisted his head around. He must've recognised a person in charge because he said, 'Where's Mrs Gallagher?'

'At my auntie's,' I lied. Some folk, like the Welfare, didnae think I was auld enough to look after three weans. Mind, he didnae look like the Welfare.

'Go get her.'

This was a problem. I could hardly go to her work and break in on the line. What would I say? *'Excuse me, my mother is needed at home. There's a strange man stuck in her bedroom floor.'*

'Can you not pull yourself up?'

'No.'

'Push yourself down then?'

Rosie started to giggle, her wee cheeks flaring strawberry red. I hushed her, and somehow that had the effect of permitting Morag to let out a guffaw.

The man's eyes narrowed into poisoned pinpricks. 'Go see if anybody's at home down there.'

If anybody had been in, surely, they'd have noticed a man the size of Oliver Hardy poking through their ceiling. But even though his glare didnae prompt me to be helpful, indeed it made me narrow my eyes, I decided it was best not to offer my opinion. At my nod, Morag spun round and clattered downstairs wi great gusto. I stood gazing at the stuck man, Martin snoring in my arms and Rosie still clutching my skirt. He'd got what he deserved, and I was enjoying his discomfort. If he'd spoken civilly to me, I might've shut the door and given him a bit of privacy, but I didnae like to be ordered around, especially by a stranger. The stand-off broke when Morag bouldered back in. 'Naebody answerin, Kathleen.'

I needed an adult, but who? Gran would be best, and

she'd take charge, but Mum would kill me if I bothered her. Gran had a bad heart.

'Go get Auntie Patsy,' I said to Morag and off she scarpered. Aunt Patsy was useless, but she was ower sixteen, and she hated walking, so she was aye in. There was also Auntie Hannah, but I discounted her right off, she was never home.

'I don't suppose you have a telephone,' the man squeaked.

I shrugged and shook my head. Martin woke up and pumped into his nappy.

'Is there a phone nearby?'

'Aye, at the shop.'

'Phone the council. Tell them the Director of Pest Control has had an accident.'

He was a high heid yin. I was in for it. 'Maybe I should get the Fire Brigade.'

'No, no, no need ...' He tried a wan smile but sweat dripped down his forehead; a bead of it hit an eyelash and spilled onto a plump cheek. Martin hiccupped, breaking my fascination, and a sliver of sympathy stirred my cold heart.

I turned, placed Martin in his cot in our bedroom where it had been taking up the floor space the last few nights, got out coats and hats from the press, tucked Rosie into her coat, buttoning it up to the collar, bumped the pram down the stairs wi Rosie stepping down one at a time behind me, went back for the bairn, wrapped him up tight in a cot blanket, hurried downstairs, slid him into the pram, his wee eyes watching me as if he knew this was a crisis, humped Rosie onto the pram seat, and rushed as fast as I could go, without bouncing Martin too much, to alert Mrs Rennie at the shop.

'The pest man's fallen through the ceiling and you've to phone the council.' I had to say it four times before the shock fell off her face. I hurried back home wi the smell from the pram making me boak, but wee Rosie was delighted wi the speed of the chase, her face ruddy as beetroot, the bunches

10

Mum had tied wi red ribbon wagging from side to side.

Even at that fast pace, it took us a good twenty minutes, and we were dizzy when we got back. Auntie Patsy was in the lobby. Her face was like a beef tomato, her ample chest shuddering as she tried to keep the laughter at bay. I peeked around her, Martin in my arms, Rosie stuck to my thigh, to see the director being hauled up by the oxters by a pair of sniggering council workers. Two others guided him across the joists to safety. He wiped his suit down, though he neednae have bothered, it was plated wi dust, and he gave me a curt nod, before turning on his heel towards the stairs. Two of the workers followed him out and the other pair got to work on the hole, aided by directions from Mrs McCann, who was now home downstairs. Morag waited in the kitchen doorway. She looked like an angel from hell, the sun turning her halo of silken red curls into a fireball.

I thanked Patsy for coming around.

'Och, nae bother, Kathleen. Jist tell oor Nellie ...' She screwed up one wrinkled eye. 'Naw, jist don't tell yer ma nothin, awright Hen?'

Phew, that was a relief. 'But will the council not ...'

'Don't think he'll be back anytime soon.'

'Mrs Rennie?'

'Ah'll have a wee word wi her.'

'Mrs McCann?'

'Good pal o mine.'

After Patsy had gone, I changed Martin's nappy and put him in his cot and wi Rosie still attached like a limpet, turned to Morag and pushed her into the kitchen. I said between clenched teeth, 'How come you let him in the room?'

'Ah didnae let him. He said, "where's the woodworm," and ah said "in there," an he stepped right in, aw by hissel.' She drew out the movements in the air wi grubby hands in her own brand of sign language.

'Did you not tell him there wasnae any floor?'

11

'Well, he said he wis the boss an ah wis tae go an get ma "*mother*". Ah wis working oot how tae dae that when he jist … drapped.' This was illustrated by a speedy rise and fall of one fist.

'Where's the sign?'

'Oh, that fell aff when ah wis shovin Martin's pram alang the lobby. There's nae room wi aw this stuff.' She fidgeted in her cardigan pocket and took out the piece of crumpled cardboard.

'Give me that.' I snatched it from her, smoothed it out, got a tack from the kitchen drawer, felt for the hole the first tack had made, and stuck the sign back on the bedroom door. Mum would go crackers and I'd be the one who'd get the slap. But worse, her temper might spill out onto the weans.

'Not a word to Mum. Right?'

Morag widened her innocent eyes, scratched her bum and said, 'D'ye think ah'm totally daft?'

Chapter 3

The Floor Falls From Under

I watched for Mum from the window and when I saw her thin figure turn the street corner, I rushed to the living room door, but she clicked up the stairs and walked past me without even glancing at the bedroom. Auntie Patsy must've sorted things as she promised, but Mum wasnae entirely stupid, even if distracted these days. While she hung her coat in the press, I shot Morag a warning look, but she only dipped her head and fluttered her eyelashes. I growled at her to watch it. Rosie took out her thumb and opened her mouth wide as if to speak. I picked her up and she couried into my neck, her hair tasting of Pears soap.

'Where's the tea?' Mum pushed past us, into the kitchen. Wi all the worry and the state of the place, I'd forgotten to start the mince and totties. Morag was already escaping along the lobby, elbows and bum scooting away like a hundred-yard sprinter. I put Rosie down and shooed her to go after her big sister.

'Oh, sorry, Mum. Been busy. I'll get it started.' I bent down to the tottie bag and as I rose, I caught it. One slap, right across the ear like the crack of gunfire. When I dared to open my eyes, I caught only a crabbit scowl. Not a word. I soothed my ear wi my palm, but it stung for a good ten minutes. The pain was nothing; I kept my ears trained on Mum moving around the house to make sure she didnae take her temper out on the weans. I'd got off lightly this time, there'd been worse, and not having the tea ready was a capital offence these days. Goodness knows what had got into my mum but it was in for the long haul by the looks of it.

Mum didnae cotton on that there'd been a minor catastrophe in the bedroom, and the council men finished the job ower the next few days. The uncles, in-between slugs of McEwan's, rolled the carpet in place, tacked it down, and moved the furniture back. We emptied the bags on the bed and Mum filled up her drawers again. There was nothing left of Dad's; no jackets, shirts or shoes. His half of the wardrobe, which used to hang wi greys, blacks and navies, was refilled wi beiges, greens and pinks. I wondered if that meant he wouldnae be coming home this time.

Mum had never moved his stuff before. Looking at her sour face I guessed it had hit the bin. And the wedding photo in its silver frame, kept on the dresser, had also disappeared. Mum looked so sophisticated in that photo, like a film star, in a long flowing dress and veil. I didnae know what colours the flowers in her bouquet were, but in my mind the roses were blood-red. Dad was smart in a dark suit, white shirt and a striped tie, his dark curls teasing his forehead. He was so lucky to have a film star's straight nose and full lips. Despite her elegance, Mum wore a stoical expression and when I thought about it more, I realised Dad was a grim version of himself, the twinkle in his eye snuffed out for this photo. They stood in parallel, an inch or two apart, yet distant. It occurred to me I should've asked her about her wedding day years ago, before it was too late to mention.

I was glad Mum was distracted, as my marks at Our Lady's werenae getting any better. Mind, she never really seemed interested in education. When the report cards came in, she just glanced and grunted, which was just as well, as I wasnae hitting the mark no matter how hard I tried.

We were back at school and this very week, I'd written

14

an essay about John Logie Baird inventing television and Mrs Richards failed it, and worse, wi a twisted scowl, she said I was in her class '*under false pretences*'. A girl in the front row sniggered and I took time afterwards to front her and shove her backwards into a desk. I glowered at the rest of them as I left the room. No pals of mine in that class. Auld snotty knickers didnae explain the problem. I thought the essay was one of my best. I'd gone to the library and read up on Logie Baird and discovered that, although brilliant, he was a bit of a loony, and so I'd discussed how the man had nearly blown himself up wi his experiments and how he'd been diddled by the Americans taking the credit for his work. I'd summed up by saying he was one of the most genius Scots in history, as television was the future, and she'd written '*utter rubbish*', across the page. How could anyone argue wi that? And I didnae understand what she meant by false pretences. I hadnae told any lies to get in her class. I guessed from the first day at Our Lady's she hadnae liked me, I wasnae her kind of pupil. She was a snob and wasnae interested in teaching girls like me who'd leave school at fifteen. If I didnae buck up, I'd have to go downstream to the B-group or the C-group. I'd been the top of every year in Primary and in Secondary One, and now I was fast becoming the bottom of my class. Mind, it annoyed me that if I was shifted, I'd lose Latin. And even though there wasnae any chance I could afford it, that meant I'd never become a lawyer or a doctor. It was all sewn up. They liked you to have Latin O-Grade to get into medicine or law, or any profession. Sometimes, I wondered why I bothered. I'd be lucky to stay on after my leaving date as we couldnae afford it. When Dad was bringing in good money, I'd harboured the notion of joining the Civil Service. You could work your way up in that job from a basic clerk and I could get enough O-Grades to get in.

Och, well, the good thing was all my pals were in B and C so maybe it was for the best.

Saturday morning came and I could forget about school for a couple of days. It was still dark, night-dark, not morning-dark, as it was quiet outside and there was none of the usual housework noise coming from the kitchen. The girls were shadowy lumps under their cover in the double bed across from mine. Morag breathed in pants as if she was running a race, or more likely, running away from somebody she'd insulted. Wee Rosie's arm was thrown ower Morag's pillow, in danger of being squashed.

The ceiling light spurted on, crackling and buzzing. I squeezed my eyes shut and when I blinked them open, Mum stood in the doorway, hair in rollers, check wool coat on ower her nightie. Snot ran down her red swollen face. There wasnae anything funny about that, but I burst into a fit of giggles. Morag sat up, blinking fast, stared at me and laughed.

Rosie stirred, turned ower, and buried her face in the covers.

Mum stepped towards me. 'Ah've been oot aw night at yer Gran's, and noo ah come in and yous are laughing.' She loomed ower me, I cowered back in the bed.

Something terrible had happened. The laughter dried up in my throat. 'Mum, what is it?'

She sucked in her cheeks and blew hard into a hankie. 'Yer Grannie had a heart attack. She's deid,' she wailed.

I couldnae help it, the sniggering returned. It just kept coming. The more I shuffled away under the covers, the more the giggles took hold. I expected her to slap me all ower but she didnae attempt to come any closer, just turned and, arms stretched ahead as if she was blind, she stumbled out of the room leaving the door wide open.

I sat up and forced my legs ower the side of the bed. Morag's eyes bulged, her face blank wi shock. Wee Rosie pushed herself up, looking from Morag to me, her lips quivering, her toffee hair tangled, the fringe sticking up.

'Mare trouble,' Morag said.

'Aye.' I tried to take it in. Grannie dead.

She'd been ill plenty of times, but she'd aye come through. She'd no right to go and die on us. What were we going to do now? My chest tightened up. Realisation seeped in. No more Grannie. It was unbelievable. No more ten-bob notes crumpled into Mum's palm, no more sing-songs on a Sunday after bacon butties … *'Ye cannae shove yer Grannie aff a bus'* … No more clootie dumplings, no more hot tarts swelling wi sugary-sweet red and green chunks of rhubarb, no more pennies for the sweetie tray, no more sleepovers in the spare room wi Grannie's clock tick-tocking all night, no more hiding behind Grannie's apron when Mum was on the warpath. No more Grannie, the one constant and selfless person in my life.

Morag slumped back against the headboard, glum-faced. Wee Rosie sat rubbing her eyes.

I stood up and reached for my dressing gown and scarf from the peg. Who'd been looking after Martin? Wee mite. Mum had been out all night. I tiptoed out of the room, into the lobby, watching for her. The bedroom door was open, but the light was off. The living room lamp was off too, but yellow light leaked from the gas fire. I guessed Mum was in there. Martin was in his cot in her bedroom, still asleep. I slipped three fingers down the back of his nappy; it was damp, and he reeked of pee, but it could wait till he woke up.

Morag had followed me in, and when I turned, I nearly fell ower her.

'God's sake, Morag, watch out,' I whispered.

She was stony-faced. 'But Kathleen, whit ur we gonna dae?'

'Go get ready, I'll see to Rosie. And then we'll have toast and go for a wee walk, awright?'

Her bottom lip quivered, but she swivelled on her heel and barged out of the room, bumping into the door as she went. When we were dressed, I got Martin up, changed his bum, sponged him down, and gave him a bottle. He was cranky, pushing the teat away. I burped him and settled him back in his cot, made toast and put the teapot on the gas, wi six teaspoons of tea in to simmer. When it was black enough, I poured three cups and put a bit wi three inches of milk and two teaspoons of sugar in Rosie's feeder cup. I gave Morag half-n-half wi plenty of sugar, sorted mine wi an inch of milk, and I put a spot of milk in Mum's.

The door of the living room was ajar, and I peeked in. Mum was slumped in the chair by the fire, her coat wrapped around her. Her head lay on the wing of the chair, but her eyes were wide open. Her glasses lay on the floor. She never left her glasses in chancy places. I almost went for Grannie, until I remembered wi a jolt she was dead. I took a step in. Mum didnae move. I took another step. The fire spurted its gas flame, the curtains were closed, and a slither of white light stole in from the street. I swallowed hard, cleared my throat; for God's sake, I had to watch I didnae giggle, or laugh, or say the wrong thing.

'Mum, I'm sorry, it was nerves.' She didnae move. 'Here's a wee cuppa. I'll take the weans out, awright?'

She raised her head a tad and pulled her eyes in my direction. 'Yer a guid girl, Kathleen. Ah'm sorry fer everythin.'

Jeez, this was bad. 'No, Mum, it's me. I'm sorry.' I was sorry I'd been a right moanin-Minny for months.

She patted my hand as I put the tea down next to her and then she let her head fall back again. A cottage from the sideboard fell out of her other hand and slipped onto the carpet. Thank God it didnae break.

I stood for a long moment, staring at my mother, the woman wi a metal spine, a razor tongue, now crumpled and defeated. I didnae know what to do so I backed out of the room, my giggles long forgotten.

After we ate some toast ladled wi creamy butter, I humped the pram downstairs and we went out in the biting cold to the park, Rosie on the pram seat buttoned up in her fur-lined pink anorak and woolly scarf and mittens Mum had knitted. Morag wavered beside me in her wellies and duffle, hood up, head down. She tripped a couple of times, and I had to steady her by the elbow. The town was already busy wi shoppers, so we took the quiet path beside the Elvern. Rosie asked to throw bread to the swans, but I'd forgotten to bring any. We stood at the railing and watched the white shapes float down the river in procession, their question mark heads dipped, their orange and black beaks mournful at their chests. They disappeared into mist at the confluence of the Elvern and the Clyde.

At the pavilion, I bumped the pram into the shelter, unclipped Rosie from her seat, and lifted her down. Her wee face was chapped wi cold and I let her burrow into me, feeling the thinness of her through our coats, her wee heart pulsing like a robin wi a broken wing. Martin was asleep again under his mound of blankets, one dark curl peeping out of his blue wool hat. Mum kept a spare rug in the pram bag, and I got that out and wrapped it ower the weans' knees, tucking it in at the sides. I stared across the greens to the Clyde running along the perimeter. I couldnae quite see to the other side, the far hills were a whiteout of mist.

There were few people around, just a couple of men throwing sticks for their dogs to catch. High oaks had shed red and gold leaves on the paths all the way down to the river. On another day, we'd run and jump through the leaves, crunching them flat, squealing when we got one to crack hard. Today, the wind stirred the leaves, sometimes whipping them into a frenzy.

Morag piped up, 'Is Grannie wi Grandpa noo, in Heaven?'

'I expect so,' I said. It was a reasonable question. Grandpa had died a few years before. I remembered days out at Havoc Shore, sitting on his knee eating chips soaked wi vinegar, but Morag and Rosie hadnae known him, other than by the photos Grannie kept of a thin, baldy man who wore check shirts.

'How d'ye know?'

I turned to her expecting she was up to mischief again but found only enquiry on her face and no sign of devilment. 'Well, it's what the priests say, and the nuns.'

'Whit dae you say?'

This was a bit too much for me. I'd often tried to work out what eternity meant. I'd held my breath and tried to imagine, but I could never keep it held long enough to get any realistic sense of dying. I wondered where Grannie was now and listened for her soft voice, felt in empty air for her secure grip. It hit me again. There wasnae an adult left in my life who I could trust. Morag thumped my leg; she needed an answer. 'Aye, she's in Heaven. How could God not take her in? She was the best grannie in the world.'

I wished I hadnae looked at her because that's when we both started, in tandem. Rosie took one look at us and bawled, waking Martin up, and we were four lost souls, sitting in the dank pavilion, the river ahead blotted by tears.

Chapter 4

The Rosary

I didnae want to, but Mum thought I should show my respects.

'Yer nearly auld enough tae leave the school, time ye learnt a bit aboot life.'

That rattled me, she hadnae actually mentioned my leaving school before, even if I expected it. I supposed it was inevitable that I'd need to earn money for the house now Dad's arse was out the window. Mind, I couldnae fathom how kissing a dead person educated me about life.

Whilst I wasnae keen on my dad as a father, and I wouldnae ever want a husband like him, if I ever wanted a husband at all, it was as if I'd been elevated to the dubious position of stand-in parent. None of my pals had to look after their brothers and sisters; they had freedom to come and go as they pleased. Mum said I could have my pals in anytime, but that horrified me, what wi Martin's nappies hanging on the pulley, or steeping in the bucket, and him girning, and Rosie hanging on to my skirts, her nose running green. And as for Morag? I shivered at the thought. My pals had teles and we didnae, which was another thing to be embarrassed about. Mum's idea of entertainment was listening to Jimmy Clitheroe's wee boy voice on the wireless. Least when Dad was here we had treats, like bags of hard wine gums so chewy they stuck in your teeth, and bottles of fizzy Irn-Bru. Sometimes he'd take Morag and me to the pictures in

Glasgow. Awright, it was aye a cowboy film, but it was still exciting to go on the train speeding along the Clyde's banks where we could see shipyard cranes and half-built boats. We got off the train at Queen Street on the smoke-filled platform under the station, climbed upstairs to blue sky and aimed for the sweetie shop across the road.

There we each could choose two ounces of sweeties from big glass jars. Then we'd visit the joke shop off George Square and Morag would choose a trick. Once she got fake vomit and placed it on Grannie's coffee table. It looked so real, as if it had been boaked up that very moment. Poor Grannie squealed when she saw it and rushed to the kitchen to fetch disinfectant to clean it up, before Morag cried out, flapping her arms up and down in glee, 'It's a joke!' Grannie took it well, though thinking of it now, that wouldnae have done her heart any favours. Then again, maybe Grannie was playing along. Course, I was too auld for that nonsense. My favourite was the café after the film, where they served a lime ice-cream drink in a high glass wi a striped straw and a twiddly spoon that chased the ice cream round and round.

I remembered that Grannie had been fond of Dad, unless she'd been playing along wi that as well. She called him Marty Son and he called her Ma, his Mum and Dad having died years ago. He'd only a sister left, Auntie Peggy, a spinster who worked in a bank someplace in Glasgow. Maybe he hadnae heard Grannie'd died. But I couldnae ask Mum, we never mentioned him now. If I didnae know that she still got a pay packet from him, I'd think he'd expired as well.

Grannie was still in her bedroom at the flat. Mum had practically raced us down the street to Grannie's for the rosary. Her worry was that we'd be late and what would the priest think? When we arrived, the house was packed wi relatives and neighbours. We had to push by on the stairs where people in black stood in a line holding onto the

22

bannister, a mighty gush of whispering men and women. They let us pass because we were close family, so there was at least one advantage in being the dead person's kin. Grannie's house, that aye smelled of baking, ham hock soup or beef and onion stew, now smelled of burning wax. Mum had fished out a blue plastic set of rosary beads for me and she had the ones that were round her dressing table mirror, wi a gold Jesus on the cross and smooth pearly-white beads. She snaked them into a round latticed box that fit in your palm and had a picture of the Virgin's face on the lid. Grannie had given her these for good luck on her wedding day. Well, turned out even that holy talisman hadnae worked.

Auntie Hannah was watching the weans round at our place and she was to come here when we returned for her chance to kiss the corpse. I'd practiced in the mirror wi my reflection, my face deadpan. But would dead lips feel as cold as glass? I tried not to purse my lips as the dead lips couldnae purse back. So, I just closed them like I was asleep and let them meet the reflection like the fall of a feather. It helped to close my eyes so I could avoid looking at the abomination glowing on my chin, spoiling what was a not bad face. Awright, the freckles were a bit annoying, but I'd been told I had nice indigo eyes like my dad's.

Suddenly it occurred that it might not be lip to lip, but a kiss on the forehead. I tried Rosie's baby doll. A quick touch above the staring eyes and away. That wasnae so bad, though I wasnae looking forward to it. Mum said I didnae have to, if I didnae want to. She said it tetchy like, as if I was such a disappointment, she'd hardly expect me to do the right thing.

So, I was going to prove her wrong, even though I was wetting myself

We wore black mantillas. Mine looked odd ower my school uniform. Morag squealed when she saw me trying it on in the mirror. 'Ye look like the banshee,' she wailed, jumping up and down on the bed behind me, her knicker

23

elastic worn so bad her pants fell to her knees and she fell off the bed in a tussle. But Mum looked better tonight than she had lately, kind of mysterious and almost human in her mantilla, not the crumpled auld bag she'd been the last few days.

The way she went on, you'd think she was the one who'd died. Sniffing about the house in a trance, not taking the weans on one bit, except to give Morag a flying slap for spilling milk or making too much noise, something our Morag couldnae help. I escaped most of that by slinking around, head down. After that first day, I thought it was a bit overdone.

There's only so much misery a person can take. I'd rather have her slap me than say stuff like '*sorry*'. She even handed me her purse to get the shopping. I decided to be the adult around here. After all, I was the brains of this outfit. My mum was dense as a pan of porridge, so she was. Her idea of a book was *Tarzan and the Apes* and *Sherlock Holmes*. Now she was at Grannie's bedroom door weeping into her frilly hanky.

Our turn came. An auld man came out of the room stony-faced, and my stomach roiled. Maybe I shouldnae have wolfed down sausages and chips just before coming out. I peeked out between narrowed eyes. The sight of the coffin was awright. Up on a trellis affair wi polished brass handles, it looked sturdy enough. You couldnae see anybody in it from the doorway, just the edge of white padded lining. Course, the room was only lit by rows of fat white candles I'd only ever seen in the chapel. The lid was set against the wardrobe, head to foot, ready to cover the coffin. I imagined being screwed down for eternity and swallowed hard. Mum stepped ower, made the sign of the cross, and leant in. Bobbed up again and turned, tears rolling off her chin. She shoved me in as she passed, and I moved close to the coffin wi one eye closed.

But even wi the one eye, I could see this wasnae my grannie. This face was both doughy and stiff at the same time, wi blushed cheeks, and my grannie never wore make-up. The hair was wiry, every strand visible, like a steel wool pad. Or maybe a whole pack of pads stuck together making an iron headscarf. The eyes were closed, as if in deep sleep, and her hands were placed on her lap wi her rosary beads tangled around them like handcuffs. When I thought of that I giggled. I bent down to hide my shame and gave her a wee wave goodbye ower her eyes, instead of the required kiss.

When I managed to stop my shoulders shuddering, I turned around. My face must've been a picture because Great Auntie Shelagh, waiting to go next, gave me a big hug and said, 'She's wi Jesus now and aw her troubles are ower.'

I nodded and blinked away my imaginary tears.

What was wrong wi me? I loved Grannie Meikle.

Mum was in the living room blethering wi a gaggle of auld women; she seemed quite animated now, and I inched my way through to her side. One or two broke from their cheer, gave me a sorrowful smile, and said they were sorry for my loss. The noise levels would've crushed your ears; Grannie would have been the first to tell them to shut up, she couldnae get a wink of sleep. Then there was a God Almighty roar from the lobby. It was Father Murphy.

'The First Decade of the Rosary,' he bawled.

After a round of coughs, the murmuring began.

I couldnae see him. He said the Rosary in the bedroom, presumably beside the coffin.

I guessed he'd have holy water to sprinkle ower Grannie's make-up, or oil to anoint her, though it would have to be her face and hands, as her feet were well covered up. The prayers went on and on and I grued when I remembered my mortifying confession wi him.

It was a Saturday not long after I'd made my first confession. Back then I was free to wander at will: no Rosie, no Martin, just Morag and me. And she was too wee to go out without Mum. Back then Mum still had her marbles and didnae make any fuss about me going out alone, though, come to think of it, I was only seven at the time.

I was so innocent, wandering past the rhubarb field and imagining a stalk in a bag of sugar, so tart it drew your gob. I passed Grannie Meikle's house and shouted up, 'Grannie.' She came to the window, grey hair in big curlers. 'Tell yer Mam ah filled the pan this morning.' I was used to passing coded messages like that and memorised the words for later.

When I got to the chapel door, I scrummaged in my satchel for my sin notebook, in-between my library books. Inside, the church was all dark wood and painted statues writhing in pain. A big Jesus, dripping blood from his side, stretched high above the altar. The place smelled foosty, and there was a worrying whiff of smoke. I blessed myself wi the Holy Water. It dribbled down my nose, and though it was ice cold, I was feart to waste it, so I rubbed it in, then dilly-dallied down the side aisle, the women's side of chapel, the best half, wi the colour on Sundays, and joined the queue at Monsignor's confessional box. The queue shifted, and I followed the row of penitents in the aisle. I was just about to step into the next pew when Father Murphy reached out of his box and clamped my arm. 'I'll hear your confession, child.' A loud whisper it was too, and what unsettled me most was the sorrowful twitter that rose and fell from the queue. I went in the box, set down my bag, slipped out my sin book and slid onto my knees, the grit of the kneeler biting into my skin. I worried I might get a skelf and there'd be the winkling of it out wi the needle and the sear of the TCP. Grimacing, I shifted my page to catch the rainbow of pinks and purples from the slit of a window.

Tuning into my sing-song voice, I started my list. 'Bless me Father for ah have sinned, it has been one week since ma last Confession.'

26

'Tell me your sins, my child.' A soft, holy murmur.

'Ah've been greedy sixty-five times. Ah've tellt lies sixty-one times. Ah've been disobedient a hundred and two times. Ah've stolen ma wee cousin's pencils twenty-five times. Ah've …' Breathless, heart thumping, I hesitated.

The bulking shadow came closer to the grille. 'Now, my child, how did you manage all these sins?'

I leaned backwards, almost sitting on my heels. 'Ah'm very bad, Father, even though ah write them doon, ah cannae keep up wi masel.'

'But, my child, how could you fit all that in, in one week?'

'Oh no, Father, these are aw ma sins since ma First Confession in May. It's been hard tae keep score. Ah've tons mare tae tell.'

The soft voice crunched cinders. 'For goodness sake, child, you don't have to remember all your past iniquities. Just since your confession last week. If that was the case, my bum would be stuck to this seat for eternity. Now, say five "Hail Marys" for your penance and a good Act of Contrition.'

I thought it might be a good idea for his bum to be stuck to that seat for eternity, but I'd settle for the time it took me to skedaddle out of there.

Now, I woke up to hear we were at the last decade and I thought my knees would crack. I also needed the toilet badly. Hannah was missing all this. Lucky thing. Very good at dodging trouble. She'd be here later, when it was all done wi.

Eventually we got to *Hail Queen of Heaven* and it was done. The wave of mourners flowed downstairs, and I rushed to the toilet before Murphy wrapped up his implements and came to give his condolences. When I came out, the lobby was empty, except for my dad leaning against the wall, coat ower one arm, handsome in a white shirt and black tie, dark brown hair combed back, just a slight wave catching the lamp light, those indigo eyes fixed on the bathroom door, and me.

'Hello, Kathleen,' he said, 'how's it goin?'

Chapter 5

Cemetery Tales

My ears filled wi a knocking sound; I thought my chest might explode. The murmurs from the living room quietened and, outside, heavy footsteps on gravel faded. His gaze rooted me to the bathroom doorway. His hair had grown, the curls he used to keep semi-tamed, curls that fell like satin on your cheek when he bent down to kiss you goodnight, now flopped in abandon ower his forehead, and one chestnut strand teased his shirt collar. Rain slashed against the stair window. In unison, our heads snapped towards the sound.

'They say a storm's blowin in.' His familiar voice was deep wi the slightest trace of a graze on the 's' sounds. He stood up straight and shifted an inch closer, his hand opening in invitation. His wedding ring gleamed in the candlelight from Grannie's room; I wanted to slap his open palm away.

The toilet light was still on behind me, my finger on the switch. I clicked it off and drew my hand to my side, bunching my fists, nails biting into soft flesh. His face darkened and the flickering light picked up a bead of sweat pearled in the cleft above his top lip. His eyes moistened, he blinked, dipped his head and stared at the whorls in the carpet. My mouth was cardboard dry.

The space between us swelled and filled wi reams of images. Picking out books at the library, him whispering jokes, attracting frowns which quickly turned to affability whenever he shot out a smile. Piling on the train after a

29

day out in Helensburgh, our tummies full of fish and chips, fingers tasting of salt and vinegar, singing *Show Me the Way tae go Home*, the other passengers joining in, him clapping the beat. Summer days, lying on the tartan rug at Elvern park, making stories out of the shapes of clouds; a convict being chased by a sheriff; a spilled bowl of popcorn; an angel blowing bubbles; an arctic teddy bear. His arm around my waist, strong and secure, as I learnt to swim at the municipal baths.

Days when we were carefree and he was my dad. Tears stung.

I glanced to the living room door, hitched my breath.

'She's away hame.' He bit his lower lip, an auld habit of his, like a wee boy, as if he was confused, looking for comfort.

I'd no comfort for him. Other times, bad times, came to mind and heat rose through my chest, flushing my neck, my cheeks.

'Sorry aboot Grannie,' he said, the familiar voice cutting through me once more.

I nodded and cleared my throat wi a cough. I'd aye been afraid to stand up to him. Nights he came home drunk, shouting and swearing, I lay in bed wanting to be brave, wanting to get up, thunder into the living room and shame him, tell him to get out and leave us be. He frightened us when he became a version of himself that, although familiar, was meaner, bitter, bullish. Like he was hard done by, everyone had it in for him, he was misunderstood. He thumped the walls, banged the doors and growled through the house, refusing to go to bed when Mum pleaded. Now, I ached to tell him what I thought of him, but my tongue stuck to the roof of my mouth. The lobby was as wide as the Clyde, and he was as lost to me as Grannie in her coffin next door. I glanced at the spare room behind him.

He raised his eyes to the ceiling in a dramatic gesture

of defeat, swung round, pushed open the door and switched on the light. I was struck wi how much he resembled me in profile. The same straight nose, our dimples in the chin and chccks, our dark curly hair, though he was weather-beaten, whilst I was pale as death. Everyone said he was a good-looking man, how he could charm the birds. His charm was lost on me, I knew him too well.

He leant ower the bed, picked out my coat, handed it to me, hard-eyed as though he knew the artifice was up. I grabbed it, steering clear of any accidental touch of fingers, and fled into a sheet of rain.

*

Mum was just back from visiting Grannie at Havoc cemetery. It was as if Grannie hadnae died, only moved to a new house. Instead of going down the road, Mum'd say, 'Ah'm jist away up the road tae see Grannie.' It was a dry hard-cold day, and she'd invited us to come a wee walk wi the pram around the gravestones. Morag and I declined while wee Rosie was quite happy to go and Martin didnae have any choice. Course, Morag relied on me to look after her and so she had to accompany them when I wasnae home. There was an understanding between us. She'd behave herself if I reduced the burden of going anywhere wi Mum.

Mum had met up wi Hannah there. A visit to the cemetery was the highlight of their social calendar. Even in winter. I supposed, other than each other's houses, and maybe the chapel hall, now that Grannie's house belonged to somebody else, they needed a new venue. Anyhow, Mum was more comfortable wi dead folk who couldnae talk back. She knew a lot of them buried there.

Now the two ghouls sat in the kitchen running a narrative on so-an-so's mother, the poor auld soul, who stuck her head in the gas oven, and that Wullie MacKay who forgot to turn off the chip pan, or someone who expired from tuberculosis, or that one who was poorly all their days and lived longer than expected. Their gab started me off on a journey imagining the lives and deaths of people buried under the headstones. I worked these into a lather of possibilities and sat up in a cold sweat. What I particularly didnae like was when Mum started on about empty lairs waiting for the next death in the family. She held a satisfaction that all was well as long as you could be buried right. It seemed a tad unhealthy and another sign of her failing mind. These signs were adding up and I was on tenterhooks all the time.

Sometimes, I thought my head would burst.

Other than Auntie Hannah, Mum didnae have any friends. She was so crabbit anyone wi sense kept out of the road. Hannah was oblivious to any of that; she just took ower the conversation, gabbing on and on. Och, they deserved each other. Except that Hannah was fashionable wi her high heels and short skirt, even though she was quite auld, maybe thirty-five. Her make-up was perfectly applied, black eyeliner and mascara like Dusty's making her eyes dark and sultry under the blonde hair she wore in a well-lacquered bob. The chatter would blow your head off. They knew everybody and could prattle off a family tree in an instant. This one was off that one, and so-an-so was this one's cousin off marriage to those ones up Bellshill, or that auld woman who was to be received in the chapel tomorrow night was the sister of that drunk that lived in such and such.

Fingers would drum till one of them got a hook. The hook would take them up hill and down dale following a lifeline until, bingo, they had the name, the mother, the father, the uncles, the aunts, the weans. It must've all been intermarriage, which would account for the number of imbeciles in this town.

Mum aye put on her good face for Hannah and acted like her auld self when she was around. Soon as she left, Mum's face fell, and she'd be back to crabbitness again. How could she change like that? Wi me she was a constant nag and a

32

happy slappy witch. She took any opportunity to skite me and Morag. Thank God, she didnae seem inclined to smack Rosie, but then Rosie was aye a good girl. Morag was far from well behaved and I wasnae a saint either, so I supposed we all deserved each other.

One thing that worried me a tad was Hannah's hatred of my dad. Sure, I hated him too, but the way I saw it, I'd every right. But she didnae, not being his wife or daughter. She was open about it, her eyes narrowing, her mouth upturned in disgust at the mention of his name. Contempt seeped from her, an attitude Mum ignored.

This afternoon, Mum and Hannah chatted wi the kitchen door open so they could hear Martin when he woke up in his cot. I was in my room reading and listening to the weans playing in the street. Morag was supposed to be taking care of the wee ones. I tutted. She could hardly look after herself. The other day she'd walked straight into a lamppost, and burst her nose, the blood spotting a whole tea towel. Now she had two black eyes. The day before she'd been sent to the shop for ten Capstan and dropped the packet down a drain. She got her bum skelped for that. But even worse was the way Mum lost it, going haywire, saying she might as well put her head in the gas oven and how we'd no money and she could ill afford to waste the cash for those cigarettes. Maybe I shouldnae have mentioned it but I breezed in wi, 'Well, you could stop smoking, it's bad for your health.' That got me a right smart across the cheek; I had finger lines for ages. And it'd only made her worse. She muttered on about gas ovens and women like her who had jumped in front of trains, and others who'd overdosed on tranquillisers. Whilst she was muttering and exclaiming, she was chain-smoking, to me a more reliable method of self-destruction, though possibly not quite in the timeframe she had in mind. Part of me didnae take her seriously, she was a drama queen, but part of me tightened up like a fist.

Now, I put down my book, got up and padded to the open door, ears perking up.

Hannah said, 'Nellie, ye should get a divorce. It's no as hard as ye think.'

Mum replied, 'Ah cannae dae that. Ah'm Catholic. It's no allowed.'

'Well, ah heard it can be allowed if ye get something called a special dispention … naw, it's a dis-pen-sation … as long as ye dinnae get married again. It's no the divorce that's the sin, it's the having it aff wi somebody else.'

'Rubbish, Hen.'

'Go ask the priest.'

'Away tae buggery, how can ah ask a priest aboot that? But anyhows, ah dinnae know …'

'Whit d'ye mean?' Here the voice was raised in disbelief. 'Ye're no thinking of letting that bastard back in. No again.'

I stood up straight.

'He's no that bad.'

'Whit?' The voice was at the ceiling. 'He's a charmer, Nellie, but loose wi his affections, and his fists. By Christ, when ah think o that …'

I stepped closer. Think of what?

Mum whispered. 'Ah've put that oot of ma heid, you dae tae, hear me?'

'Ah, awright. But ah'll say this, he's far too fond of the drink.'

'Aye, but he's a guid provider and ah've got four weans.'

'He's no providing much the noo.'

'Naw, that's true.' But there was a note of regret in Mum's voice that sent my heart trilling.

After Hannah left, Mum was in a frenzy. Up and down the stairs wi the bin, getting the washing done and she even cleaned the step, all the time reeling off complaints about this one or that one, as if demented. Then it was the ironing. Every garment had to be ironed so there were creases in the right places, in the centre on the run up your arm, four squares neat on your chest, knife edge pleats in your skirts.

That evening we all got our hair washed. Every hair on your head had to squeak. In the morning there'd be the application of the ribbon. No one could wrestle wi a ribbon like my mother. It was a feat of engineering so complicated that it stunned the eye. She aye wet the ribbon first, a good soaking. She never used elastic bands because they ripped your hair to shreds. She got the ponytail in one hand, a big fat chunk in the centre of your head and she made it ride to the top of the crown wi a squeezing action, her fingers rubbing your skull. Secure thus, she slapped the ribbon around the join, and when it took purchase, winding and pulling would ensue until every strand was tightly wound in the ribbon, some strands pulled so tight and so hard, it was as if they were being pulled out. The ribbon would circle the shaft maybe ten times or so before being tied into a double bow. At the end of all that, your eyebrows would be straining northwards in a terrible tension and from the front you looked like a boy. All day you'd be stretching your eyes to loosen your forehead, but relief only came wi the untying of the knot and the freeing of the ponytail. You had to run your fingers through the sheaf of hair to separate the locks again and bring them south. It was a misery.

That night I had the recurring nightmare that came on me after the funeral. I woke up panting and parched, my chest rattling like jiggies in a box. Grannie didnae look too well in death. She had on a Virgin Mary frock, white wi blue, and funny enough, she had the Sacred Heart of Jesus pumping away, totally visible, on her chest. Red and wet and pump, pump, pump. She could hardly walk, lifting her foot as though it was made of brick, clamping it down and then bringing up the other, slow like. When she came close, you saw that her skin was melting off like she was in the fires of Hell. But my grannie wouldnae have gone to Hell.

Not wi all those holy medals stacked in her hat. And she was aye saying, '*Jesus, Mary and Joseph*' this, and '*Jesus, Mary and Joseph*' that. I had to do something desperate, so I made a pact wi God. I said, 'God, I promise I'll be a nun when I leave school if you take these nightmares off me.' And they went away, the very next night. If I had to be a nun, I planned to become one like the Sisters at school, the long black dress and wimple variety. It was a good job and you didnae have to worry about having babies or making the tea for an oily man coming in from the Yards, drunk and spending all the wages. No dirty smelly men or nappies, and no wee sisters reading your diary on the landing steps wi their pals. Only last week I'd heard Morag and her pal giggling. The pal had come round to ask Morag out to play, but the rain came on, so they holed up on the landing wi orange squash and Jammie Dodgers. Normal giggling had a rhythm to it, but this had an edge of exclamation that roused my suspicions. And Morag couldnae be allowed to get out of hand, she needed her more daring traits clipped, so I tiptoed down to see what was going on and caught them reading my diary. When they sensed me behind, they turned, and the pal scarpered. Morag just closed the book and handed it to me, saying, 'Kathleen Gallagher, ye're a dark horse.' I skelped her as she passed, but she just laughed.

There was a lot to be said for celibacy.

*

Thank God, money was still coming into the house from Dad's wages, though it was less than what we were used to, Dad having to keep himself as well. Mum did as many shifts as she could, and I was given the rest of her work to do at home. Mouth tightly zipped, she hurried out of the house alone every Friday at quarter to six and returned, mouth tightly zipped, wi the pay packet at half past, and put it in a teacup inside the china cabinet.

On Friday, after I got in from Our Lady's and had changed,

she sat me down at the table. Slices of fish were already breadcrumbed, and fat white chips sat in the basket waiting to be fried. Gosh, I didnae have to do them. Something was sorely awry.

'Sit there, Kathleen.'

I frowned, then wiped it off in case she objected.

'Off ye go, Morag.' Morag's eyes narrowed and she peered at me sideways as Mum shooed the weans into the living room. Mum came back in and shut the door. During this time, my mind raced through any possible infringements I'd been party to, or Morag had been involved in, or – my heart sank – surely she hadnae found out about the Pest Control man. Mind, for all her faults my mother didnae hold grudges, everything was immediate wi her. She sat down to my right, took a deep breath, smoothed her apron, and said, 'Ah've a wee job fer ye, Kathleen.'

Chapter 6

Kitten Heels

'Mum, Amy Roberts is having a birthday party. Can I go?'
I'd already said aye to the invitation, but Mum was still a
hissing serpent and the negotiation could end in a sting.

She was busy wi the wringer and the kitchen belched
steam, but at least her hands were fully occupied. 'When is
it?'

'On Friday ...'

'No.'

'But Mum ...'

'Nae buts, Kathleen.'

I didnae often resort to wheedling but I stuck my head
inches under her roseate cheeks, taking a blast of heat on my
neck from one of Martin's nappies.

'Mum, I can still do the job, come home and go back to
the party. Please.'

She sighed, dropped the nappy back into the tub, and put
down the tongs. 'Whit time is it at?'

'Five o'clock till eight o'clock.'

She winced. 'Amy Roberts, eh?'

'I can still go. I'll leave the party at quarter to six, dash
down the road, pick up the packet and run back here. Then
sprint ower to Amy's again. No one will notice a thing.'
Mum couldnae do it, and she was far too affronted to ask her
sisters. I sensed possible leverage. I could work this and use
some of the credit I'd run up.

Her eyes narrowed and for a moment refusal set on her lips, then her face relaxed, her shoulders drooped, and I knew I had her. Maybe it was the eagerness in my face, or some memory of fun-times past (though that was unlikely, this was my mum), or maybe she was just worn out. I pretended to be anxious wi anticipation, to give her the satisfaction of the indulgence. It wasnae often she had any of that. Finally, she said, wi the slightest glimmer of a smile behind the eyes, 'Awright. Mind ye've got tae be there on the dot or else …'

I knew the critical nature of my task and the consequences of failure. There could be no *'or else'*. I was living two lives; one responsible parent-in-lieu and the other would-be party girl in nylon sheath, kitten heels, and flick-out hair. Those kitten heels sure took some getting before Grannie died, when Mum was just about approachable. I'd nagged for ages and she'd finally let me have them on the Provident Cheque, so I wasnae about to sprint in them.

Instead, I'd have my sannies in my pockets ready for the dash.

On the day, all my lies were suitably concocted to avoid failure. The excuse had to have the appearance of immediacy. I couldnae be called away. For a start there wasnae a phone in my house. A ridiculous idea but one I'd imagined many times … having a telephone in the lobby, able to call friends, the library … that would make the librarian woman sit up on her skinny arse. But there wasnae one, nor could I ask anyone to rush up to the door and fetch me off on some emergency as this was only between Mum and me. I could've blackmailed Morag but I let that idea go as foolhardy, ransacked my brain and the obvious scenario fell into place. It was perfect.

Amy's house was on a private road, where people wi money lived who knew nothing of scrimping and saving for shoes or relying on the Provident for your school uniform or the Saint Vincent de Paul for a pram for your wee brother. Mum was her sternest that day of the charity pram. The SVP man was a plumber by trade, soft-spoken and kindly, but Mum was sour, like, '*Okay, ye've brought me whit ah need, but dinnae fer a moment expect gratefulness or even a cup of tea.*' I sighed as I approached Amy's building, fiddling in my inside duffle pocket to double-check my Snow White watch. The other pockets were tight wi my sannies and I couldnae actually display this relic from a younger Christmas.

I strolled up the crazy-paved driveway, jagging myself on a stick of purple heather protruding into the path. The house looked smart enough, a semi-detached Victorian building, bay windows, blackened brick and brass knockers, one of those types my mum cleaned when she got the chance. She complained that the dirt in those houses was a mortal sin.

I bit off one glove and knocked the maroon door three times. There was no answer, though people milled around in the big front lounge. Brightly dressed, teenage girls were giving it laldy to Elvis Presley under an actual crystal chandelier. I patted down my yellow straight up-and-down, pan-collared number. I was a skelf, and probably looked like a colouring pencil, and to add to my misery, elastic bands held up my knee socks making my legs itchy, so I had to lean down and massage the angry red circles. It was about time I had stockings, but they were expensive.

After a few minutes shivering, I realised the outer doors led into an inner wee sanctuary where you're supposed to ring a bell. I rang and rang and just as I was about to leave, Amy appeared in the hallway and opened the door. She was bright in a red velvet dress, but this didnae help her startled eyes and pale twitchy face. Normally she was dressed in school uniform like me. We both stood staring at each other in a kind of trance.

Gathering my wits, I strolled past her, head held high remembering what Mum had said when she'd taken a precious minute out of her chores to lecture me. 'The Roberts think they're posh, but dinnae ye think anything of it. Ginty

40

Roberts was Ginty McLeish before him, and he's an odd-bod. English Catholic, no the same as us. Rod up his arse.'

In the lounge, I was greeted by a bunch of girls from my school, but the rest were strangers, most likely from the private school up the hill, neighbours of Amy's. I joined in the dancing for a while, gyrating to *The Loco-Motion.* It was all a bit loud and Amy was absent, so I smiled my way through the throng and found her on a stool in the kitchen.

'Where's your Mum?'

I'd expected to find Mrs Roberts in the kitchen, but there was no sign of her. The noise in the lounge was growing louder; two of the girls were dancing on the coffee table. I'd never been to anything unsupervised, unless you counted babysitting the wee ones. My mum would have a fit if she found out. More high jinks and squealing came from the lounge and girls started to spill into the hall and kitchen, one shamefaced wi a broken ornament in hand. I took it from her and laid the pieces on the counter. Amy's eyes twitched like she had tics and she kept rubbing her hands together, bending back her fingers as if they were rubber, all red white blotchy as though blood pooled underneath.

My own house was a stress pit most of the time, and I recognised trouble when I saw it. Sure enough, Amy burst into tears. I took her by the arm and shut the rest of them out, closing the door wi my heel and stared at her.

She blurted out, 'Oh, Kathleen, my dad will be home soon and …' She drew a hanky from up her sleeve and blew into it hard. Now, balloons were bursting to squeals of laughter.

Mr Roberts would be scandalized; he was in the Knights of Saint Columba.

I repeated, 'Where's your mum?'

Amy's face scrunched into ridges and folds where tears puddled. She pointed to the ceiling.

'Righto, I'll get her.' I took the stairs, two at a time.

'Mrs Roberts,' I called out. 'Mrs Roberts, Amy needs you

down the stairs.'

At the end of the hall a grandfather clock chimed the half hour, its gold hand quivering ower the Roman numerals. I'd need to get out of here in ten minutes, tops. There was a toilet ahead, the sheen of white porcelain winking in the semi-dark. Amy's bedroom door was open, her uniform discarded on the floor, a teddy bear wi a tartan bow helpless on its back on the pink coverlet. A few hardback books were scattered at the side of the bed. The ceiling light was on and I pushed the door open a tad more, out of nosiness. This was a fine room, not like mine at home wi the beds close together and cupboards busting wi stuff. My books had to be kept well under the new bed for fear of damage and an unaffordable fine at the library. A bump to the right jolted me out of my jealousy. I turned and stepped down the hall, recognising a strong peaty smell that caused me to pinch my nose. I stopped at another door, this one only open a fraction, soft light spilling through the gap, wishing I'd never come to this blasted party. And what had possessed me to come upstairs? Something must've been up if this woman hadnae heard the racket. Maybe she'd taken ill. I knocked. 'Mrs Roberts?' I pushed the door open.

A Johnnie Walker bottle, without its plug, balanced on the lip of a large ashtray on the bedside table, three or four inches winking like honey. One black high-heeled shoe lay on its side on the Chinese rug and the other pointed toe-up to the ceiling on the nylon foot of the figure prone on the bed.

Mrs Robert's lilac party skirt had slipped down in abandon, hip bones nudging the material either side like wee rounded pebbles. Her white silk blouse had loosened from the waistline and slipped up to rumple ower her bra. A line of blonde down ran from breastbone to belly button ower flushed, milky skin. One hand was flung ower her head and blonde curls rioted around a doe-soft face. Her daughter's features were there, but without the mousiness. The other hand drooped ower a crystal glass upended on the floor, which had dripped a wet stain on the rug. Women didnae get drunk in our social set. My mother liked an Advocaat at Christmas, I'd seen the aunties wi a Babycham and Great Auntie Shelagh liked a wee tipple. I stood there far too long for decency, the sight oddly captivating, my senses banging in my ears, drowning out the noise from downstairs. Maybe she'd expired. I'd heard of men who drank themselves to death.

It was only when she turned, lashes fluttering, a little pop escaping from her lips, that I backed out of the room, shutting the door fast behind me. I picked my way downstairs despite the clock on the landing telling me to get a move on. The girls were playing a tag game, falling about, pulling and shoving, a sight I saw as ridiculous. Amy stood at the kitchen door, her chest rising and falling as if she'd just climbed Ben Lomond.

I said, 'Er, your Mum's sleeping.'

Her eyes widened, the irises so gray they were almost colourless.

I wanted to tell her not to worry, but that would be a bare lie, as opposed to a white lie which was perfectly acceptable in my book, so I planted my feet square in the doorway, stuck two fingers in my mouth and drew out my best whistle. That stilled the melee and I went ower and turned off the record player. All eyes were trained on me; if I didnae act fast this could get out of hand.

I shouted, 'Right, you lot. Party's ower. Mrs Roberts is sick. Get your coats and leave. I need to go for the doctor.'

A fox-faced madam sidled to the front of the group, but when I took a step forward and gave her my mother's serpent hiss, she backed off. Within five minutes the place was cleared.

Amy stood at the kitchen door.

'You'll need to tidy up, there's something I forgot,' I said.

She sniffed and nodded, her hands shaking. Out of the blue she planted a kiss on my cheek. I smiled, and high-tailed it out of there, changing my shoes at the gate before I took to my sprint.

Outside, it was icing up, the ground glowing wi frost. At first my feet were cold in the sannies, but they grew warmer as I ran across the Common, past the empty footbaw fields either side, past the public baths and under the railway bridge. Amy was a nice girl, I liked her, maybe we could be best friends. Slowing down, the idea flushed my cheeks. Ower my head, up in the rafters, invisible pigeons cooed, warbled and fluttered. I sped up when I thought about the white pooh that aye decorated the tunnel's walls and pavements.

I slowed as I reached the East End where the shipyard siren was reaching a crescendo announcing the end of the shift. The boiler-suited men hadnae yet begun to burst out of the big gates to make their way to the High Street pubs to spend their week's wages, so I was in time to catch him and get the pay packet for Mum. She couldnae do this job anymore. It had to be me. I sped down George Street, the gates now swinging out to empty the tide of working men into the lanes, alleys and streets of the town. Huddles of women, some wi prams, some wi toddlers, some wi curlers under their scarves, waited on the roadsides and pavements ready to relieve their men of their pay packets before too much damage was done. I slid in and out of these clusters, some of them enjoying a good blether, others wan wi cold and anxiety. At last I reached the prearranged spot on a corner and waited.

I'd shame him into it if I had to. 'So, we're to starve while you drink our suppers away.' Or 'You're a big man, so you are, taking the food out of the mouths of babes.' I'd heard that one in the chapel. Or, if pushed, I'd resort to wheedling. So far, he'd cooperated but I knew fine and well he still entertained the idea Mum would have him back any time he liked. Despite her moment of doubt wi Hannah she had steadfastly acted as though he was dead meat. Once he realised that reconciliation wasnae going to happen, he wouldnae cough up. I stayed in the shadows until I recognised him amongst the crowd. He swaggered while others walked, he surveyed whilst others watched, he commanded space whilst others pushed and shoved. As he came closer, a street lamp picked out the pale sweep of his forehead and the glint in his eyes, his oil-blackened lower face split by a grin, and he waved as he located me skulking at the corner. This was a job I could well do without. I gritted my teeth as he fell away from the crowd and jogged ower to me.

'How's yer Ma?'

'Fine.' I glanced at his pocket.

'An the girls?' He was going to string this out.

'Aye, fine.'

'Wee Martin?' He bit his upper lip.

'He's getting big.'

'An yersel?'

'Awright.'

He put one hand on the wall and leaned forward, hemming me in. I twisted my head away and blinked back the sting behind my eyes. He smelt of the yards: Bunsen burner, oil, sweat, and that thick peaty undertow that was aye on his breath.

'How's the school?'

'Give's the message.' I slipped under the extended arm and shoved my hand out.

He shook his head. 'That's ma girl awright, jist aff yer Mam's back.' But he fished out the pay packet, bust it open, took out some notes, and crushed them into his pocket. He passed the still fat packet to me, narrowing his eyes as if about to say something else. Instead he laughed and backed away, soon jogging after his pals.

I turned towards home, jamming the packet in my inside

pocket, shivering now, my brain jiving. Soon as Dad realised the game was up, I'd not be getting any pay packet. Mum seemed to think we'd manage; I didnae know how. But it was good to be able to go to bed and not have to listen for him coming up the stairs garrulous wi the drink. Sometimes after tea, we'd all lie on the carpet and listen to a story on the wireless as long as Martin was asleep. Mum would knit and she'd seem normal again. No, we didnae need Dad or his measly pay packet.

I pushed open the gate and hurried up the path. Mum was waiting in the kitchen doorway, the wee ones sober-faced at the table behind her. Even Martin's eyes were question marks. I slipped the envelope into Mum's hand and she emptied it onto the sink counter, counting it out.

'Off ye go, Kathleen.' She smiled.

My heart jarred. This was my auld mum.

The party? I'd almost forgotten about that. I hesitated. There was one errand left. I slipped into our room and panned beneath my bed for the parcel. It was only a box of Maltesers, a hand-stitched handkerchief I'd made myself, and the glittery birthday card that said '*Happy Birthday Amy*' in my best italics.

Chapter 7

Blood and Bone

Mum had yet another job for me. I'd have to live wi this particular nightmare for three days. She got up, patted me on the shoulder wi a lopsided smile, nodded to the weans, took her coat and bag from the press and left for work as usual. Morag sat big-eyed on the couch, mouth zipped. Wee Rosie leaned tight against her big sister, thumb in gob. Martin was asleep, his wee stripy-blue chest rising and falling in the pram. When the front door clicked shut, Morag piped up, 'Jings, Kathleen, glad it's you and no me.' She waltzed both eyes around her head.

'Your time'll come, believe you me,' I said, still in shock.

'Don't think so. This is a one and only.'

Saturday finally arrived after three nights of weird dreams. The bus let us off ten minutes early at Church Street, by the town clock. Ten to nine and the square was deserted. Frost whitened roofs and pavements, and tall fir trees in the graveyard were cobwebbed silver, but all I saw was blood and bone.

My fingers yearned for the red double-decker as it slid away round the corner at a snail's pace. I could've ran after it, caught the bar, and hauled myself aboard, but instead I swallowed back bile and stepped the other way, terror springing in my throat as we picked our way ower cobbles. I chanced a sideways peek at Mum. She hadnae spoken a

47

word since we left the house. Hannah had come in early to watch the weans.

I'd asked, 'How come Hannah wasnae chosen?'

'Yer Aunt Hannah's lily-livered and wouldnae cope.'

I wanted to shout in both their faces that I was only thirteen and couldnae cope. But saying that aloud would only get me a skite.

We approached the mouth of the close. Mum stepped in first, disappearing into the yawning gloom, her footsteps echoing through the building. I followed her up the winding stairs, holding onto the bannister to steady myself. A huge stained-glass window dazzled my eyes as I turned onto the first landing. It was as if someone had thrown a bucket of stars at the jewelled panes, they so shimmered wi frost. We climbed the second flight to the next floor where yellow lamps lit up chequered linoleum. A heavy door greeted us wi a sign above the knob in italics. *Open*. Bunching my fists, I stepped back when Mum turned the knob. 'Come on,' she said, frowning. We entered a bright reception hall wi brass pots and green rubber plants, white walls and a horrid whiff of antiseptic. 'Wait here,' Mum said. I stood quaking in the hall as she spoke to the receptionist behind a desk. The woman stepped out of her cubicle and gestured Mum through a door. Mum nodded for me to follow. We went into a waiting room and sat down.

More brass pots, half-collapsed rubber plants, an auld square dining table stacked wi tattered magazines, and on the walls paintings of austere buildings. No other patients. I tuned into sounds coming from somewhere close. Drilling, suction, metal clanging on metal. My stomach seesawed, my mouth filled wi sourness. I gagged but managed to hold it down.

'Mum, I don't feel well.'

'Me as well, Hen.' She peeked out from behind her glasses wi a look so lost, so desperate, that I was driven along the road to adulthood in one fleeting moment, never to return.

I shimmied closer to Mum and laced my arm through hers, feeling the rise and fall of her chest through our coats. How could this have happened? The hospital said she needed to have her teeth extracted, the gum disease could cause major health problems, and she was anaemic. The new baby had further depleted her reserves. It'd have to be false teeth when her gums healed. I shivered but stilled myself. It was time to man up. Mum relied on me.

'Listen, Mum.' She turned to me. 'It'll all be done in a half hour. You'll get the gas, you willnae have a clue. And don't worry, I'll get you home.'

She'd counted out precious shillings for the taxi. The receptionist would phone when ready.

'Aye, Hen. Course it'll be fine. Yer a guid girl. Go tae the toilet if ye like.'

'No, it's awright, it's calmed a bit.' I clutched my tummy.

The one window had frosted panes wi *HAVOC DENTIST* printed across. Who would advertise such a place? The sign might as well say *COME INTO HELL*. Something rose from deep inside and I wanted to smash the glass. But I still had my arm through Mum's, like auld times. Maybe I should be more helpful to her, stop dodging her company. Must've been hard for her these last few weeks.

Folk's voices carried up from the street. Shopfront grilles were being unhinged for the day's business; a car tooted, a boat on the Clyde shrilled its horn. But it all seemed so far away from us here. Together. Waiting.

'The wireless weatherman thinks it might snow.' Mum shivered, though it was warm in the waiting room.

I hugged her tighter, her wool coat chafing my chin.

She laid her head on my shoulder and gave out a big sigh. 'Ah'm glad ah didnae huv tae come here by massel.'

'Would Grannie have come?'

'Aye. She'd huv come wi me if she was still here.'

The door opened and the receptionist announced, 'The dentist is ready for you, Mrs Gallagher.'

Mum patted my knee and we got up. I managed to hold back tears until the door clicked shut behind her, and then they poured out. I lost control of my imagination as well.

The sounds coming from beyond the door seared into my head. An air pump and whooshing sounds, cutlery pinging, and ding after ding which I imagined were teeth being dropped into a bowl. I panicked, my breath coming in rapid gasps. Remembering my first aid class, I sat down and put my head between my knees. It helped a lot and once I had my breathing under control, I prayed. First the *Our Father*, then a *Holy Ghost*, and by the time I was on my forty-something *Hail Mary*, the door opened and the receptionist came in.

'Your mum's all done now, she's recovering well, and I've telephoned for the taxi.' She must've seen the state of me, because her business-like face fell and became full of concern. 'Are you okay?' she asked. 'Do you need a hanky?'

I shook her off wi a head shake and got to my feet.

'I'll come down the stairs and get you both into the car. Let me get my coat. But, don't worry if she's talking a lot of nonsense, that's the gas. Just put her to bed for the day.'

I followed the woman through the hallway and into a wee anteroom, glancing into the dental theatre as I passed. A raised seat tilted backwards beside black gas canisters wi tubes and knobs, a tray full of instruments of torture sat on a tall cabinet, and ower a deep white sink, the dentist, a huge hairy man wi bulging eyes, was removing a face mask. I knew he'd never leave my nightmares. The wail that rose from my belly reached my throat, but I swallowed it back, like every other screech busting to be heard.

Mum was sitting on a low stool wi a basin on her knee and a handful of bloodied gauze at her face. She hadnae on her glasses and I almost didnae recognise her as she swooned and moaned, her face blanched white. Her free hand fluttered about her head as if unattached.

I turned to the receptionist. 'Where's Mum's glasses?'

The woman stared at me a moment, turned on her heels, and returned wi them in her palm. I placed them on Mum's face and she blinked and sighed.

The receptionist took Mum by the elbow and teased her to her feet. Mum's eyes rolled back and I thought she'd collapse, but her helper knew her stuff, had her in a vice grip. I hurried in and took the other arm. Between us we got her into her coat. The receptionist wrapped a roll of bandage around Mum's head, pinning it at the back so it covered her ears and held a cotton pad in place loosely at her mouth.

'Just keep this at her mouth until you get home; the bleeding will stop soon.'

'Kathleen,' Mum whispered, 'my lovely girl.' I knew then she wasnae herself, was well under the effects of the gas.

We half carried her downstairs to the taxi at the kerb. The driver looked a bit sickly as he helped Mum in. I shimmied in beside her and we drove off, the kind woman waving to us, concern darkening her face. Mum slept during the taxi ride and thankfully didnae say anything else. I kept my head straight ahead so as not to look at her face.

At the gate, I asked the driver to peep his horn to alert Auntie Hannah. But he got out, gave me a lopsided smile and helped Mum out of the car and up the stairs. Hannah appeared as we rose. Instead of gathering Mum up, she stopped dead, dithering. 'Oh my, oh my, Jesus Christ …oh my …' I wanted to slap her, but she took to her feet and scrambled back upstairs leaving me and the driver to manage Mum's ascent between us.

At the top, the weans crowded the lobby. Morag's eyes were tea plates, her mouth opening and closing like a fish, and wee Rosie burst out greetin when Mum leant against the bedroom door. Hannah shepherded them away into the kitchen and shut the door.

I reached in my pocket for the shillings, but the driver waved them away. 'Naw, it's awright, Hen. Nellie wis a guid pal tae ma mam when she wisnae well. God bless her. Ye awright?'

'Aye, thank you.'

He was gone, the door slamming, leaving me alone wi Mum whose bandage had slipped. She smiled at me fondly, her mouth a gaping beetroot hole, empty of teeth. My mum's teeth hadnae been pearly white for a long time but this gummy, bloodied vision made me cuff my fists to my cheeks. I closed my eyes, took a deep breath and when I opened them, Kathleen Gallagher had run for the hills, and standing in her place was a doppelganger, one who'd grown ten years older in as many seconds.

I took a firm hold of my gas-drunk mother, manoeuvred her into the bedroom, sat her down, dragged off her coat, unpinned the bandage and pad, and took her glasses off. I placed them on the bedside table, sat beside her and stroked her back.

She said, 'He willnae love me noo, will he?'

'Who cares,' I said wi immediate understanding, now that I was twenty-three years auld, 'that bastard can rot.'

'Aye, he is that, a bad bastard. The things he did … Dae ye know he tellt me ah was an ugly cow? Well, noo ah really am.' She made a cackle. My spine contracted.

'No, Mum, once you get your new teeth you'll be hunky-dory.'

'Ah'm bad, a bad woman, a fool, ye'd aw be better off withoot me,' she wailed.

'No Mum, don't say that.'

She fell back onto the pillow, her eyes fluttering. Her poor mouth open, red raw, cheeks sunken, deflated like thumbed dough.

I felt my way to the toilet and wet a clean towel under hot

water from the geyser. Was this what being an adult meant? Clamping down on tears and growing a backbone? That's how it felt. I had to be the dependable one, Mum wasnae up to it. I peered in the mirror at my thirteen-year-old self. I didnae want to be grown up yet. But I went back, and wiped the blood and spew from my mum's face and throat, my tears brimming. One dripped onto her cheek. I wiped it away wi all the rest.

Chapter 8

Shelagh's Virgin

The doorbell rang its shrill alert and a neighbour of my Great Auntie Shelagh came up the stairs before Morag could beat her way down and have the privilege of announcement. That's what they did, knocked and came right in as they liked. That aye annoyed me, what if you were up to something you didnae want folk to know about? Our lives were a public library, that was for sure. So, Joe McFadyen comes in, like he's our best pal, puffing wi gossip, filling the doorframe.

'Nellie, Hen. It's yer Auntie Shelagh, she's taken no well. The doctor's been and he asked fer a relative tae come.'

There's nothing like somebody else's bad fortune to take you out of your own. My mum's face fair lit up wi curiosity. Maybe an iota of concern as well, if I was giving her the benefit of the doubt. She rolled up her ball of wool and stuck the navy cardigan into her sewing bag, rushed to the press, pulled on her coat, got her bag from the kitchen, her purse from where she'd hidden it under the cushion on the living room settee, and instructed:

'Right, Kathleen, ye get on wi the tea and ah'll go see whit's needed.'

'What's needed here?' I wanted to say, but kept my mouth firmly shut. As if I didnae have important matters to see to myself. Like homework, like exams, like listening to Helen Shapiro on the wireless. Like going out wi my pals to walk the streets. My social life was just beginning and here

54

was my mum leaving me in charge of three weans again; her weans, no mine, by the way. The neighbour shepherded her downstairs. An auld man too, but I saw the lecherous way he looked her up and down. I didnae know if I was most shocked by him being a dirty bugger or that my mum could merit such attention. I supposed she wasnae that bad looking if you discounted the crabbit mug. And the new false teeth, although slightly too big for her face, had actually given her a whiter smile than she'd had before, on the odd occasion she deigned to show them.

I did as I was told, spitting bullets all the while. Morag saw to Martin, sitting him on her knee, feeding him as many rusks as he could stapp down, his wheat-wet fingers stuffed down his throat. Wee Rosie sat on the kitchen stool, swinging her legs as I tidied up after tea.

I gave her a big kiss on her silky crown for being a good girl and she said, 'Is auld Auntie Shelagh deid as well?'

And I thought she took nothing in.

'Naw, Hen, course no. It'll just be one of her wee turns.'

'Whit's a turn?'

Well, there was a question. What was a turn exactly? Another mystery I had to get my busting brain cells around. 'I think it's fainting, lack of oxygen to the head.'

She looked at me vacantly, so I picked her up and swung her around. Jist a wee turn, aroon and aroon and aroon until she laughed up her baked beans.

Mum came back at eight. She took her tea and fag into the living room where I was studying. 'Kathleen?'

I looked up. 'Aye?'

'Got another wee job fer ye.' She rolled her eyes. 'Yer Auntie Shelagh dyed her hair the usual black, but it went royal blue and she wasnae leaving her bed till it was fixed. So, ah sent one of the neighbour's boys tae fetch Hannah and we got it dyed right again.'

'So she's awright, no had a turn?'

Mum flicked ash into her saucer. 'Fit as a bull, she is, no like poor Ma. Nae pregnancies, nae heavy hoosework, nae men tae savage her hert. Though, come tae think of it, yer Grannie tellt it different.' She pursed her lips as if the information had to be drawn from her wi pliers.

I played the game, glad of a rare chance to have a chat wi Mum, and let my mouth fall open in shock. 'No?'

'Aye, some soldier efter the war.'

'What, she'd have been auld even then.'

'No, daftie, the First World War, when she was a lass, mibbe eighteen.'

'Was he killed?'

'Ma said he went back tae Canada and Shelagh followed him.'

'Jeez. How did you not tell me this before?'

Mum nodded solemnly. 'Ma tellt me it in confidence, but she's no here noo. Ma said she wasnae gonna tell tales aboot her sister, but … She went efter him is aw ah know. Ah dinnae know whit happened tae bring her back here, but she was hertbroken. Wasnae right since, aw they turns. Took tae the chapel, holier than thou.'

'Maybe he did die then.'

'Or mibbe he got fed up wi her. She did get merried at some point. Some Irishman.'

We both sat for a minute thinking this through. My respect for Shelagh was growing.

To have gotten out of Havoc and away to Canada on her lonesome. I didnae know any Canadians, but to me they were just Americans who lived north of New York. I looked up at Grannie's cameos of Jack and Jackie Kennedy on the back wall, sent by Auntie Ina from Buffalo, and Mum's now after she'd cleared out Grannie's house. Jackie Kennedy looked lovely in a white pillbox hat and pearls. The president was awright for an auld man.

Shelagh's lover would've been more exciting. Elvis

56

Presley came to mind, making me gasp.

I must've made a noise, maybe swooned a little, because Mum realised she'd forgotten she'd a job for me, deadened her fag in the saucer, gathered it up with her cup, and dropped the bombshell.

'It's been agreed, on yer behalf, that ye'll visit Auntie so she has regular company.'

Of course, I didnae get a say in that arrangement.

Despite the revelations, I wasnae happy. It might've been sufferable if Great Auntie Shelagh didnae talk about sin constantly. Like a tap running, it came out of her mouth unfiltered. And she was aye complaining of being not well, though she looked hearty enough to me, if a wee bit geisha under the coal black hair. The scarlet smear across her mouth didnae help, though who was going to tell her? So, I wasnae looking forward to this job.

Mum made me visit the very next night.

I strode up the hill to the last development in town before fields and crags. Like us, Auntie was in a flat, though she was downstairs, and the entry was by a close, no like ours and Gran's wi our front doors leading to the stairs. First thing you saw at the front door was the Virgin's downcast head on the doormat. Thereafter, the place was littered wi memorabilia from Lourdes, fetched by the town faithful ower the years. Indeed, the house was a shrine to the Virgin Mary, but it was Auntie's own personal Virgin, who appeared when the dark drew in, that gave me the shivers.

After she got out a slab of bun and a lemonade for me, she went to the cabinet and lifted out a half bottle of gin, unscrewed the cap and poured herself a good two inches. Despite the hair and lipstick, she was quite striking wi light tanned skin, dark brown eyes and lovely white teeth which looked natural. Not like the false ones Grannie used to leave lying around the place, or Mum's new pair that lay in the cup by her bedside table. Auntie settled herself on the chair at the window and said, 'Turn off the light, Kathleen, and if ye're lucky and we kneel here at the window tae say a decade of the rosary, ye might see her holy self.'

'What do you mean, Auntie?'

'The Virgin appears here every night when darkness falls, ye can only see her from this spot at the window.'

I rolled my eyes but did as I was told. It took ages, my knees throbbed, bare that they were, seeing as I was still in my school uniform and top hose. Auntie was on the second decade when it happened. A figure appeared on the trunk of one of the trees that skirted the road down the brae. She stood in profile, hands clasped in supplication, under the nicotine glow of a street lamp. I gasped and Auntie nodded, pleased as punch. After a moment I'd worked it out. It wasnae an apparition. It was only a weird reflection, but the worst of it was, I'd have to pass her in the dark, on the way home, all alone. I told Auntie I was a wee bit feart, and she tucked my hair behind my ear and whispered, 'The Mother of God loves ye. It's the de'il ye need tae watch oot for.' Then came all the stories of Hell and Damnation for any sin that's mortal.

When my shift ended, I sprinted down like my arse was alight, just in case the Holy Mother noticed me and took an interest.

Despite all that, ower the next couple of weeks I came to enjoy my visits to Auntie. She told a lot of good stories and because she never had children, she hadnae learned bad habits like no listening to them, or expecting them to do the housework, or treating them like imbeciles. If you led her the right way, she'd forget about the Virgin and ask you about yourself. That was new to me.

I got to know about shaving my legs from Auntie, and how to iron my hair straight without singeing my scalp. It was a matter of the precise placement of brown paper, not too close or the metal rim would burn your skull, not too far or there would be a demarcation line between straight

58

and crumpled locks. She also knew a lot about men, and I learned that she'd been quite a gal in her day. Her version of emigration to Canada after the war confirmed Mum's, but only to an extent.

One evening I stayed on quite a bit later, having lost track of the hour. Auntie was on her third medicinal gin and was more thoughtful than usual. We sat close to the coal fire as flames spat and wavered in the grate. Only the wind keening outside and the occasional splat of rain on the window interrupted my rapt attention.

It began wi her jewellery box. After pouring herself a gin from the bottle in her cabinet she'd lingered. Instead of bringing ower the glass she came back wi a jewellery box and sat down balancing it on her knee. I got up, retrieved her glass and set it on the side table at hand's reach, but she ignored it, intent on the lacquered wooden box. At first, I thought it was a sewing box like Mum's, but it was too well made and far more substantial. It had a filigree metal key in a gold lock, and its design of red poppies on glowing ebony told me this was special.

She turned the key and opened the lid. Clasping one hand to her chest, a tender wistful smile softened her face.

'Auntie, what is it?'

She looked up as if surprised I was there. 'It's my anniversary, darling.'

'You mean a wedding anniversary?'

Her eyelids drooped, and she laid her head against the chair. 'I was married. Twice. This is the anniversary of my first wedding day.'

She sat up, fingered through the box and withdrew a ring between thumb and forefinger. Raising it to eye level, she twisted it around. 'Doesnae fit me noo.'

Teasing my fingers open she placed the ring on my palm. Then she turned to the box, placed it on the side table and picked up her glass.

While she sipped her drink, I slipped the ring on my middle finger and held my outstretched hand under the glow from the table lamp. The ring had a rectangular blue stone that deepened when you rolled it, wi some shiny stones all around.

'Art Deco sapphire and old cut diamonds, made in France in 1915,' Auntie said.

'It's beautiful.' The cut glass stones really did look like diamonds, each of which was bigger than the one Mum had in her engagement ring.

'Emile gave it tae me on our first anniversary. I have a wedding ring too, which I'll wear in my coffin. Ye remember that wish, Kathleen.' She threw me a look that would've frozen Hell,

'Awright, awright.' Gawd, that was a bit maudlin. 'Did you not have an engagement ring as well?'

'No, we wed too quick, there wasnae any engagement. This ring was tae make up for that.'

'And do you not want to wear this one then, like, when you're … dead?'

'No, this one will stay in the world for a guid cause.'

I handed it back, reluctantly. She placed it on top of the jewellery box. Oh, how it shone. Might be fake, but it was the prettiest thing I'd ever seen.

Remembering her wedding story, I said, 'Auntie, what happened?'

'Oh, that's a long story, but I'll make a start on it tonight, if ye like?'

'Aye, that'd be great.' I wasnae that interested but the martyr in me bent double.

'My mother, yer great grandmother, was Rose Riley, Irish Catholic stock, came ower wi Saint Patrick hissel.'

Goggle-eyed, I drew in a breath, that was something. She winked. Another tall story!

'But that aside, my mother was a great seamstress. And

she taught me well. See there, those linen table covers.' She pointed to the white, scalloped edged linens draping the sideboard and the bigger centre table at the window.

I hadnae noticed them before, but I went ower and trailed a finger along the stitching.

'I made those masel, as well as my ain petticoats, dresses and blouses. Like this one.'

She fingered the collar of her pink floral blouse and for the first time I realised I'd never actually seen one like it. Not in fashion, well, not today, but it suited her, was tailored ower her small bust and into the waist and had luminous pearl buttons fastening it, matched wi a pair each on both cuffs.

'I didnae know my great grannie was Irish and could sew,' I said, wondering why I'd never thought of her before.

'Most of the folk in Havoc are Irish stock, at least most of the Catholics, but yer great grandpa was a Highlander. Came doon from Oban after the clearances. Pitched oot of land and livelihood by the Duke of Argyll.'

'What were the clearances?'

'My oh my, Kathleen Gallagher, and here I was under the impression ye were a clever girl.'

'But Auntie, we don't get Scottish history in school, it's all English kings and that, and sometimes the American Revolution.'

'Aw a way tae control the masses.' She shook her head in disgust.

I didnae know what she meant but chalked it up for later, interest spiking for the love story. 'What about Emile? How did you two meet? Have you got a photo?'

'Aye, I have. Go look in that drawer and bring me oot my album and I'll show ye yer kin and my darling.'

I belted ower to the cabinet and opened the drawer to reveal a large white book wi '*Album*' written in raised letters on the front. I handed it to her, and she gestured me to kneel beside her. She opened the book on a page wi two black and white photos of a severe looking couple. 'My mother, Rose, and my dad, Craig. Ye can see the rest in guid time, but here he is, my Emile and me on our wedding day.'

I drank them in. Here was Shelagh looking gorgeous in a pale skirt suit, holding a trailing bouquet, gazing out of the photo in what could only be described as rapture. At her side stood the most handsome man I'd ever seen. He was dressed in a suit and tie, twenties style, and had a chiselled face, wi high cheekbones and deep-set eyes. He wasnae looking directly into the camera but at Shelagh as though she was treasure.

'Emile,' she said. 'Emile Caron.'

'French?'

'French Canadian.'

'How'd you meet?'

'In Dieppe during the war, the First World War ye understand. They've taught ye aboot that, I'm sure.'

'Aye.' I was slavering now. She was in the war?

'Awright, Kathleen, I think I've tired masel oot tonight. But I'll tell ye more next time. Listen now, something important afore ye go.'

Disappointment flushed through me, but it was nearing ten and I'd be in the soup if I was home much later. I stood up. 'Night, Auntie.'

'No, here.' She picked up the ring from atop the box and handed it to me.

I was confused as I took it in my open palm.

'Now, I have a note in the box that says this ring is yours when I pass, but knowing that Hannah, she'll strip the place and take it aw when they empty the house. So, I want ye tae have it now. Keep it safe till ye need it. It'll be worth a few bob, I expect.'

'But Auntie, I couldnae …' But already I'd folded my fingers ower it, my heart thumping wi excitement.

62

She smiled. 'Oh aye, ye can, and ye must. Now, off doon the road, Hen. And I'll tell ye aw aboot Emile another time.'

Chapter 9

Christmas Doldrums

Christmas loomed, and Mum was back to her usual glum self. The girls and I sat around the kitchen table, drinking up our orange drinks after tea, loathe to move from the damp heat of the kitchen, the windows steamed up from the hot water in the sink. Martin contented himself by banging his feeder on the tray and thumping his feet against the legs of the highchair.

Mum washed up pots, elbow deep in suds, her neck red from the effort.

Morag started it. 'Whit d'ye want fer Christmas, Kathleen?'

'I don't know.' I hadnae thought that far ahead, but it was only two weeks.

'Mibbe ye'd like a boyfriend.' She stuck her lips out in kissing fashion, smacked them together and batted her lashes.

Wee bugger, that was in my diary. Not that I wanted a boyfriend for Christmas, she'd twisted my words. I'd written about gorgeous Adam Faith and how I'd like to kiss him. I wasnae interested one bit in the boys round here, tedious oafs. I kicked her under the table, hit home, but she just sniggered.

'Is Santa coming?' Rosie's eyes were round wi expectation.

Mum turned, opened her mouth to say something, and I

sent her a pleading glance. In her mood, she could give the game away. Morag's eyes narrowed cannily. I couldnae tell if she still believed in Santa or not. She'd know that not to believe might be chancy in this house as you might never get a gift at all. So, on that premise, she wouldnae let on. But she might still be a believer at her age. Hard one to crack. But Rosie believed, and I wasnae going to let Mum spoil it for her. Mum was still itching to reply when I barged in wi, 'Course, Santa's coming soon. He'll be down the chimney wi his big bag of toys on Christmas Eve and you just wait to see what's in it.'

Rosie shivered wi anticipation, her china-blue eyes wide as the sky. Morag jumped up and down, whooped, then picked Rosie up round the chest and stalked her, both giggling, into the living room. Martin shot out both arms and wailed. I picked him up and cuddled him, but he kept pushing against me wi sticky fists, anxious to follow the girls.

I didnae blame him. Mum wiped her hands on the towel, sour as lemons. 'Ye shouldnae get their hopes up, Kathleen. We huvnae got cash tae waste.'

Balancing Martin on my hip, I shut the kitchen door on the girls, and whispered, 'We can get second-hand, clean them up and pretend they're new. It cannae be that hard.' She tutted and turned back to the sink.

Last Christmas, we woke to a stocking full of sweeties tacked on the window ledge, and a big thick-skinned orange each. Three bundles of gifts sat on the fireplace. I had *Bunty*, *The People's Friend* annual, a Lucky Bag, and red wool gloves Mum knitted, somehow without me knowing. A silver bangle was my special. Morag had a knitted blue scarf, *The Beano* annual, a Lucky Bag, and her special was a watch wi Mickey Mouse on it. She got a footbaw too. Wee Rosie had some colouring-in books, crayons, a pink wool hat wi a pompom, some plasticine, and her special was a baby doll.

Martin brought me back to reality as he wriggled and pushed, his fists like hammers on my side. I turned him around, so his back was on my front and he could kick out safely. His fine, dark, baby hair smelled of lanolin and tickled my nose as I kissed his head. He hadnae been here last year but Dad had, and as soon as Morag was happed up, they'd clambered downstairs wi the footbaw. Mum, me and Rosie had hurried to the kitchen window where I perched Rosie on a stool, so we could see them turn up below on the frosted green between the washing poles. He dribbled and dodged, his back to us, tricky as treacle, never letting Morag score. She didnae seem to mind, a permanent grin splitting her face, but I did.

Mum did too, she tutted and shook her head all the time we watched them. They ran back up when it got so cold, Morag's face glowed. Or maybe it glowed, not from cold or exertion, but from the unusual attention given by our father. Though, his attention was on himself, not her. How come he aye had to be centre stage? It was as if, because he was a man, he was entitled to privileges.

Sour wi the memory, I turned my mind to this year's problem. How could I replicate all those presents? And then there was the dinner. We aye had a roast chicken at Christmas wi stuffing, links, roast totties and Brussels. For afters, we had a shop-bought gâteaux wi cream.

That would cost a lot of money. Who had money? Dad? Mum would never let me ask him, and anyway I could hardly ask upfront, 'Give us money for Christmas,' when I met him on a Friday. I shivered at the thought. Mum was right; it would be a climb-down, and waste all the months we'd shown him that we could manage without him. And we could.

Auntie Hannah? Mum was too proud to ask her; she'd never hear the end of it. She might pass ower some cash, but there'd be strings. Hannah never gave away a penny, despite

66

Uncle Jack having good money coming in. I wondered what she did wi it, apart from look great in all her new clothes. I'd asked Mum one time and she said Hannah hoarded money in case of catastrophe, like unemployment or divorce. Mum said, 'Ye cannae plan fer that, there would never be enough.'

Patsy? Aye, Aunt Patsy would keep the secret, if I asked her. And not think badly of Mum. But she didnae have much herself. Uncle Joe had a war pension and did some caretaking jobs, but they'd three mouths to feed. They were as hard up as us.

Maybe I could get a job? Christmas was only two weeks away. I wouldnae earn much but I could ask Mrs Rennie at the shop if she needed an extra hand.

I decided that might help, so I took Martin into the living room, dumped him on Morag, who held him at arm's length, his legs dancing, told Mum I needed a sharpener and ran up the road to Rennie's. She'd still be open, it wasnae yet six.

The two big shop windows shone in the dark, even from as far away as the play park. I hurried towards them and clenched my fists in determination before taking my place at the end of the queue. It moved fast when Mrs Rennie was at the counter. The place was stuffed wi colour: groceries on shelves, fruit and vegetables in crates, sweeties in jars – my eyes lingered on the lime green soor plooms, my mouth watering – tobacco and cigarettes behind her on the slim shelves, and toys. Lots of toys displayed and stacked high overhead.

'What can I get you, Kathleen?' She smiled wi perfect rows of false teeth. They were too big for her wee face, and I often worried they'd fall out into the sweetie tray, but she was a nice woman, and aye let people in the scheme use the phone in emergencies and without charge. She was strict on tic though, there was a big sign in the window to that effect.

'I was wondering if there was any work going, seeing that you'll be extra busy coming up to Christmas.' I smiled my most endearing smile. Before setting out, I'd practiced briefly in the hall mirror even though it was a bit smarmy like Dad's.

'Well, we usually manage, Jim and I ...'

She hesitated just enough for me to bowl in.

'You wouldnae have to pay me much. Actually, I'll work for that doll up there.' I pointed to the toy shelves. 'And that tennis set ower there, and throw in a few colouring books, pens and maybe *The Beano*, and you can have me for the next two weeks.' She looked doubtful so I added, 'And after as well.'

'I could do with someone who could actually count,' she said, turning towards her son, Jim, who stacked shelves to her left. He stopped mid stack and grunted, then returned to his task, lifting huge cans of peaches up to the highest shelf effortlessly.

'Count? I'm a whizz at arithmetic and maths.'

'Alright, Kathleen, you're hired. But your Mum needs to sign to agree as you're under fourteen are you not?'

'Aye, but it won't be for money. It'll be like voluntary work, for experience like, and you'll just be rewarding me wi items. I don't want to bother her. She's still ...' I screwed my face up, hopefully in an attitude of grief.

She screwed up her face, mimicking my misery. 'You're a good girl.' She smiled 'Alright, it's a deal.'

That was some of the gifts sorted, but there was more to think about: food, cards, decorations and a Christmas tree. Gawd, how did Mum do this every year? Dad was no help at all, just sat on his arse swirling whisky in a dimpled glass all day and expected to be fed. I doubt he ever shopped, or even gave a second thought to Christmas. No, we'd do it without him.

I also had to get around Mum. She wouldnae care about me working, but she'd need me to help around the house wi the weans and Mrs Rennie wanted me for two hours after school each day. I walked home in the dark wishing I'd worn a hat as my head was freezing, my hair stiff wi frost. Maybe I didnae need to tell Mum. Morag was coming ten, she could watch the weans. It was only a fifteen-minute sprint away. I discounted that as desperate and foolhardy, then I had a thought. I could come before school. It was accounts, packing and a bit of cleaning that could be done anytime. I charged back up to Mrs Rennie and renegotiated the contract. She huffed and puffed, but in the end gave in. I was to come at quarter to seven in the morning, leave at quarter to nine and run to school directly. When school broke for holidays before Christmas she was willing to be flexible.

When I got home, and got a minute between chores, I fiddled through the woollies in my drawer for the jewellery box wi last year's bangle inside. My nails hit leather and I fished it out and opened the lid. The bangle shone. I twisted it ower my knuckles and raised my arm to the ceiling light. It was the nicest present I'd ever been given. Things were so different last year. I pushed back the ache that came in my chest. So what? The bangle was too nice to wear. I wondered if the pawn shop would give me anything for it. I was fond of it, but it was just a thing. A thing the likes of which could be bought another time when I was well off, when I grew up and became someone else, someone wi a job, and easy cash. Maybe you had to be an adult to pawn stuff. I didnae know, but no harm in finding out. Also in the box was Auntie Shelagh's auld ring. I placed it in my palm. I'd memorised what she'd said. It was a sapphire and old cut diamond ring, made in France in 1915. Well, it was awright for an auld lady, a blue stone that deepened when you twirled it, wi some shiny stones all around.

Probably fake, but might be worth a few pounds.

It was destined to save our Christmas. Auntie Shelagh would approve. No, not just approve, she would be proud of me and encourage me in my Christmas Saviour Project.

Course, I needed to hedge my bets and omit telling her. She might not actually agree, and I'd be scuppered. Why was life full of secrets?

On Saturday, Mum took the weans up the cemetery. Morag's face was at her knees when she realised I had plans to go out and she would have to weave in and out of frozen gravestones in her woollies, listening to Mum read the names and dates, exclaiming about the manner of death, imagined or lettered on the stones, taking delight in it. While they were out, I took my ring and bangle to the pawn shop in the high street. The sign saying you had to be sixteen jumped out at me as I was opening the door. I marched back home and made myself look years aulder. It wasnae hard, I was tall, and worn out wi work, and had steely eyes when I tried. I also put on a pair of Mum's high heels and padded one of her bras wi auld stockings. My own bras were just cotton flaps. Sitting in front of Mum's mirror, I added pink lipstick, mascara and Panstick, and I was the works. Except the lipstick tasted like cough medicine. Transformed, I wrapped the sophisticated package up in a checked wool coat of Mum's. I turned in the mirror; this wasnae me, this was somebody mature and confident.

What a difference clothes made. I clicked my way downstairs and slipped out, head down and in a hurry just in case anybody recognised me.

The town was quiet for a change. After hanging about outside freezing to death to make sure the pawn shop was empty, I tapped my way in. It didnae look much like a shop. Everything was behind bars.

'Here's a ring and a bangle I'd like to pawn, please,' I said to the jowly man at the grille.

He looked at me wi naked suspicion, and something else I couldnae put my finger on, but his half-gloved fingers were already fidgeting wi the items, and I expected in his line he wasnae interested in provenance.

'The ring is from Canada. My aunt left me it in her will. And this bangle was given to me by my fiancé, my late fiancé.' I lowered my lashes demurely. I enjoyed being this mysterious woman.

He picked up a magnifying glass and examined both, quickly dismissing the bracelet.

'Silver,' he said, 'quite nice. Can't give you much …' I held my breath. 'Ten shillings?' He looked at me enquiringly, tilting his head in a curious way. I hadnae expected that much. That would buy a chicken, totties, a cake …

But being pushy like, I said, 'How about twelve shillings?'

'Done at eleven.'

'Awright.'

He placed the ring on a gold plate. 'This is a nice little piece,' he said. He was drooling, licking his blubbery lips. 'How about five pounds?'

Lordy, I needed to hold my nerve. Five pounds would buy a lot of treats. But something nagged at me. Why was he being so generous? Of course, it was worth much more. I had the toys, I had the meal, and another card up my sleeve. I didnae need to sell the ring.

I took the ring and eleven shillings from sticky fingers that didnae want to let go, zipped the ten-bob note and a shilling piece in my purse, went home, and examined the ring under my lamp. It shone wi different shades of blue, depending how you twirled it and sometimes it even looked dark as midnight in the middle. All the little crystals surrounding the centre dazzled my eyes. I tried it on. It was a little too big for my third finger but fitted the middle one quite nicely. I returned it to its box, wrapped the only item I owned of any value in a sock, and hid it at the back of my drawer. For the first time I wondered where Mum's rings were. She hadnae worn them for ages.

Chapter 10

Christmas Fairies

The day before Christmas Eve, that something I had up my sleeve appeared like my fairy godmother. I was beginning to worry that I'd miscalculated, and that because of Dad, she wouldnae come. Mum was in the kitchen hanging the washing on the pulley, the girls were sitting on the carpet at the fire, and I was changing Martin's nappy on my knee when Morag shouted, 'Somebody's at the door.' She jumped up, fled along the lobby and clattered down the stairs, Rosie on her tail. Soon I heard an adult woman's voice, one I was familiar wi, and relief flooded through me. I scooped Martin up in his clean nappy and stepped into the hall. A fuss of bags and weans climbed upstairs. Rosie, smiling from ear to ear, gripped the biggest lolly I'd ever seen, shaped like a Catherine Wheel and covered in glitter. Morag was laden down wi two shoppers from which poked various shapes wrapped in Christmas paper. Her eyes bulged wi excitement. Behind them was Auntie Peggy, trailing in snow.

For the first time, it struck me how much Peggy looked like Dad, even though she was eight years aulder. The same dark curls, hers tamed to a wave in an old fashioned, bouffant style, the same features, strong nose and full mouth. Of course, she was smartly dressed in a mid-calf grey checked wool coat and sensible black boots. I had a sudden realisation that she was the only link I had left of Dad as Grandpa and Grannie Gallagher were both dead. Memories rose up as I watched her approach. Dad holding my hand as we climbed up a dank staircase in a close wi red tiles and the strong smell of onions. Sitting on his knee in a tiny living room wi a black iron range which took up most of one wall, two winged chairs either side where Grandpa and Grannie sat. Holy pictures of Jesus and Mary hanging under smoky glass above the fireplace. Grannie's spine bent as she tottered about, hunched up, in a brown apron. Brown, brown, brown … all around; the walls, the floor, the curtains. Grandpa in his bunnet, thick grey curls escaping underneath, smoking a pipe, puffing away like he's sucking in the smoke, putter-puff and the smoke fanning out ower his head. I blinked the memories away as Auntie Peggy came nearer.

She looked nothing like her parents, being tall and slim. They were very wee people wi bandy legs, and it was only after they died that Mum told me they both had rickets as children which had stunted their growth. Dad never talked of them after they died. I wondered if he missed them and then realised that he must've done. They loved him, and he wouldnae have visited so often if he hadnae loved them back. It was sad to me that when people died, they werenae spoken about and remembered. I resolved never to forget Grannie Meikle. I'd looked up rickets at the library to find it was linked to poverty and lack of vitamin D and was shocked that it was a common problem even now and that was why we had to take that thick, smelly cod liver oil every day. When Gran and Grandpa Gallagher passed away, one soon after the other, Auntie Peggy started to visit us, every Christmas, Easter and sometimes during the summer holidays. She'd never married, and I remembered Dad saying if she were to marry, she wouldnae be allowed to keep her important job at the Royal Bank in Glasgow. Something to do wi a marriage bar. A ridiculous rule but definitely the right choice for her. I imagined her at her grille, flicking notes, like a Las Vegas moll, gentlemen in three-piece suits hanging on her every word. The aroma of cigars, success, money …

Morag broke into my dreams, announcing, 'It's Auntie Peggy,' bringing Mum from the kitchen, hands and face still puffed red from the steam of the washing as she fed it through the roller.

Peggy smiled, the moll image replaced wi a straight-laced persona. 'Hello, Nellie.'

Mum stared, narrowed her eyes and said wi her usual charm, 'Ah didnae expect you.'

'But I always come the Sunday before Christmas Eve, no reason why I shouldn't this year.'

Mum tutted and turned back to the kitchen. I stood wi Martin in my arms, uncertain in the moment. I wanted Peggy to stay, there were the gifts after all, but I also wanted to make sure she knew how bad things were here. She was the only reliable person in the family. But Mum wasnae going to make it easy. Why should Peggy put up wi that? But Peggy merely turned to me and Martin. 'Kathleen, look at you, you're all grown up. And the bairn, the double of his father.'

My eyes darted to the kitchen. Mum wouldnae like that one. She was drying her hands and arms in the doorway; the face on her would have curdled milk. But Peggy was made of stern stuff.

'Come here Rosie, so I can see you.' She pulled off leather gloves, picked Rosie up and hugged her tight, placed her down, and put one arm round Morag's shoulders. 'I hope you've been suitably misbehaving, young Morag.'

Morag grinned. Started to tell her stories of what she'd been up to. How she'd battered that weasel boy who lived down the road, how she stuck her tongue out at the teacher, how long she could suck a gobstopper …

To my surprise, Peggy managed to keep smiling under Mum's disapproval, making her way into the living room, instructing Morag to put the bags down, shedding her coat and scarf, and plucking Martin from my arms, before settling herself on the settee. Morag was too busy watching her to notice Mum's temper, but I kept a close eye on Mum's movements.

When she went into the toilet, I sat down.

'How's things?' Peggy looked ower Martin's head, pulling on his pyjama top, which she'd spied lying ready.

Morag and Rosie sat on the floor watching us both. Morag was listening intently, catching up wi the mood now.

'Not great,' I said.

'Your Dad paying up?'

'Aye, but …' He hadnae turned up on Friday but I was to try to catch him again on Christmas Eve. I wasnae sure if I should tell her that.

'Right.' She reached down and picked up Martin's bottoms, expertly turning him ower whilst she got his legs inside. Not bad for a woman wi no kids. I was becoming more and more sure that not having children was a good way to live.

'And her?' She nodded to the toilet door.

I looked at Morag. She shrugged as if to say, '*tell her*'.

I scrunched up my face and shook my head. My eyes filled, despite myself. Morag chewed her top lip and scrunched her face, making her look a hundred.

Peggy cuddled Martin for a bit. 'Kathleen, she won't take it from me, so in my bag, there at my feet, there's an envelope. Alright?'

I leant down. Picked out a sealed envelope wi no markings and slipped it into my pocket just before the toilet flushed. I indicated to the girls by a slight shake of the head this was not to be spoken of. I knew it wouldnae be. Morag knew the score and Rosie would die rather than upset me.

Mum came in, hair brushed, face washed. She leant down and took Martin from Peggy, sat him in the pram at the back of the couch, gave him a rattle which he quickly threw out, then sat down on the armchair at the fire.

'The house looks festive, Nellie. Very nice.'

'Kathleen's doing.' She stared straight ahead at the wall, drumming her fingers on the arm of her chair, tight-lipped, the bile coming in waves. I couldnae work out if it was resentment, jealousy, or anger, but she was fizzing. I supposed it had to be strange to have your errant husband's sister sit there, pretending nothing had happened, going on as usual.

But they used to get on well. And it wasnae Peggy's fault. Mum sure knew how to freeze someone out. My heart was fluttering, I didnae know how to fix this. She needed to accept any help Peggy could give us.

Peggy ignored the angst. She smiled broadly, looking around as though this was Santa's grotto. 'Freezing out there, but you're all warm and cosy in here. And just look at this bairn, he's coming on great.'

Maybe it was her optimism that thawed Mum out. She turned, raised an eyebrow and said, 'Aye, he's a guid wee soul. Like ma three girls. Kathleen's done wonders sorting oot Christmas. Sure, we're aw set.'

I had the weans' pressies all safely tucked away in Mum's wardrobe. When Mum found out I was working for Mrs Rennie she only nodded slowly and blinked. When I told her not to worry about the presents, she nodded slowly and blinked, when I came home wi the presents she nodded slowly and blinked. I didnae know what that meant, there was no '*what a dear girl you are Kathleen*', or '*how wonderful that you've got me out of another hole*'. No, not my mother. Missus Inscrutable. And here she was, singing my praises. There was no sense to be made of her.

I didnae care, I was excited about Christmas. I'd even got a teddy and a sleepsuit for Martin and a couple of second-hand books for me, to show Santa was real. Morag, Rosie and I had made decorations out of gummed paper I'd asked Miss D for at school. As the secretary of Our Lady's, she was a useful sort to know if you needed anything at all. She had keys to the storeroom and wasnae above a bit of imaginative redirection of resources.

The place looked festive and colourful wi the gummed rings laced together and slung along the four walls of the living room pinned up wi tacks. I hadnae managed a Christmas tree though. I'd looked longingly at Mrs Rennie's in the shop, imagining it in our living room. It would be a good fit, but short of actual thievery that was not to be.

I'd harassed Uncle Jack, the butcher, for a deal on a chicken and sausages and they were promised for tomorrow. At first, he'd said no, special prices for family werenae allowed, but I told him to put it through as part of his own employee discount which Auntie Hannah was aye boasting about. He tried to argue that had a limit, but I stood at the counter refusing to move until he laughed, shook his head and promised. He was glad to be rid of me. Mum had the veggies in the larder and would do her usual grocery shop in the morning. We were all ready, though I was sure exhausted wi the work, and once fell asleep ower my desk in class, only to be wakened by the lash of Mrs Richards' ruler on the back of my hand.

'Well done, Kathleen.' Peggy kept her voice light, presumably intending to wear Mum down wi cheer. It seemed to be working. Mum's stiff face had relaxed. 'Morag, take these parcels and put them in Mum's room until tomorrow, there's a good girl. Rosie, pet, you go help.'

The girls jumped to their feet and dragged the bags out.

'Don't peek,' I said, my words already drowned by their giggles.

Mum turned to me. 'Kathleen, go and make a pot of tea and there's some biscuits in the larder.'

Dismissed. There it was again … Kathleen the skivvy. But I went, taking care to leave the door ajar. Firstly, I checked on the girls. They were having alternate licks of the lolly.

'Didn't Auntie Peggy give you one too?' I said to Morag, knowing fine she must've got a gift.

'Aye, but ah'm saving that fer Christmas.' She began to hop from one foot to the other. 'Need a pee,' she cried and bolted.

I shook my head. 'Wire in, Rosie,' I said. 'Go in our room and play till I get the tea.'

'But Kathleen, it's freezin in there,' Rosie protested, eyeing Mum's fire. There were only two fires in the house and our room would be much colder than in here.

'Awright, but no peeking in the bags.'

Morag ran back in and they both scrambled onto Mum's bed wi the sticky lolly. I tiptoed slowly to the living room door and stood wi my ear to the gap.

'Listen, Nellie,' Peggy said, 'there's no use going on at me. I can't tell him what to do. Well, I can, but it makes no difference. He's always gone his own way.'

'He's asking tae see the weans, did he tell ye that? Is that why ye've come?' Mum asked.

'No, I haven't seen him in months, Nellie. He knows what I'd say if he came near me.'

Mum raised her voice. 'He's no getting near them.'

Peggy cleared her throat. 'That's between you and him. But … what about Kathleen and Morag? They're old enough to say what they'd like.'

'They hate him.'

'Well, maybe now but …'

Mum's seat squeaked. 'Ah'll go see where that tea's got tae.'

I scarpered into the kitchen and put the kettle on the gas double-quick.

Mum calmed down and, by the time Peggy got up to leave, was even smiling, wanly, but a recognisable split of the lips. Peggy gave us all hugs, and as she left, she pressed a note into my hand wi a knowing look. It was a phone number. 'For emergencies, Kathleen.'

Although I might be hard-pressed, I'd never use that. Mum would kill me. Peggy was Dad's kin and as such no matter how kind she was, she wasnae one of us.

I put the weans to bed, and they went off fast. As I was organising my clothes for the morning the doorbell rang. I slipped downstairs to find Mrs Rennie and her son. And in his frozen mitts was the Christmas tree from the shop.

'I wondered if you could use this, Kathleen,' she said. 'It was just going to be thrown out after the season.'

Being lost for words, I grabbed her hand and shook it. She pulled me in close and kissed me on the cheek wi cold lips. Poor woman's coat was stiff wi frost.

We traipsed it upstairs and Jim managed to straighten it up in the corner whilst Mum and Mrs Rennie passed a civil time of day in the lobby. After they left, I found a plastic bag they'd dumped behind the couch. It was stuffed wi decorations. I hung bells and stars on the tree, wound tinsel all ower it and placed the angel on the top. Mum and I stood staring at it for ages.

I was worried Mum might be mad because this was, after all, charity, but she said, 'Well, Kathleen Gallagher, ye never fail tae amaze me.'

I nearly bust wi pride. Deciding this might be a good moment, I slipped my hand into my pocket, pulled out the envelope and handed it to her. She looked at me suspiciously as she opened it. I held my breath until she let go a half smile and pulled out four five-pound notes.

Chapter 11

Red Patent Bag

Auntie Ina's crate, stamped *Buffalo, New York,* arrived on a snowy Saturday in January. Too late for Christmas, but I soon shed my irritation when it shed its promised delights. Auntie Ina meant *rich* to me. Meant glamour and sophistication. When she'd visited Havoc two years ago, I could hardly believe she was Mum's sister. Mum of the thick glasses, the wax apron, perfuming all in her wake wi the whiff of Domestos. She of the red-raw wash-day hands that scoured your skin on contact, while Auntie Ina was a flower, an orchid or a magnolia, clad in silks and cottons of the purest whites and creams, perfuming all in her wake wi the floral notes of Chanel No. 5. Her lips were delicate pearl, her nails coral, her skin lightly tanned from regular *vacations* in Florida. She spoke wi a slight Scottish accent, the hint of a burr, nothing like the harsh dialect spewed out by my mother. The voice had a delicious Yankee overtone, which spoke film star to me.

When I'd said so, Mum laughed out loud. 'Ye should see her going tae her bed, Hen, withoot her wires and girdle, her fat mug creased wi face cream, her heid in rows of curlers.' Mum was such a moan.

Ower the years, Auntie had sent trunk after trunk to Mum for distribution as she saw fit amongst the family. The most memorable gift had been white leather ice skates, their blades sharp, bright and ready to go. Too bad *I* hadnae been ready to go, and they slumped in a corner of the wardrobe, like two floppy ears, for two years while my feet grew big enough to fit them. When the house was quiet, which was seldom, I'd take the skates out of the wardrobe and dream. Kathleen Gallagher in a tutu, arms rotating above her head like the fairy on the jewellery box in Woolworth's window, going faster and faster until she spun into a netted pink ball and sank her belly onto the ice, arms akimbo, spellbinding her audience into stunned silence.

Unfortunately, my feet tended to grow in fits and starts and one day the white boots were too big and, what seemed like the next, far too small.

Somehow, they'd skated right past me.

Now, a red patent handbag emerged wi a flurry. Before Mum could claim it, I barged past Morag's outstretched arms, reached ower the silken heads of the weans, and plucked it out of Mum's hands.

She raised her eyebrows. 'Och, awright, Hen, you huv it.'

I planked it in the wardrobe to examine later, thinking how the pressure of Christmas might have been relieved if the crate and its special envelope had come sooner. Auntie Ina had sent a spray of wonderful dollars too.

But I supposed Christmas Day hadnae been too bad in the end. Dad didnae turn up, but I hadnae expected him to, given that he'd deserted me on that last Friday before Christmas and no pay packet had been delivered. When Mum sent me to the Yard gates again on Christmas Eve, I stood there at the corner waiting until the place cleared, and the last of the men had disappeared into the white for the holiday. The bosses' cars rolled past, the noise of chattering women died away, and I shivered despite my anorak, boots, and the two scarves wrapped around my body tied wi a pin under my chest. My eyes nipped wi the cold as I watched the snow dance in circles around the yellow street lamps, reluctant to leave, not knowing what to say when I got home. But when I got back, Mum nodded her head as if she wasnae surprised.

'What we going to do, Mum?'

'After the holiday, ah'll sort out Assistance. We've enough wi ma Family Allowance and wages, and wi Peggy's cash, tae keep us the noo.'

I couldnae tell her about the plan to pawn my ring, but I could offer it. 'I've got Auntie Shelagh's ring we could sell, Mum. It might be worth something.'

'Och, no, Hen, it willnae come tae that. Anyhow, Shelagh? She'd no huv parted wi anything worth keeping.'

I knew better, it was worth at least a fiver, but part of me didnae want to give up my emergency stash. 'Why d'you think Da didnae turn up? Oh, maybe he's not well, and will send something.'

She slumped down on the chair opposite, frowned, screwed up her mouth as if making a decision and said, 'No, ah've been tae see the lawyer, Kathleen. He sent him a letter aboot a legal separation. That's why ye had tae go meet him aw they weeks. The lawyer said ah wasnae tae huv any contact. Noo it's at the stage of court. He'll huv took it bad.'

'Mum, you mean it? He's not ever coming back?'

'Aye, Hen.' She got up and busied herself at the sink, and I knew that was the end of that. Relief surged through me.

And it stayed wi me through the holidays despite the fact it meant we were even poorer than before. On Christmas morning, Morag had been up first and was almost to the presents before I could wake Rosie. I had to wave her bright red stocking in front of the wee one's eyes, before she came to, and realised what it was; 'Christmas,' she breathed. After that we were all set to go, wi parcels ripped open and sweeties munched. Mum got up wi Martin to a mountain of paper and we quietened to check out her mood. Morag did it more theatrically than Rosie and me, by maintaining her position, like a stone statue, a table tennis bat in an arc ower her head. Rosie dipped her head and shut her eyes tight as if about to be eaten, and I sidled in front of them both, ready to deflect the blame.

After a lull a century long, Mum smiled and, one by one, wished us a happy Christmas. She kept cheerful most of the day, and even lingered outside chapel in the snow to blether wi a few of her auld pals. She laughed once, that sharp guffaw that I hadnae heard for a long time. It stabbed me through and through to hear it.

It was at nightfall, oily darkness pressing at the window, when I noticed the tears. Mum was turning the chicken out of the oven, eyes glistening, and when she saw me looking, she blinked and tried to sniff the tears away, but one trickled down her cheek. She couldnae wipe it as her hands were occupied.

'Are you sad for Grannie?' I said. We were alone for a moment. The kitchen was warm wi comforting odours of roast chicken and stuffing.

'Aye, Hen, sometimes ah cannae believe she's gone.'

'Me too, maybe she can see us.' I smelled burning. 'Maybe she's gonna tell you off for burning they peas.'

She rushed to the hob and switched off the gas. 'That was a close one.'

As she turned towards me, I took a step forward and we banged into each other. Instead of moving away, she hugged me. I thought my heart would burst. She stepped back and gazed into my eyes. Hers were still wet wi tears and mine welled up too.

'Och, Hen. Ye must miss yer grannie as well. Especially the noo, at Christmas.'

'Aye, I do. Why did she have to go? It wasnae fair, she wasnae that auld.'

'There's nae rhyme nor reason tae it. God must've wanted her.'

'He could've waited a bit longer until Martin was two or

three and we were back on our feet.'

'Nae time would be a guid time, Kathleen. Cummoan, we need tae get finished up here.'

The moment passed when Morag barged in, blowing a whistle, Rosie behind her.

No, despite my errant father, I couldnae complain about Christmas. And the dollars were more than welcome. I returned to the emptying of Auntie Ina's crate, satisfied to receive chocolate, silk knickers wi rosebuds on and two novels. One looked particularly interesting, about The New Wave, some sort of women's liberation. We could've done wi some of that around here.

Later, I retrieved my new bag, set it on the chair under the window and looked out ower backyards to the play park along the boundary of the scheme. Outside, weans squealed as they played snowball fights, and a bicycle bell trilled. Huffing, I swished the curtains close, stepped to the door, and ear to the wood, turned the handle, teasing it shut wi a squeak.

The room took on a glow, an in-between day and night seclusion.

I rested the bag on my lap, turned it around, fingered every nook and cranny, zipped and unzipped the compartments, raised it to my cheek, let the gloss slip-slide ower my skin, and breathed in the tang of elegance. Twin compartments wi two zipped inside pockets were separated by a stiff divider, the handles erect strands that met at the apex, not quite long enough to go ower my shoulder, and it was the red of strawberries when they were fit to bust. The bag itself, if you didnae count the handles, filled the space from my knees to just under my chest. I raided my bedside drawer: my comb, a tangle of elastic bands, Kirby grips, a box of mints, two pencils, a grubby rubber, a sharpener emptied of shavings prior to inclusion, and a bluebell hanky I'd chain stitched in Primary 7. I added several red notebooks from Woollies and my buttoned-up purse in which there was one thrupenny bit and a couple of pennies, put in fake cigarettes, the ones that tasted of icing sugar, and a sachet of shampoo.

I unfurled my socks, rubbing at the red lines circling my calves, pulled my jumper ower my head, unbuttoned my blouse, slipped out of my skirt, and waltzed up and down in front of the mirror in my slip, feet arched to replicate high heels. I held the bag on my arm, fingers splayed at my cheek in the way catwalk models posed.

I flounced down on the bed.

The bag was clunky on my arm. Mum would groan if she saw my antics. I emptied it out on the candlewick cover, inserted it in a pillowslip, handles sticking out in protest, and laid it on the top shelf of the airing cupboard. Like the skates, it was no blooming good to me.

The dollars had put Mum in a better mood. We couldnae get them changed at a bank, as we didnae have an account, but Mrs Rennie did that for her customers, so we had a bit of a windfall.

Mrs Rennie had let me away wi working my debt off after Christmas, but asked me to get Mum's signature, which I duly did, and she paid me cash after that for any hours I could come in. Any earnings went to Mum, of course, but I didnae mind. We were hard up, and I enjoyed the work. Mrs Rennie and her son were cheery souls and there was aye grand banter going on as they worked. They'd discuss what was on the tele, the news, and local gossip wi cheery optimism as if the world was a place of endless entertainment. Even particularly vile subjects like the debate about hanging ended up painted wi gallows humour. Though Mrs Rennie did throw a pack of toilet rolls at Jim's back, when he joked about them having to make an extra big trap for him after he'd murdered her for nagging. He didnae even notice. It was like pitching a feather at a mountain. It amazed me that people could be so content in work and I was pleased to be around them. Besides, it was more time away from home and the chores.

Mum gave me half a crown from the dollars, a fortune. But I was worried about taking it as I knew we were skint. But she pressed it on me, and I bought three pairs of stockings, two to keep as new for when needed. It was aye a worry not to have stockings now without runs at the weekends.

Mum had claimed Assistance as a single parent. Well, actually she fell into the deserted wife category. Anyway, that meant Morag and I could have free school meals. Of all the events in the last few months, this was the most excruciating. Other than Grannie dying, of course. It meant queuing up each morning before the bell rang at the secretary's office, wi the whole school walking by for assembly, to be allocated a free meal ticket which you handed in at the door of the canteen.

I got used to it, but only after I squared up to two or three titterers who thought it was funny to be in that queue. After I got my ticket I chased after the loudest of them and slapped her hard on the back, so she stumbled along the corridor and fell on her bum. It was strangely silent, not a breath to be heard as I loomed ower her and asked her if she'd anything to say to me, she seemed to be taking an interest in my business and I'd like to know what exactly was concerning her. Her pals stayed well back as she muttered, 'No, no me, nothing, honest, Kathleen.' I pulled her close to me by the tie, so the blood ran to her face. She was terrified, blubbering now, and to my shame this gave me a deep sense of satisfaction and power.

Pushing her away, I turned on my heel, thinking this must be what violence felt like.

I had no more trouble, but it still galled me to have to stand in that public queue. It didnae seem to bother our Morag. Mind, hers was a different queue, wi wee-er sniggerers. Only after I saw her squirreling jam pieces in her schoolbag, did she own up to selling her ticket for pennies. I wished I had her guile.

Chapter 12

A Mockingbird

We were on Assistance but there was an upside. Mum wasnae allowed to work more than two nights a week, or she'd lose the extra wages from her Assistance. I thought this was a bit daft, myself, even though it was an advantage to me. They didnae give you enough to live on, and when you tried to make it up, they took it back. I imagined we must be the poorest family in Britain, so I read up on it. There was absolute poverty which was they poor folk in Africa suffering famines, and there was relative poverty. We were relatively poor, not starving, just hungry most of the time, and freezing in this Arctic weather, which was okay wi they government tossers who were in charge, who lived in central heated mansions and drove Bentleys. But the good thing for me was that I had most evenings free, or relatively free. There was no absolute freedom in my house. I still had to help wi the tea, the washing up and bedtime.

Hockey became impossible in the frost, so I took up netball. Being fleet on my feet and a higher jumper than anyone else in my year, they made me welcome. It meant I could stay on after school, get some peace on Mondays and Wednesdays, miss the teatime shift, washing up, and the noise. Martin was teething and his wee gums were red-raw. When he bawled, Rosie bawled as accompaniment, and Morag thumped around as chorus. Though not keen on it, netball was a sacrifice I'd conjured up as a rescue plan, though I didnae sell it that way to Mum. What I said was that Sister had personally asked me to help her out as there was a low take-up of the sports this year and I was very athletic. That wasnae true but the gym teacher had said I was the fittest girl she'd seen for a long time. That was down to hoisting prams, hauling bags, and dodging slaps. Added to that my diet was a subsistence one, mostly relying on school dinners. At home, Mum could barely make us a sandwich for tea, or we had to make do wi boiled eggs or tottie soup. She couldnae be bothered wi anything, but at least she hadnae the energy to give you a skite.

Somehow, I was popular at school, possibly because I was mature for my age, playing Mother most of the time. My powers of negotiation had advanced by having to get myself and our Morag out of scrapes on a regular basis. I liked School and School liked me. My grades were up, and after the Rennies, it was the one place I felt appreciated, if you left out Mrs Richards and the poor man's queue. Schoolwork wasnae difficult and I had a flair for science and maths. My English wasnae bad and I liked French. Mum never came to parents' nights, or to sports days, which suited me fine. Anyway, we couldnae both be there, and I could represent myself.

Pals I had a-plenty. In fact, it was getting quite difficult to please all of them as I was part of several groups; the sporties, the brainy-bugs, and the rough kids. The brainy-bugs included Amy Roberts and I liked her company. Amy and I hadnae spoken about the party. She gave me a shy smile whenever we met in class and we'd pass the time of day. I shrugged the whole business off. Other girls were mean and sniggered behind her back. How I hated those two-faced snobs, but I hadnae the time to waste fighting other folks' battles. The best I could do was ignore them and take Amy's arm now and then for a confab. That showed them not to mess wi her, as she was now a pal of mine. She was smart, got a hundred percent on tests that I could only manage ninety on. And she knew all about American politics and Art, pictures and that, by the great masters. She read as much as me and was the only one I knew who'd read *To Kill A Mockingbird*. We both loved Atticus and she planned to go to Glasgow University to study law. One day at break, she asked me what I was going to be.

I laughed. 'Me? Probably end up in the factory, sewing cups, like Mum.'

She was appalled. 'You need to be more ambitious, Kathleen.'

'I *am* ambitious, but have no money, unless the ring my Auntie gave me is worth a few pounds, and even if it is, that'll go to support the house.' University was out of the question for the likes of me.

'There's bursaries and grants coming in, Dad says.'

'It's not only that, I need to earn to help keep the house.'

It was a terrible worry though; a fist took a grip of my insides, so I gathered my stuff and made the excuse I needed the loo before class. My future felt like a long, hopeless trudge through stagnant water, which, like Mum, would eventually drown me.

The pressure to have contact wi pals after school was rising. This was something I couldnae easily do, not having the freedom I deserved at my age because of a crabbit mother and neglectful father. Mind, I was glad he wasnae coming back. The place might be a madhouse, but it was better than the horror show it had been when he was drunk. We didnae have a tele like most of my pals so I had time for homework and reading, so long as the weans were asleep. For a while that sufficed.

Then Chrissie joined my class.

Chrissie was nearly a whole year older than me. She'd been held back at her previous school due to her *misfortune*.

I hadnae the nerve to ask what this might be, putting it down to the fact that her parents were divorced. Actual divorce was unheard of in my social circle, and this was a Catholic school. Separation was common, but not divorce. No, you were tied wi shackles to the bastard you'd been foolish enough to marry for the rest of your days. Apparently, it said so in the bible. Something along the lines of what God has joined together let no man put asunder. And that was another thing, where was the woman in this equation? Anyway, Chrissie's Mum must've got some sort of dispensation for her daughter to be allowed in.

That first day in class, Chrissie stood at the blackboard, hand on hip, toe pointing forth, the pink tip of her tongue darting between top and bottom lip, and announced wi a smile, to Teacher and a room full of bored thirteen-year-old girls, 'Hi guys, I'm Chrissie Hall.'

Hi guys. To the teacher. How mature was that?

A frisson sizzled through my spine as Chrissie tossed back her silver hair. It was like frost on a windowpane, and her eyes were sharp green, like two polished emeralds, the effect startling. She had a figure too, a bust that thrust from the V of her cardigan. Mine was like two fairy cakes, even in the bra Mum got me from the factory.

We became friends. I ditched the sports nights to go around to Chrissie's where we talked about boys, experimented wi her mum's make-up and imagined lots of grown-up things we would do when we reached sixteen.

Chrissie lived a few streets away and far enough to ensure our parents didnae meet casually. I couldnae bear the thought of Mum showing me up in front of Chrissie's much younger and more with-it mother. I was welcomed like a daughter in Chrissie's house. Her stepfather worked all sorts of shifts and her mother, Jackie, did her catalogue selling from home, often going out in the evenings to take orders and collect payments, leaving we girls, '*my little angels*', to ourselves. Jackie had the same silver hair and startling eyes as Chrissie but fine lines on her face were patterned like a spider's web. 'It's the fags, girls. Fags and sex, puts years on you,' she said, focusing a moment on the cigarette poised between two fingers. Chrissie smothered a snort, but my face burned.

Sex was unknown territory. I'd just had my first period, which of course I'd expected at some point, but the reality was disgusting. It happened in the toilet after I peed, blood pinking the water. I stacked toilet roll in my knickers, but the blood just ran off. I had to call mum into the toilet, and she moved like lightning to get me one of those awful sanitary towels, like insoles for big men's feet. 'Mind and keep it well up in front,' she said, fastening the sanitary belt around my waist. Even wi that they wouldnae stay put, and there was aye that nagging worry you were leaking. Not to mention the cramps that rippled through your belly like fire. I knew some boys, of course, two second cousins about my age and one much older, but I couldnae think of them as potential boyfriends, the thought made me grue. Otherwise, there was only the boys at chapel, or those who ran in packs downhill from the boys' high school. An uncouth, ugly tribe, lacking brains or any sense of manners. The men I liked played in pop bands, had even, white teeth, were scrupulously clean and well-groomed, or much older. No, the men I liked knew how to treat women.

Chrissie and I went around arm in arm. She told me she'd had loads of boyfriends. When I told her I liked an aulder more sophisticated fella, she scolded me. 'Kathleen, older men are dangerous. I'm sure we can find you someone just a little bit older and wiser.'

That took the wind out of me. I had a lot to learn and Chrissie was just the girl to guide me.

Some of my mates didnae like her and kept their distance. It was only jealousy because she was so good looking. And because they thought I should go around wi boring auld them and talk about what was in the Co-op window this week, or play jacks, or skip, for Gawd's sake. They were all so childish.

Even our Morag was better company. She kept me on my toes. I'd hidden my diary where she couldnae find it, back of the red bag on the high shelf in the airing cupboard because it had loads in it from my conversations wi Chrissie. I couldnae chance that coming into Morag's hands. And I made sure Mum didnae notice the jam pieces disappearing into my annoying wee sister's schoolbag. I couldnae do anything about the nits though, and we all ended up wi the antiseptic shampoo from the health clinic and the bone comb that took a layer of skull wi it. We had to wash our hair wi the special shampoo. I did Morag and Rosie's in the bath before doing my own in the sink. Then we knelt down on a towel in the living room whilst Mum scraped the bone comb ower your skull again and again. The good bit was when she scraped the back of her thumbnail across the comb and you heard the crunch of a nit getting its due. Mum said nits preferred clean heads and that's why we had them, but I knew for sure that Morag's pals were all mockit and that those nits didnae discriminate when looking for a new home.

Morag was blind to lamp posts, walls, and other such obstacles most people could see a hundred yards away. Her face was a multicoloured rainbow of bruising. For most of February she sported two black eyes. The penny fell when she sprained her wrist running into a postbox. A postbox on the edge of the play park that had been there for a century, bright red wi a big white sign in front. At the hospital, after they examined the arm, the doctor suggested an eye test, and lo and behold, she was so short-sighted it was a miracle she could see her jotter. Turned out she wasnae as stupid as she looked, she hadnae been seeing what was on the blackboard her whole school life. Why, oh, why had no one ever noticed that?

Probably because she wasnae teacher's pet at school and had been written off as the class clown. Another thing that wasnae fair in our lives.

Chapter 13

In the Soup

The weans were in bed asleep whilst Auntie Hannah and Mum gabbed in the kitchen. Hannah gabbed for Scotland, only took a breath to blow out smoke. The kitchen was thick wi it, swirling and banking at the ceiling like fog. Mum had cut down because fags cost good money, and Hannah didnae help, lighting up one after the other. I aye had to pick up the ashtrays after she left, dribble in some water to avoid fire, and dump the ash and stubs in the bin.

One good thing about Hannah being around was that I found out what Mum was up to. The pair acted as though I was invisible, like a servant girl in one of Kipling's stories, wafting about in a sari, appearing blind and deaf to the antics of the rich and powerful, saving up nuggets of information to use against them later. Course, I was in the living room in my navy school skirt and jumper, wi the door ajar, studying, my jotters and textbooks fanned out on the floor on one side of me. The other side was stretched out toasting at the fire. My ears perked up when I heard Hannah ask:

'So, whit did the lawyer say?' She said it casually, as though it was an everyday occurrence to talk to a lawyer.

Mum replied, 'Cause the hoose is in his name he could throw us oot anytime he likes.' There was a strong hint of bitterness in her tone, that fatalistic edge she had.

'Ye're kiddin, Hen.' I detected a breathy fascination wi bad news.

'Naw, the rent book's in his name. That means ah've nae rights.'

'Huv ye asked him tae sign it ower?'

'Naw. Ah'm no going near him.' She paused and then … 'Ah'm gonna let sleeping dugs lie.'

'Whit aboot the Cooncil? Will they no get him tae sign it ower?'

'Ah huv tae be legally separated first. Depends who has the weans.'

Hannah was silent; I imagined a waft of smoke billowing up and around her. What did this all mean? Who was paying the rent? Mum, Dad or the Council? What did she mean, who had the weans?

Hannah piped up, 'Who's paying the rent?'

'The Board's paying me an allowance fer it. As long as ah'm living in the hoose wi the weans. But the lawyer says ah've tae apply tae the council fer a change of tenancy.'

That was a relief. It'd surely be a formality. But then, Dad wouldnae just hand the house ower. He was mean that way.

Hannah said, 'How'd ye no jist get a divorce and be done wi it?'

'Father Murphy says ah'm awright getting this separation as long as ah dinnae go fer a divorce. That's no allowed. Ah'd be excommunicated.'

'Jeez. But that means ye cannae get merried again.'

'Whit? Ah wouldnae entertain another man in ma life as long as ah live.' She shouted this out.

'Aye, right enough, Nellie, right enough.'

The gab went on to a monologue from Hannah about her weans.

I put down my pen; I hadnae written anything anyway. Mum was a dark horse, I knew she'd been to the lawyer but she hadnae cracked a light about the priest. The house was in Dad's name and she didnae have any right to it. So far, that was awright as he wasnae asking for it, holed up as he was wi this other woman. But he could do, if he wanted. That wasnae fair. Mum was in danger of returning to her worst self. Already she was having headaches, shouting at us weans, and I could do nothing right for doing wrong.

Hannah peeked into the living room to say goodnight but lingered long enough to frown. 'Keep a wee eye, Kathleen. She's no looking guid the day.' This worried me further.

Hannah never made comments about Mum to me.

After I went to bed, all the possibilities raced around my head. What if we were thrown out of the house, where would we go? No one else had space to take us all in. Worse, what if we had to stay wi Dad, and Mum was someplace else? Who would watch out for her? And wee Martin, he didnae even know Dad. No. I wouldnae go to live wi Dad. What happened to families like us who had no place to go?

I couldnae find answers and worried myself to sleep, waking up next morning wi a sore mouth. I must've bit the inside of my lip during the night; it stung like hell.

Saturday lunchtime, I lugged the shopping bag upstairs. Then went back for the pram. It was to be tottie soup again. 'Blame yer father fer that,' Mum said. I did, it was self-evident. But I didnae see how that would do any good when he wasnae here to face the consequences. Once Martin was settled, I made space to sit down, moving a book from the armchair and Mum spat out, 'What good will books dae ye, ye'll leave school and help keep the hoose.' It was as if Dad's meanness was my responsibility.

Mum was working herself up to a temper, and her whole demeanour had set like stone. Morag hung back behind me whenever I moved, and Rosie watched me like a hawk, in case I might disappear. I picked Martin up on my hip where he was unlikely to make any noise that would send Mum scurrying in to slap us at random. She busied herself making the soup in the kitchen but she wasnae content. The veggies got chopped to smithereens and she muttered while working, her voice rising and falling, reprimanding some invisible entity. I wondered, not for the first time, if my mother was demented, and that sent a spike of fear through me as we couldnae do without her and those that were in charge might see fit to take her away in a straitjacket. That wasnae a random thought. It had happened to other women in the scheme, women known for their 'nerves'. Carted off to the loony bin, never to be seen again. Unless they'd already gassed themselves or thrown themselves under a train. One woman had tipped herself off the town bridge, breaking her neck, leaving three wee weans without a mother.

It was odd that you never heard of men doing those things. Seemed to me women aye had the short straw, or maybe men just drank away their woes.

Morag scratched her head, 'Whit's the matter wi her noo?'

'Money.' I grabbed the scratching hand and forced it away.

'Can she no jist go and ask Dad?' Fingers from the other hand dug into the matted curls.

I sighed. 'Done that, nothing came.'

'Ah hate him.' She had glasses now that made her eyes twice their size and they were brimming dark blue like the sea. She didnae hate Dad, she had aye been his favourite.

'Aye. I know, but never mind.' Not much of an answer that, but my attention was elsewhere.

Mum was still clattering and banging in the kitchen, and I kept the weans in the living room, busying myself changing Martin. No point waiting to be shouted at for not doing it. Morag pulled out her board games from the cupboard and whined at me to play wi her. I shushed her, as whining would just set Mum off, and told her to set up snakes and ladders. I threw a few rounds, and then got Rosie to take ower, even though she couldnae count and Morag would cheat her silly.

There was an almighty roar. We froze, the girls' eyes

locked to my face. I put Martin down beside Morag, and tiptoed to the kitchen, worried that Mum had hurt herself, but even so, she could still be dangerous. She stood at the sink shaking but seemed all in one piece. A fire? No. Her fists were bunched at her sides, the veins in her neck knotted like pipe cleaners. 'Mum, Mum…' I stepped close and reached out to her arm as she slumped forward ower the sink, letting out a great quiver of a breath. Then she drew herself up, turned and rushed past me. Her bedroom door banged. I went to the kitchen door to see Morag and Rosie peeking out of the living room. Morag chewed her lip; Rosie was breathing hard and I could hear the beginning of a wail. I caught her up in my arms and hushed her. When Morag saw the coast was clear, she edged along the wall into the kitchen. I put Rosie down and fetched Martin who was sitting on the snakes and ladders board. We followed Morag.

'Whit is it?' she asked.

'I dunno.'

Carrot stalks, turnip and butcher's paper lay on the counter and after I slipped Martin to Morag, I automatically started to clear them into the bin.

'Gies a bit of turnip,' Morag said, cautiously watching the door. I cut her a slither off the hard rim.

The pot on the stove was bubbling, its lid off. Mum wouldnae leave the lid off the soup pot. I picked up the spoon to give it a stir while I turned down the gas and that's when I noticed the green slime. The soup had something odd in it. The washing up liquid was next to the cooker, the salt was ower on the table. Both were alike, white, plastic tubes. 'Oh Lordy,' I said, 'there'll be no supper tonight.'

Morag poked her nose in. 'Is that washing up liquid?'

'Aye.'

Rosie's wee face lit up. 'Is there bubbles? Can ah see?'

I lifted her. Her eyes widened when she saw the damage.

Morag said, 'Mibbe we can start again.'

For once, she had a good idea. 'Right,' I said. 'Out the road. Morag, see to Martin.'

She yanked him up from her hip, slipped him into his chair and the girls sat at the table while I got the sieve and poured the liquid into the sink.

I rinsed the hock thoroughly, and the hard veggies; totties, carrots and turnip. I let the onions go, they looked greenish. I chopped more onions, added a couple pints of clean cold water, pepper and proper salt and set it all up again. It smelled good and there were no bubbles. The weans ate pieces-n-jam to keep them going, and Martin a rusk, and then I thought about Mum. A cup of tea might help.

'Morag, take the weans into the living room, till I go and check on her.'

Morag's face fell. 'Ur ye sure? She might still be mad.'

Another astute comment from Morag. I was terrified, but someone needed to be the adult here. 'It's awright.'

I poured a cup of tea, added milk, tiptoed to Mum's room, and tapped on the door.

There was no reply. Maybe that was enough. By tapping she'd know I was concerned. I didnae need to go in. Pressing my ear to the door, I listened. The sound of sniffing. Gawd, I nearly ran out of the house. But instead, I steadied my hand, so the tea stopped shaking, took a deep breath and opened the door.

The curtains were closed, the wardrobe and dressing table bulky shadows. Mum was lying in the darkened room, fully clothed on the bed, her chest rising and falling too quickly.

I stepped in and, thinking of Auntie Peggy, pretended cheer. 'I fixed the soup, Mum. It's awright. Here's a wee cuppa. Have a good rest, I'll see to the weans.' Even to my own ears, I sounded manic. Avoiding her gaze, I put the cup down beside her on the bedside table.

I was fixing to leave, my heart drumming, when Mum groaned and got up on her side.

'Ah cannae believe ah done that,' she said, staring at the floor.

'Naw. Well, they look the same, easy done.'

We peeked at each other, me biting the inside of my cheek. She looked terrible, her hair ruffled, her eyes swollen. When she started to cry, I stood there, aghast, unable to conjure up a miracle, unable to move. She reached out her hand and I let her pull me down onto the edge of the bed beside her where she continued to grip my arm until the tears subsided. Then she let go and blew her nose. I was afraid to breathe so I just sat there, saying nothing. It was only a pot of soup, not that important, my brain told me. But I knew it wasnae only the soup. It was the whole bloody mess.

'Kathleen, it's awright, Hen. Ah'll be fine in a minute.' She sniffed and raised herself on one elbow.

'It's all been too much, Grannie, Dad, the money and everything …' A tear welled up, spilled and I wiped it wi my sleeve.

'Aye, a run o bad luck. Just got tae me there, whit, wi the soup and me being so stupid.'

'You're not stupid, Mum. It was just a wee accident. It's sorted, anyhow.'

She patted my hand. 'Off ye go, Kathleen. I'll jist rest here a bit.'

I got to my feet, heart thumping, and crept out of the room.

Chapter 14

Egyptian Mummies

It was five when Mum got up; we'd just finished our soup. She looked like an invalid tottering up the lobby, fingers splayed to the sides, eyes deadpan, hair sticking up. As she came closer, she tried to smile. I noticed the skin on her face was tinged blue and a vein in her neck throbbed. Whilst my mum was never a great-looking woman, this was a travesty of her former self.

Morag said the soup tasted of bubbles, but she ate it up awright, dipping in four slices of plain loaf thick wi margarine. I'd kept some soup warm for Mum, but she said, 'Couldnae stomach it, Hen,' and lowered herself down on her usual chair only to stare out of the window. Morag took one look at Mum's blank face, lifted Martin out of his seat, and scarpered. Rosie clambered down, stood stock-still, and at a nod of my head, fled. Mum fumbled in her cardi pocket, took out a pack of ciggies and her lighter and, after three attempts, managed to light up. I poured her a cuppa and let her be. I didnae know what else to do.

As the days went on, she got some of her energy back but was closed off and sullen. There were no more half-hearted smiles. I wasnae able to read her moods. Morag became hypervigilant; she'd lost her spark and although that was a pain, it was better than this stalker creeping about the house. Wee Rosie had taken to scratching and pulling at her clothes. Her buttonholes were so stretched, Mum, slack-faced, stitched them tight. And when Rosie's hems came down, where she worried at the stitching, Mum just sewed them straight again without a word. Rosie took to holding her breath until her face became puce and someone had to slap her on the back. Martin was Martin, crabbit and clingy, but he was just a baby.

On Sunday afternoon, I sat on my bed, the quilt around me, my homework abandoned in its valleys and hills, so distracted by the rain battering the roof and thrashing the windowpanes, that I couldnae concentrate on my work. But at least Spring was around the corner and I was warm under my covers.

This relative peace and quiet gave me space to think, but Dad's face intruded and I couldnae push him away. Tears rushed to the back of my eyes but I didnae let them fall. He didnae deserve the privilege of my tears. Course, he wasnae here to see them, anyway. I thumped my pillow and lay down.

I tried to nap, but the sound of the rain trickling down the window and the weans clambering around the living room kept me alert. Mum was round at Patsy's. She'd wanted the weans to go wi her, but Morag whined about the weather, and Mum just turned away, shrugged and took Martin, happed up in the big pram.

Dad's face loomed again; jovial, satisfied, and I wanted to punch it. At least he wouldnae be coming home. In the past, Mum had aye changed her mind and let him back in, but this time she was determined. Of course, this time he hadnae asked to come back. He had other priorities.

I sat up and hugged my knees against my chest. I was being childish. No one was all bad. It was easier for me when Dad was around, at least when he was sober, as he looked after the weans when Mum was out, might dry dishes if in the mood, carry the heavy bags and entertain us when it was raining, wi jokes and stories of the fairies and spirits

103

of the town. Did he take the pram up and down? I couldnae remember. No, he left soon after Martin was born.

That had been a bad night. I lay my head on my knees. Most Friday and Saturday nights he came home drunk, sometimes on his own, sometimes wi his cronies, men full of the drink, sucking up to the big man, and I'd wake to his rousing and teasing of Mum.

Mum, a woman who was not one to rouse or tease without repercussions. That night he brought company, trailing the salt and vinegar smell of fish and chips and the stink of whisky into the house. There was laughter, interspersed wi Mum's complaints that they should pipe down, Martin and the girls were asleep. Later, after the mates had gone, it was only his voice I could hear effin and blinding. There was something about the tone of it that scared me; the effin and blinding had become personal to Mum; it was her that done effin this or effin that, her fault, the bitch, he couldnae keep his hands to himself. I'd sat up, my ears cocked, and didnae relax until I heard Mum flush the toilet and pad into the bedroom. I waited till I was sure they'd be asleep, got up quietly so as not to wake Morag and Rosie, tiptoed into the kitchen and surveyed the damage. The place smelt of fag ash, sour whisky and congealed fish batter. Dregs of flat beer left in glasses littered the table. I tidied it up to avoid more bad tempers in the morning, boaking at the stains left on plates and glasses mixed wi ash and doups. Leaning down to wipe the floor, I spied blood spots on the linoleum. I pressed one splat wi my forefinger; it was oily, thick, a dark crimson, one of an array of splats. My heart banged in my chest even as I wiped it up and wrung out the cloth in the sink.

Next day, I stared Mum up and down but couldnae see any cuts. Could've been one of the visitors cut himself, I supposed. Maybe it was Dad's blood. No, I discounted that. Even though Mum was slap-happy wi us weans, she'd never hit an adult. That was a norm that she kept to. Hitting weans

104

was the way you brought them up. Hitting Dad could be fatal when he was drunk. Mum wasnae daft.

He'd left that morning and I hadnae seen him until … aye, at Grannie's rosary.

Now, I lay back and listened to the rain beat down on the roof. The snow had finally cleared, but then the rain had come. We were aye soaked. Rosie had a permanent snottery nose. But at least we'd survived the winter. Mrs Rennie told me three auld ladies had died of pneumonia and I'd heard talk of bairns who'd been found dead in their beds. Lucky for us, Mum had prioritised the shillings for the meter so both fires could be used, and Martin was aye snug. She said we were lucky in Havoc as the houses were well built, some folk in Glasgow were still in slums.

Dad came to mind again. He could tease Mum back into a good mood easily, the only person I knew who could do that. How could that be? I certainly couldnae. I sat up. Mum needed to see the doctor and get some pills or something. Who would know? Maybe I could ask Auntie Shelagh or Aunt Patsy. Or Auntie Hannah. But, no, I dismissed that. This was Mum's own personal business and anything that went on in this house stayed in this house.

I flopped back down, recalling better times when Mum used to laugh and play wi us. She liked draughts and listening to plays on the wireless and sometimes we even had parties where she would lead the sing-song. My mum had a good singing voice, high and sweet and she could fair hold a note. I'd forgotten that. We went every week to Grannie's, to eat cake and drink squash, and run about her back green. Sometimes Dad came too, and he'd chase us down the street to howls of laughter. No, that hadnae been me, now that I thought of it, that had been Morag. I'd stood watching at the gate.

It occurred to me that I didnae like my own dad. I tried to love him, to get along wi him. It would start wi some teasing and then he'd go too far, and I'd get annoyed wi him and go off in a mood, hearing him call out, 'Run run scaredy-cat.' He was too loud, too full of himself; he'd say the wrong thing. Like the time he said he didnae know where I got those brains from, couldnae be him, and certainly wasnae Mum, she was a stupid cow. He laughed at that, full of his wit, but I'd already turned away, my face flushed. And he'd go too far wi the games. He had to win, and he'd cheat. He aye had a trick up his sleeve. And he was unreliable wi the pocket money. We were supposed to get a shilling on a Friday, and sometimes it was left on the mantelpiece and sometimes it wasnae. You went to fetch it and it wasnae there. Morag bawled and I shrugged, sour as lemons, just like Mum. He'd said that very thing to me, when I met him the first time at the Yards. Just like Mum. Could that possibly be true? Naw, I wasnae like my mother, so crabbit, so ... unappealing.

Morag adored Dad. Crikey, I wondered if she missed him. She said she hated him but maybe she just hated him for leaving.

She was better off without him.

I sat up, lifted my jotter and worked on an equation for a minute, but couldnae get it to balance.

Sure, it was scary having a dad like Marty, but wasn't that normal? Lots of my friends had Dads who drank. Seemed to me our town was a drunk's paradise. Every second shop was a public house. And there were the whisky factories too, where the stuff seemed to flow into jars in men's pockets, which they drank, or sold for a fraction of the price in the pubs. I didnae know how the bosses allowed it; surely if it was common knowledge, why did they do nothing to stop it?

Morag startled me, thudding down on the bed. 'The sheet's fell aff the tent, Kathleen.'

I shifted ower, kicked down the eiderdown, swung my legs around and sat up. 'Aye, I'll sort it. But wait a wee minute. Here, budgie up.' I patted the cover.

Her eyes narrowed, but she edged nearer. 'How?'

I realised she expected a row; she was up to something, but I let that go for the moment.

'It's awright. I just wondered if you missed Dad?'

'Naw, don't be daft.' She dropped her gaze to the carpet, crinkled her forehead and twisted her mouth to one side, but she didnae move to leave.

'But you really got on wi him, not like me.'

'Aye, that wis when he was guid, noo he's a bad man.' She screwed her eyes shut.

'Well, he's not any different really. Would you like to see him, maybe?' I shimmied closer to her, our shoulders touching.

She chewed her lips. 'Dae you want tae see him?'

I hadnae anticipated that. If I said no, she might take that as the end of the matter. But I didnae want to see him. Course not.

'I'll see him if you will.'

'Who says we can, anyhow?' She turned and looked me straight in the eye.

'Well …' She was right, he hadnae asked. Was probably glad to see the back of us.

Morag was wiser than me; I was raising a dead donkey.

She let me off the hook. 'Naw, it'll only make Mum mad. She cannae stand any talk aboot him.' She got up. 'Cummoan, the tent, Rosie's stuck underneath.' She pulled my arm and I groaned.

Wee Rosie was wrapped up in the bedsheet so tight she couldnae get up on her feet. She looked like an Egyptian mummy rolling in half-turns on the carpet, her mouth sucking at the sheet for breath. I unrolled her and thumped her shoulders so she could breathe. Morag hunched her shoulders in her 'wisnae me' pose. So much for losing her sense of mischief.

Although I was glad to see that, I couldnae let her away

scot-free.

'Jeez, Morag, wee Rosie could've been smothered.'

'Don't be daft, Kathleen. Ye'd never let that happen.'

Total trust filled her eyes and I was ashamed of how I'd been thinking and acting about our dad. Morag thought he was a bad man but he wasnae bad, just vacant, like there was something missing. I had two parents nothing short of disturbed and there was nothing to be done about it. But Morag was right about another thing. Mum didnae mention Dad by name anymore. If he had to be mentioned it was aye '*him*', or '*he*', never '*your dad*' or '*Marty*'. He'd been wiped off the slate, that was for sure. Probably for the best.

Chapter 15

Nae Winchin

Daffodils had dared to peek above the ground, and I'd taken a hike myself, growing at least two inches taller than Mum. I'd filled out a bit too, my bust reaching a size 32A. It was Saturday afternoon and the house was empty, they were all away to the cemetery. Wearing only my knickers and bra, I turned in Mum's full-length mirror, stretching my neck to examine two evenly spaced dimples at the top of my bum. I wondered if that was normal, maybe only people like me, who had dimples elsewhere, got them. I pulled on my dress, socks and cardi, closed the door, dragged a stool to the airing cupboard, stretched up and pulled down my red patent bag.

Anticipation bubbled up as I drew it from its pillowslip, kissed it and imagined myself walking into the Odeon wi my date, looking like Helen Shapiro, a sophisticated woman. This evening I'd have a real use for the bag, instead of the occasional outings in front of the mirror. Excitement brought nerves to my tummy and I needed to pee.

After tea, I filled the bag wi my bits and bobs. Oh, glamour indeed. Mum had agreed to me going out to the pictures wi my pals. What she didnae know, wouldnae hurt her. Between the pram, Rosie's pushbike, and various other obstacles, I levered myself along the lobby. Mum shouted, 'Dinnae be late.' My delight was brought up short when I encountered Morag sitting on the bottom step, picking her nose, waiting for me. She rose as I shrugged past.

109

'Ye don't look like ye're goin tae any picture hall,' she drawled, her head nodding coyly. She exacerbated the strange sight wi a pout and a knowing glare. I ignored her and banged the door closed behind me. How come she'd got wind of my plans?

Soon Chrissie and I were scurrying down Main Road arm in arm, Chrissie's pearl lips luminous in the dusk, my eyes heavy wi her mum's mascara. We giggled about the date this evening. We'd arranged it that afternoon in Capaldi's. Packed to the gunnels on a Saturday, we'd squeezed our way in, heady wi the hit of coffee, vanilla and dark tangy chocolate. I was quite overcome wi the chance to be in the café. We never went to cafes or restaurants. The highlight of a meal out was fish n' chips in a poke, or a scone before a concert in the chapel hall. Mrs Hall gave Chrissie pocket money every week, without fail, and had given me a shilling, pressed into my hand for a wee treat.

Chrissie gave me a push. 'Get a move on, Kathleen. We'll miss those seats at the back.' A party of four were vacating a booth and I twisted through tables and slid onto the bench, Chrissie bagging the place opposite.

She leant forward, her cleavage misted wi talc as she sloughed off her jacket. 'Did you see those guys eyeing us up as we came in?'

Before I could fully turn around, Chrissie grabbed my hand. 'Don't, you'll look too keen. Let me reel them in.'

'Oh, right.' I concentrated on Chrissie's face, those emerald eyes, the perfection of her cheekbones, the full lips. She was gorgeous and far more sophisticated than me. She'd had loads of boyfriends and knew how to flirt.

'Two Irn-Bru ice creams please.' Chrissie's ice-eyes glinted ower the waitress's shoulder as she wiped our table. It wasnae long before those eyes swept two good-looking fellas ower to the booth. They slid in while I pretended fascination wi my orange infused bubbles. Before I sooked up the last of my Irn-Bru, a date had been made for that evening.

Now, I scanned the queue at the picture hall. People waited in pairs for the evening show, their conversations billowing up and down the line. Mum would kill me, and these days she really would actually kill me. We didnae know anything about these boys, they werenae local; maybe they wouldnae turn up anyway. I jumped at a tap on my shoulder and turned to a wink and a lopsided grin. Under the lamp light, I didnae recognise the face.

Chrissie was allowing her date to kiss her full on the mouth. This one had to be mine then. Bill. I smiled in a manner that was just right.

Funny, but I could have sworn Bill was much younger in the café, maybe the half-light had tricked me. This fella looked … well, ower eighteen. A whole five years older than me. He might expect a kiss like Chrissie's date, Tom. No way was I going to kiss him in this queue. Or maybe even at all. He wasnae that good looking, his face red from the cold and his chin pitted wi acne which became angrier at his throat. Chrissie was acting all Brigitte Bardot, pouting and flashing smiles. I wished she wouldnae do that, there might be local folk who knew our mothers. How did we even know if *Bill* and *Tom* were their real names? I hurried on into the dark hall, breathing again once we found our seats. But not for long. Bill nudged my arm and passed a flask.

I whispered, 'What is it?'

'Vodka.'

What if someone noticed and we got thrown out? I'd die of shame. 'No thanks.'

'Suit yersel.' He took a slurp.

That's what was wrong wi him. He was half-cut. I sat forward and tried to concentrate on the screen, my heart pounding at my ribcage. When he slid his arm around my shoulders, I stiffened.

'It's awright, Doll.' He breathed booze into my face.

Caught between the urge to get up and run, and the embarrassment of appearing a fool, I decided to sit it out. And besides, I couldnae leave Chrissie alone wi them both. I glanced ower. Tom's arm was around Chrissie's shoulder and his hand flopped far too close to her breast. I flushed from my forehead to my knees.

It took me a few deep breaths to calm my nerves and I held fast to the handbag on my knee. Bill seemed to have got the message when he withdrew his arm and settled back. He was absorbed in the film, some war story. When the lights went up at the intermission, I tried to catch Chrissie's attention, but her eyes were glued to her date as though she was desperately in love. Bill asked if I liked the film. I nodded and tried to smile. He wasnae so bad, he seemed to have sobered up, was being relaxed and polite, and he fetched me an ice cream tub. But I couldnae concentrate on the rest of the picture, being sandwiched between Bill and Tom, alert to every squeak and shuffle at either side.

As we left the cinema, I tried to shake off my date. 'I'll be off home now, thank you, goodnight.'

He laughed and caught my arm. 'Ah'll take ye hame sweetheart, don't want ye gettin intae any bother noo, dae we?' There was a wheedling in his voice that gave me the heebiejeebies but I didnae want to cause a scene wi the crowds milling around. He had me firm by the arm. There was no sign of Chrissie.

'Maybe we'd better find Chrissie and Tom?'

'Don't worry about them. They're huvin a great time. Least he is.' He laughed.

What happened between that and being wheeched up a close, I had no idea.

My back was being driven into the freezing tiles on the wall. The bag bit into my leg under the weight of him; his breath and tongue were all ower my face. 'Cumoan, relax,' he kept saying. I tried to scream but his mouth muffled that soon enough. Someone had to come home from a night out, return from work, go out on the night shift. I tried to kick out, only for him to wedge a knee across my thighs. My arms were pinioned to the wall by his chest. He stank of cloying aftershave and sour sweat. When his hand crept under my skirt and groped my bum, I bit his tongue and he yelped, but he still held me tight.

A door opened, spilling light into the stairwell. A man's voice. 'Hey, whit's goin on here. Nae winchin up this close.'

I wailed, but it came out like a snort.

Bill said loudly, his hand relaxing, 'Only havin a wee kiss o ma girl, nae bother auld yin.'

'No. No. I'm not his girl.'

The man went back in. I gave Bill a shove, got an inch of space, freed one arm and drove my bag hard under his chin, caught him off balance, swung the bag again at his head and registered a crack as he squealed. I stumbled out of the close mouth, scrambled up, looked around for someone, anyone, but the street was empty.

'Whit the …' His voice propelled me on.

The street was a line of tenements wi dark, yawning closes, only the occasional spangle of light breaking four storeys of stone. I raced away, only turning at the corner to see Bill sway and stamp in the middle of the road clutching his head. Like a two-bit actor in a cowboy film.

I kept running, past streets of tenements until I reached the play park. Though it was inky black ahead, I'd have to risk it. Tendrils of misty breath flickered into the darkness. Clouds patched the night sky, masking the moon. I stepped gingerly through the gate, fingers fluttering at arm's-length to feel my way, and tripped. Steadying myself, I inched forward on the path and as my eyes adjusted to the dark, made out the slide on my right and the swings on my left, eerily glowing under the row of lamps on the far side. When

I heard footsteps approaching me, my throat tightened. I stumbled again and was steadied by a hand at my elbow.

I looked up, terrified.

It was Mum. 'Hen, ye're awfy late. Ah came oot tae look fer ye. Cumoan the way hame.'

When we reached home, I took off my boots at the door, and climbed up to the lobby. Mum was already stepping into her bedroom, curlers under her scarf, wrapped against the night. She made no attempt to flip the switch and there was only the yellow tinge of a streetlight seeping into the space between us.

'Och, Hen, get tae yer bed noo, and dinnae wake the weans.'

The third degree didnae come. No explanation was asked for; where were my pals, why I was alone, why I was late, how come I was made up to the nines? It was as if she just couldnae be bothered. A bit of luck coming my way at last.

I dropped the red bag, fumbled for my flannelettes from under the pillow, went to the toilet, stripped, and scrubbed my skin red-raw. My cheeks flushed cherry in the mirror, partly from the freezing water and partly from the roughness of the facecloth. When I switched off the bathroom light the house pitched into darkness, and I felt my way into bed to the sound of my two wee sisters breathing. I hoped my thudding heart wouldnae wake them. Mum might not be interested in my shenanigans, but Morag's nose would sniff out my shame.

I lay awake fretting about Chrissie, and when sleep finally came I dreamt that her body was lying face up in a ditch near the Common, her silver hair matted and tangled in weeds. Her eyes were closed but sprang open when I leant down to touch her cheek. She whispered, 'It's all your fault, Kathleen Gallagher. You left me on my own.' Worse, I woke up during the night, my heart racing from the effort of running along the banks of the Elvern, trying to keep abreast of Chrissie's body as she floated downstream, soaked and bloated, extremities nibbled by the fishies.

Chapter 16

Aftermath

On Sunday morning I woke wi a splitting headache and could hardly open my eyes to the light. The house was up, the noise levels pierced my ears, but I rose, dressed and kept my head down. Though Mum threw me some long looks, she didnae say anything. Morag noticed Mum's attitude and copied that, so even longer stares came from my sleekit wee sister's bespectacled midnight-blue eyes.

She fished, 'Wis the pitcher guid, Kathleen?' Her whole body adopted an attitude of disbelief, her toes pointing one way, head inclined in the other direction, nose in the air, one hand sweeping away imaginary supplicants behind her.

'Aye. It was.'

'Whit wis it aboot?' Now she gave a knowing flutter of the eyes.

'War story.'

'Och, whit did yous go tae see that fer?' Her jaw dropped.

'It was what was on.' My voice rose wi every reluctant answer.

'Don't need tae shout.' She adopted her poor-wee-me look.

I washed the breakfast dishes in a fury. For once I was glad to be going out to Mass.

It was aye a rush job, there wasnae time for conversation.

Whilst I worked, I planned. I had to find out if Chrissie was okay. She didnae ever go to Mass, so I'd have to go to

116

her house after lunch, but that was a long time to wait. It was only half past nine. What if someone had seen me last night? What if Bill told people that I was easy?

My heart jarred in my chest. Mum was going to kill me yet. I needed to talk to Chrissie. Assuming she hadnae really been murdered, she'd know what to do, how to handle all this.

Mass was a trial; the murmured prayers, the over-loud choir, the priest's bawled-out sermon. My nerves almost shattered. We were in a pew next to the Virgin's statue. Her beatific face looked down on me wi pity as her foot crushed the long, winding, fork-tongued, red-eyed, mottled snake. I prayed for assistance; surely the Virgin as a woman wouldnae condemn me, whereas I knew God, a man, would be happy to throw me through the gates of Hell. I even thought of missing Communion, but that would raise eyebrows, and anyway, what had I done wrong? Only lied to my mother, lied to my friends, lied to myself. I wasnae prepared for dates, if this was what dates were about. All this raced through my head as I said the *Our Father,* as I knelt at the communion rail, as Father Murphy looked down on my bowed head, eyes drilling through my skull.

Could he see what was running like a movie in my mind: the sleezy rubbing of my backside, the putrid stink of breath, the rasping of an acned chin on my cheek? I shivered as I rose, and nearly tripped ower the next communicant. Mum, next to me, threw a question. I shook my head, *it's awright.* I could swear auld Murphy narrowed his eyes in denigration. He could spot a mortal sinner from five-hundred yards and here was I in front of him receiving the good Lord's body, my soul black as thunder.

'Teach oh teach me how to die' gave up its final breath. Even Mum sighed in relief at the end, and we filed outside. The sun shone, the sky was largely blue, and the daffodils sighed in their clumps, but all of that only served to make me

feel exposed. I would've rather had cloud and rain, a storm even, so I could muffle my face instead of having to arrange my countenance into something that would pass for equable. Morag sidled along beside me, stealing glances all the way home. She'd quietened and that worried me because it meant she'd realised this was more than a teasing matter.

At noon I could bear it no longer. I called to Mum from the lobby. 'I need some homework pages from Amy Roberts.'

'Awright, Hen, dinnae be long.' Whilst my mum showed no interest in my schooling, she never interfered when I mentioned homework or books. Using Amy worked as Mum easily accepted that she had study materials, whilst the rest of my pals wouldnae have pages of any kind.

I ran all the way to Chrissie's. When I turned the corner, I slowed, caught my breath and tried to think straight. Was she okay? Was she alive? Of course she was. It would've been all around the town by now if she wasnae. All the same, I needed to check. Images of her poor abandoned body still cluttered my mind and now, despite my reasoning to the contrary, her eyes, mouth and ears were attracting pond life.

I knocked the front door, noticing for the first time how worn it was, the green paint peeling, the glass in the window cracked, the net curtain blotched and stained yellow wi age. My mum would die of shame rather than have her front door greet visitors in such a state. But Chrissie's mum had better things to do. Maybe my mum needed to widen her horizons.

Feet thumped down the stairs, a key turned in the lock, and the door creaked open. Through the crack, Chrissie grinned at me. She was wearing a pink baby-doll nightie that sloped across her breasts and swung about her thighs. I was mortified, my face burned.

'Kathleen. Come in.' To my horror, she swung the door wide. People would see her nakedness from across the street. She peered in my face. 'Are you sick or something?'

She seemed cheerful enough as she dragged me by the

arm upstairs to her bedroom. I tried not to look at her bum rising before me. I'd been in that room many times and it was still untidy and dishevelled, but I hadnae noticed actual dirt before. The once beige carpet was blackened in places, and stained in others wi orange juice. Silver hairballs billowed ower the clutter on the dresser. The window was dust-caked and her bed looked as though the wrinkled mustard sheets had never been changed. There was even a dark faded blood spot the size of a half crown.

She slumped down onto the squeaking bed and the nightie slid up her swan white thighs. I didnae know where to look.

'Is your mum and dad not in?' I glanced at the door.

'Gone out for the day. We have the place to ourselves.' She patted the bed and I perched on the edge, careful not to land on the sheet, but keeping my seat firmly on the coverlet, the soles of my shoes slip-sliding on the filthy carpet. And there was a sour smell too. Sweat certainly, and body odour, but not Chrissie's. Hers was a sweet perfume, probably the Coty L'Aimant she liked.

What was the matter wi her? I thought she'd be as distressed as me. Of course, maybe her date was fun and she didnae know about mine. But there was something else. She was acting – well – like a harlot. I laughed at myself. What exactly did a harlot act like? This wasnae a movie or a love story. But she was flouting her nudity. And she was batting her eyelashes and smiling coyly at me. I didnae like this new Chrissie. My eyes filled.

'Chrissie, that Bill attacked me last night.' I burst into tears. To my shame, they came in floods. She hugged me tight, the cool flesh of her bare arms and chest making my skin crawl. And from her breath I smelled sherry. I turned, gasping through my tears. On her face was a knowing smile. A smile that belonged on a woman of more advanced years, a smile I associated wi loose women I'd met in novels. Not a fourteen-year-auld school pal.

'No, he didn't, Kathleen. He told me you became hysterical when he tried to kiss you. You got the wrong end of the stick.' She thumbed away my tears.

'You spoke to him?'

'Yes. He caught up with us at the bus stop. Me and Tom were… well …you know…'

She stroked my hair. I cringed.

Looking her square in the face, I shimmied away, appalled. 'No, I don't know.'

'We'd just finished doing it, you ninny.' She giggled at the memory.

Shock plastered my face and I could hardly move my muscles to speak. I whispered, 'Chrissie, but you don't know him. Them. They're strangers. Anything could've happened to you. I was worried sick.'

'Don't be daft, Kathleen. I know how to take care of myself.'

'But what if you get … you know …?'

'He used a rubber, silly.'

'What's that?' Shame seared my cheeks.

'Gawd's sake, Kathleen! It's a rubber sheath, you know, for …' She looked pointedly downwards.

Shock upon shock was coming in waves. She was an expert, knew all about sex. Well, that was awright for her.

'But Chrissie, it wasnae like that, he tried to force me …'

She tutted. 'I should've warned him you were a virgin. He probably just went a bit too fast, sweetie.' She patted my arm again and I shivered.

She was still smiling, sitting there in her see-through nightie, roseate nipples plain to see through the sheer fabric, quite relaxed, totally believing what this arsehole had told her instead of what her best friend was saying. I'd been stupid all along.

I got up and backed out, ran downstairs and out of the front door to high pitched laughter, unable to dislodge new images of Chrissie's exposed breasts under the lamp light.

Chapter 17

Free Spirit

After calming down, I figured that no one was ever going to find out about Saturday night. Chrissie would hardly tell anyone she was easy, and those fellas werenae local. It was a narrow escape. I'd learned my lesson. Though it occurred to me I should've known better. Going out wi a stranger was foolhardy. What had I expected? Romance? I laughed at myself, if anyone knew romance was a fantasy it was me. Though, I was confused about my friend.

She was a sweet girl most of the time and I'd grown fond of her. But who was this minx in her bedroom on Sunday?

Chrissie didnae appear at school all the next week and finally on the following Monday, it was announced at assembly that she was moving away and wouldnae be returning to school.

Somehow, the bad stuff faded, and I was left wi this peculiar longing to see her. I couldnae shake the notion that something was badly wrong. Being too damn curious for my own good, I took another chance and went around to her place after tea when her parents would normally be out, hoping she hadnae moved yet. At the very least I had to say goodbye.

I knocked on the peeling wood. The net curtain quivered, and the door opened a crack. Chrissie's pale face filled the space. 'Chrissie, you awright?' I tried a weak smile. She opened the door and gestured me into the empty living room.

The television was on low, figures moving about the black and white screen. I stood in the doorway; she sank down on the couch and I sat across from her on a wing chair. She wasnae her usual bubbly self; she was morose.

I said, 'Teacher said you werenae coming back to school?'

'My schooldays are over.' She pulled her legs up beneath her. Tonight, she was well covered up in brown cord dungarees and a polo neck sweater. She rolled her eyes upwards, blinked, and to my horror a tear fell, then another, until they ran off her cheeks in fat drops. I held my breath, paralysed, until she wiped her face wi her sleeve, sighed and looked straight at me.

'Got preggers, haven't I?' She dropped her gaze and twiddled her signet ring.

I watched it burl and twist on her finger, not knowing what to say. Pregnant. There might be worse things, like death, but even that ... I finally managed a garbled, 'Does your Mum know?'

'Yes. I'm to go to my Aunt's in Newcastle tomorrow. I'll write you when I get there, I don't know the exact address.'

The loss of her welled up in me and overflowed. I wiped tears away wi damp fingers. She looked up, stopped twiddling, came ower and knelt in front of me, her bright eyes now locked wi mine. Again, I was struck by how beautiful she was, all silver and light.

'I'm sorry, Kathleen. I'm not the person you thought I was. It was good being her for a while, though. Being your pal was the best thing. I'm sorry I spoiled it all.'

'No, Chrissie, you are who I thought you were. I'll miss you.'

'I'll miss you too. You're the best friend I've ever had. Shit, you're the only friend I've ever had.' She laughed through her sniffs.

'Go sit down, you eejit,' I said through mine.

She sat back down and brought her knees up to her chest.

'I was careless. Now up the spout. Serves me right.'

'No, it disnae. It's not your fault.'

'Tell Mum that. And him.' She spat that out.

'Who?'

She bit her lip, curled up tighter.

I was lost. How could he know? 'You mean the father?'

Still no reply. My heart was thumping but I was afraid to stir. She was looking out of the window at nothing, just street lights breaking the smoky-blue dusk.

After a long moment I said, 'But you don't know Tom, we could try and find out …'

'No silly, not him, he has nothing to do with this. That was only days ago. I'm much further along than that.'

She blew out a breath, caught my gaze and held it. I was terrified. This was ower my head; pregnancy, sex, babies.

'James, my so-called stepfather.' She looked directly at me, eyes wide, hammering home some point I wasnae getting.

'Oh, he won't be happy I guess, but …'

She laughed. And it was in the bitterness of her laugh that I heard the truth. I clapped my hand to my mouth, and she nodded.

I started to shake, and a chill shot through me. That slimy bastard, his hands on her lovely skin, his mouth … My stomach turned making me gag. Chrissie rushed ower, pulled me up and led me into the downstairs toilet. I knelt at the pan and heaved but got up after nothing came. 'Sorry, Chrissie, the last thing you need is me being a wimp.' I washed my hands and face and spotted them dry wi the dirty towel from the rail. She took my hand and led me back into the living room.

We sat together on the couch. I said, 'You must tell … the polis.' Images flooding in showed me how ridiculous that was. How could anyone talk to loud Sergeant Brown in charge down at the Town Hall? I saw Chrissie at the public desk accusing her stepfather, Brown's ridicule caked on his face. 'Your mum, Chrissie. For Gawd's sake.'

'She knows, pretends she doesn't.' She sighed heavily.

'Tell her, make sure she understands. She'll kick him out.'

'Oh, Kathleen. My mum isn't like yours. She's afraid of her own shadow.'

I'd no idea, Jackie aye seemed confident to me. 'Chrissie, come home wi me.'

'That'll be right.'

'You cannae stay here.' Somehow, I knew Mum would take her in. A bolt of pride shot up my spine; for all she was a witch at times, my mother had plenty of spunk. She wouldnae let a pal of mine be left in danger.

'I'll be fine at Auntie Lisa's. She's okay.'

'Does she know?'

'I'm preggers? Yeah. She'll help me. I won't keep it.'

'No, I mean does she know about …'

'Oh, you mean, know about him? No chance, and I won't tell her. But I won't ever be back here. Don't you worry.'

'How could this have happened and I didnae know.' I was greetin now, like a wean, a poor excuse for a pal, but I couldnae imagine a worse predicament to be in.

'Honey, it was a secret, still is. I don't know why I'm telling you. He'd kill me. He's sly too, he's hurt Mum before. Said he'd kill her if I told anyone. And I believe him. Look.' She rose from the couch and hurried into the hall where I heard her rummaging. When she returned she held out her hand. Something glinted, it took me a moment to recognise it as a blade. My stomach tightened. It was the sort wi a bone handle and serrated sharp edge. 'He has several of these, and the first time he threatened me with this one.' She shivered.

'Put it back.' I couldnae bear the sight of it, and I panicked that he might come home any minute.

I followed her, ensuring she slipped it into the inside

pocket of a duffle coat.

'When did it start?' I asked.

'When he moved in … oh, three years, maybe.'

She was eleven. Just a bit aulder than Morag. Morag, for whom the world was a giant playground. I wanted to scream. I didnae. Instead I made myself buck up and hug her tight.

We sat down on the couch and stayed squashed together for ages.

I said, 'When's your Mum back?'

'Soon. You better go, Kathleen.'

'Aye. Listen. I'll write down my Auntie Shelagh's address. I don't want to lose touch. Write to me at Shelagh's so my mum doesnae open it. Awright?'

Her face brightened. She hurried to a drawer, pulled out a notebook, tore off a piece of paper and found a pen. I got up, scribbled the address, folded it into her hand, kissed her cheek and we hugged again.

'Oh, and you, Kathleen Gallagher. You do great things. Right?'

'Right. Chrissie, let me know how you go. If I don't hear from you, I'll be worried sick.'

She closed the door softly behind me. I turned back to ask one more question, but it was too late. What had she meant she wouldnae keep the baby?

Chapter 18

A New Pal

I was packing my kit after hockey when a weight pressed me into the bench. Wi the riot going on around me, I assumed somebody was being pushy, shoving me out of their road, and I pushed back. Turning, I saw Amy Roberts fall back a few steps into two other girls, her eyes full of alarm.

'Sorry, Amy, I didnae hear you there,' I said, grabbing my bag. I fastened myself to her arm and led her through the throng.

At the door she said, 'I just wanted to say I'm sorry that Chrissie's left. I know you were close.'

Talk had gone around school that Chrissie had fallen out wi her parents. When they asked what was going on, I said it wasnae anybody's business but hers and I glared at them making sure they got the message.

Chrissie was unique. Others didnae understand. I hoped she was okay and tried not to think about that sod of a stepfather. Or that night at the pictures. I was in no hurry to repeat that fiasco. The promise I made to become a nun was less of a worry now; on the contrary, it was an attractive prospect.

I took Amy's arm and walked her across the playground asking her all sorts of questions to change the subject. Did she like hockey, I could get her on the team, and how about a game of jacks at interval? She was all smiles at that, and when she smiled her wee pale face lit up. For the first time

I noticed that she was pretty in a quiet way; pale, thin and mousy, aye, but her hair was fine silken gold, and her grey eyes actually a light shade of blue wi darker flecks.

I liked her. She was smart, didnae fool around like a lot of my friends and we were in the same boat as far as parental problems were concerned. We didnae have to say so, we just knew.

We started to go about at school. My other pals werenae happy. 'Whit ye dain wi that snob,' they said. 'Mind aw that English disnae rub aff on you.' As if someone's dad's nationality was a disease. I began to see my pals in a new light. They had no ambition in life except to leave school and work in the factory or in a store, until they got hitched. Which was fine for them. None of them had bothered to ask me how I was coping now my dad had left us. Nobody seemed to think anything of it, and I supposed in a lot of ways it was the norm round here. Women just got on wi it. Thinking about it, I took the same attitude when other families broke up. But mulling it around more, that wasnae very nice of me. Seemed to me this was a deliberate policy of those in power, mostly men, to keep women down. It was clever, get the women to keep each other in the gutter by accepting their lot.

I walked the jagged edge of loyalty until I was forced to choose between Amy and one of my roughest mates, Jeannie Blair. Jeannie was a tough cookie, bottom of the class and content to stay there. She aye teased me about my books and going to the library, but I just smiled and kidded her on that I could get her a baby book anytime. She sniggered at that but took it in good spirit because she liked me, followed me about like a puppy and it was Kathleen this and Kathleen that. But I knew she could be vicious if cornered and liked to keep her tough reputation in good nick.

It was morning interval and I was on my knees playing jacks wi three pals, and winning, when a rush of legs came into view, and a gaggle of girls threw themselves into the circle. 'Kathleen, it's Jeannie. She's battering Amy Roberts' was what I heard first off, followed by, 'She's got her in a heid lock and Amy's face is aboot tae bust.'

I jumped up and raced around the corner to the other side of the building where there was a concrete yard we used for ball games. A row of girls stood in front of a pair who were conjoined in an odd dance. I pushed myself through the line, which was strangely quiet – these fights usually occurred within a circle of noisy baiting – grabbed Jeannie's forearm, my face in hers, and spat out, 'Let her go, you big dope.'

Jeannie's attention span couldnae deal wi both Amy and me and her grip on Amy's neck loosened enough for her victim to squirm out and stagger away. That left me to deal wi Jeannie. Red-faced and breathing heavily she looked like that fat jowly dog her Dad kept tied up wi rope in their yard. Her pea soup eyes glared at me and I knew reason was beyond her. I had to fight her.

*

Sister Philomena's office was as dark and dire as the confessional box. There wasnae a grille, but there might as well've been, it was so bleak, poky and terrifying. Especially when you were standing there wi your enemy, shaking like a pair of leaves under that wimple-bordered inscrutable face. A sash of wooden rosary beads circled Sister's waist, wi a cross of Jesus the length of your palm, a talisman of her righteousness, swinging from the centre. And the broad leather belt in her right hand wasnae there for effect.

'Kathleen Gallagher, I cannot believe you are standing here before me in this condition, fresh from what can only be called a schoolyard brawl, a dogfight, a …' She drew herself up, seeming to have run out of breath, apparently wi the shock of discovering her one-time star pupil wi blood on her hands and no alibi or possible defence to offer. All I was thinking about was the beating I'd get from Mum and how I could possibly endure the shame.

The strap was nothing. I'd had it before in primary school, everyone had.

Jeannie had the cheek to giggle and I leant against her shoulder to calm her shakes as that wouldnae go down well for either of us. We werenae hurt really; I'd scraped my knee on the concrete when I fell under the weight of Jeannie's body as she hurled herself at me. It had bled profusely, but that had stopped. Jeannie had some scratches on her face, but that could have been either Amy or me. After the first round, I got back on my feet and we circled each other, wi plenty insults flying and the odd jab landing, the audience standing well back, silent no more as witnesses to a fair fight, throwing in encouragement to one or other of us, until someone shouted, 'Sister's coming.'

'Well, what have you to say for yourself, Kathleen Gallagher?'

It was an odd question. What could I say? So, I said that. 'Nothing.'

That seemed to be the right answer. She turned to Jeannie.

'And you, Jeannie Blair?'

'Me whit, Sister?'

Sister sighed heavily; her shoulders slumped. 'Off you go, Jeannie Blair, back to class, wash your face first, and I don't want to see you in this office ever again. Do you hear me?'

Jeannie scarpered, but not before giving me a worried glance. We both knew I was in for it because, as in everywhere else in my life, I was the one who should know better.

'Sit down, Kathleen.'

She put down her strap. It slithered from her hand to the floor, well out of reach, as I sat down on a chair in front of her. It was odd being on the same level as her; although she sat ramrod straight, my chair was a bit higher. Maybe it was so she could look directly into your eyes and see your soul.

All the dark splotches of sin spattered there.

This made me want to giggle so I closed my lips tight and tried to think of sad things, like my grannie in her coffin. That sobered me up. Tears pricked and I felt a rush of longing for my poor grannie. And I felt a rush of pity for poor me. I took a breath. Sister's eyes bored into mine. I looked away; this was unfair. Why didn't she just get on wi it? She was known for her quick decisions, and although a bit of a battleaxe, I'd aye found her fair. Not a likely disher-out of torture.

She folded ower a page on a notebook in front of her. It had her own neat writing on it, a lovely italics, a style I couldnae quite get right myself. She folded back another page as if looking for an entry in a diary. 'Ah, here we are.'

I stiffened.

'Your grades are down, Kathleen. In maths, physics, yes, even chemistry. Mr Abernethy isn't happy. He wanted to put you forward to represent Our Lady's for the interschool cup.'

Jings, I didnae know that. I nearly jumped for joy, before it set in that my grades were still down.

'I can do it, Sister. I'll work harder.'

She closed the jotter, sighed again, in that way I knew only too well. Kathleen Gallagher was a big disappointment.

'And now this … brawling. Kathleen, this is not like you. Tell me what is wrong.' Her eyes lasered into me. For the first time I noticed how pretty they were, a sage green wi very light lashes. I wondered if her hair was blonde under the wimple. Maybe it was shaved like a penitent and the image of her in undies, prostrated in front of a giant cross, intruded.

'Kathleen.' She raised her voice.

I caught up. 'Nothing.' What did she mean what was wrong?

'I've had reports from your teachers that you are … let's say quick to … offer your opinion whenever you feel someone is being critical.'

What was wrong wi that? 'Just standing up for myself.' I realised I was pouting and forced my lips upwards.

'Problems at home?'

Lordy, I was squirming now. You didnae say anything about what went on in the house to anyone outside.

'I'll have to get your mother and father in.'

'Oh, no, please, Sister, don't. I'll work harder, honest.'

'Kathleen, I can help you. I'm not asking you to betray a secret, only to share a problem. One you have, not anyone else's.'

I considered this, head down. I could do wi some advice. Maybe I could put it in a way that didnae mean telling my worst family business.

'Hmm, well, I'm not getting a lot of sleep, Sister, at the minute. The baby cries a lot …' That wasnae enough, she sat waiting implacably. 'And my grannie died, you know, Mum misses her a lot …and she's sad. You know.'

'Ah, I see. Maybe there's some help she could have for her sadness. It's not uncommon.' She stood up. 'Kathleen, no more brawling and we'll say no more, alright?'

'No, aye, definitely, Sister, thank you …' I was crawling now, but I backed out of the cell, blowing out in relief, and hared it back to class.

Amy was beside herself, worry carved into her delicate features. I sat down across from her and winked. I was feeling rather pleased wi myself having got the better of Jeannie, though that wasnae anything to brag about really, and Sister had let me off the hook.

Jeannie caught up wi me at home time. I strode on but she ran-walked beside me.

'Kathleen, did ye get the belt? How many straps?'

Hers was an open face, albeit a bit squinty, and on it I saw respect. Time to lay down the law.

'Jeannie, I took a few belts but it's fine. I said it was all my fault. Seeing as you got off scot-free, I want you to

131

promise me something.'

'Aye …' Suspicion leaked from that one word.

'Lay off Amy Roberts, right?'

She twisted her mouth from side to side, trying to weigh up the pros and cons, but Jeannie had no sense of balance in terms of decision making. So, I just told her. 'Touch her and I'll belt you.'

'Awright, then.' She thumped me playfully on the forearm.

Jeez, I was nothing but a punchbag, that was for sure.

Chapter 19

No Trace Left

I trundled upstairs wi my bursting schoolbag to a quiet house which made me suspicious. I peered round the living room door expecting there'd been a gas attack and my family had expired. But Mum was sitting on the couch gazing at the table in front of her. I'd never seen a ten-bob note escape in this way, it was either tightly clutched or hidden in her purse, not open to prying eyes.

Morag and Rosie stared as though it might bite. When I came in the room, Morag did her big *oh* mouth and stared even more pointedly at the note. I wondered if it was a dud, and if so, we'd be in hot soup.

Mum looked up and said, 'Joe McDade from the Saint Vincent de Paul was roon. Said this was tae keep us going and he was sorry fer ma trouble. He said he'd be back every Wednesday. How'd he know?'

Gawd, Sister Philomena. To distract any possible link to me I said, 'Mum, you aye say you cannae keep a secret in this town.'

'Aye, right enough.' She swept the red bill into her purse, patted it and smiled.

Morag squinted a question through the thick glasses; she could winkle out any hesitation in me at forty paces.

I left Mum to it, and Morag followed me into the bedroom, sat down on the bed, her head cocked to one side. 'Was it you that got it fer her?'

133

'Course not, how could I?'

'A wee word in auld Murphy's ear, mibbe.'

'Wasnae me.'

She stood up and laughed. 'Liar, liar, pants on fire.' Then she rushed at me, pushing me onto the bed, planting a big slabbery kiss on my cheek.

Things were tough, but at least we didnae need to depend on Dad's wages and Mum got her National Assistance and Family Allowance every week. The factory manager was good and set her hours according to the amount the Board said they would disregard. I babysat the weans at night when she went out, but had three nights in the week off, which was fine for now. We were independent of Dad and never saw him. He wasnae mentioned in the house, and the photo album had blank spaces where photos of Dad had once been. His stuff was gone of course, clothes and shoes, but now even his shoe polish had disappeared. Whisky and beer glasses had been thrown out. All traces swept away as though he had died, or worse, had never lived. But he had lived; I saw him every day in wee Martin, who was his image, and even in my own face when I looked in the mirror. Especially wi my ponytail when I looked more like a boy than my trendy teenage self. I couldnae talk to anyone about him, not Hannah for sure, or Mum. Whilst that would've been a recipe for a broken jaw a few weeks ago, now she'd likely burst into tears. I'd rather have the broken jaw. Or maybe I could talk to Patsy. No, she would only tell me to never mind. She ignored you unless you spoke right into her face. I sometimes wondered if we had a genetic link missing in our family. One for brains.

Becoming more and more worried about Mum, I was tempted to phone Auntie Peggy.

But that seemed disloyal given she was Dad's sister and, given what I'd heard Mum say at Christmas about him wanting to see us, it might look like I missed him. I considered

Shelagh, but she was an anomaly, was too wise and would ferret out my very soul. Hannah wasnae a possibility, she would pooh-pooh it, and I couldnae go to Sister Philomena. She'd sent the SVP, but they were all fellas and though the money was welcome it didnae solve the 'sadness' problem. Mum was getting more and more gloomy. The slapping and shouting had stopped, which really concerned me, despite the relief. It was like a kind of exhaustion, a couldnae be bothered wi anyone or anything stupor. She slept a lot more too. Either in the chair, or in her bed before going out to work, and she sent me and Morag for the shopping now. Most early evenings, I took Martin out in the pram for his walk.

It was a Saturday when, on one of these walks, I ran into Amy in Elvern Park. She was wi her mum; it was the first time I'd seen Mrs Roberts awake. They walked hand-in-hand laughing, and Mrs Roberts flung her head back as though she hadnae a care in the world. She even twirled around, right there on the path, her dress billowing out around her lovely slim legs. They approached me as I pushed the pram, Rosie on the front, Martin bouncing against his reins. Morag had elected to stay home. She announced that she was getting kind of auld to be seen wi the likes of us in public. I did worry that she might get up to some mischief, but she aye wore me down, or had some blackmail at the ready.

Amy grinned and peered into the pram. 'Hello, little man,' she said.

Mrs Roberts cooed at Martin and patted wee Rosie on the head, laughing jovially. I wondered if she was quite awright now I could see her up close. She looked a bit demented. Her lipstick was askew, and her Panstick wasnae rubbed in right, giving her a blotchy skin tone. Her cardi was buttoned up wrong, so that the hem was uneven by a whole button's worth. Amy saw me staring and reddened. I looked away and when I turned around again, Mrs Roberts had gone off to look at the fountain. Amy watched her closely until a man's figure came around the bend. He hurried to Mrs Roberts and took her arm to steady her. She dipped her head onto his shoulder and let him lead her to a bench. They sat there together holding hands. It made me smile to see that, and it occurred to me that I'd never seen my mum and dad hold hands. I was overcome wi the vision of Mum and Dad fighting in the kitchen, her baiting him wi insults and him growling back, the growls becoming fiercer and fiercer until he slapped her, and she screamed. That time I must've been quite small, watching at the kitchen door, struck dumb. Mum rushed by me and he sat down heavily on a stool, head in his hands. Whose fault was it? Should Mum have shut up? Did anyone deserve to be assaulted? They should never ever have been married. But if they'd never been married, I wouldnae exist, and neither would Morag, Rosie or Martin. It was doing my head in trying to work it out.

Amy broke into my thoughts. 'Can't take them anywhere.' She looked ower at her parents.

'Is your mum awright?'

'Not really.'

We sat together on a bench. When I let Rosie down from her perch, she ran onto the grass and flopped down to watch a brown spaniel chase a ball. Martin was content to stare at the sky. Ower at the swings a boy stood on the seat of a swing, got it going high, jumped off backwards, ran underneath, and steered clear when it swung back to stop it hitting him. It was a new game called Jumpy and the trick was to catch it at the critical point. This boy was like a circus acrobat as he skipped off backwards and sailed under the arc of the seat. I tutted because it was dangerous and foolhardy.

Amy was speaking. 'She has depression. It's called manic depression. Sometimes she's blissfully happy, and other times she's suicidal. The doctors are trying to find the right balance of pills, but that's not working at the minute.

They're talking about more ECT.'

'What's that?'

'Electroconvulsive therapy. It's so horrid. They have to strap her down and put these wires on her head and literally shock her.' She squeezed her eyes shut.

I was heart sorry for Amy and her mum. 'Dear God. That's awful.'

'Yes, but it does help for a while.'

I couldnae see how that could possibly be, but I didnae want to interfere. We sat watching Rosie play for a moment. I wondered about my own mum.

It came out before I realised. 'My mum might be depressed, I think.'

'What makes you think that?' Amy watched Rosie pick daisies.

'At first, it was like she was angrier than usual, she'd slap me about, and shout. Morag too. Don't get me wrong, she's aye done that. All the aunties do. But it was much worse after Dad left. You know my dad left, don't you?'

'Yes, I did wonder.'

'But lately she's just gone into herself, as though she's not tuned in.'

She turned and met my eye. 'How do you mean?'

'Like, today. She gets up, doesnae get changed, tells me to see to the weans, go to the butcher shop, get sausages, and maybe some eggs, gives me some money, doesnae look at me once and then goes back to her bed. That's happening a lot at the weekends and evenings when she's no at work. In the daytimes when I'm at school, I don't know …' It occurred to me I didnae know what she did or how she looked after Martin and Rosie on schooldays.

'Sounds like depression. How old is Martin?'

'Nearly ten months.'

'Could be postnatal depression. Some women get it after having a baby.'

137

'I think she was fine after that. And she was okay too after Dad left. Relieved maybe.'

'When did it start?'

I thought back. It was hard to pinpoint, but maybe … 'After Grannie died, I think. Not as clear cut as that, she has rallied from time to time, but then something else happens and she goes down again.'

'What's happened recently?'

'I don't know. Nothing. Well, actually she had all her teeth out. But she was fine after that. Except maybe it could be the money.'

'Gosh, all her teeth out?'

'Yeah …' I shivered and licked my teeth all the way round wi my tongue.

'And she hasn't any money?'

'Not enough. We're on Assistance now, Dad isnae paying, and Mum's only allowed to earn twelve bob a week. She cannae work full time because of Rosie and Martin so it has to be National Assistance.'

Amy drew herself up straight. 'That's not fair.'

'No.'

She smiled in a sheepish sort of way. 'We're not really experts, Kathleen. You could ask one of your aunties to talk to Mum, or even get them to take her to the GP.'

'I don't want her getting TCP.'

'ECT.'

'Oops.' I clapped my hand ower my mouth.

'That's a last resort for extreme cases, like Mum.'

She looked so sad, I hugged her. 'Thanks, Amy, I'll think about this and see if I can come up wi something.'

'Don't think it'll get better on its own. It won't.'

Mr Roberts was waving, and Amy waved back before turning to me. 'Fancy going to the pictures sometime?'

'Yeah, that'd be good.'

I watched her slip in-between her parents and link her

arms in theirs. Then, I pulled myself up and collected Rosie and her bunch of daisies from the grass, stuck her on the pram, and thought about the Roberts as we walked through the park to the river. Despite their problems they were a close family. They enjoyed each other. That was something to admire.

Somehow, we'd lost that in mine. We were too busy surviving, working out how to get by, and being vigilant. First of Dad and now Mum. It wasnae fair on the weans. Martin lay back in his pram watching the sky and my heart did a quickstep. My beautiful wee boy. And here was Rosie clutching her bouquet as she bounced along, a wee sweetie. Things had to get better somehow.

Chapter 20

Sin Expert

The paper on the desk was pure white and unscored, as blank as my mind. Pens scratched all around me, as if on some furious race to the finish. I looked up at the clock ower Sister's head. I'd wasted fifteen minutes already.

If Chrissie didnae write soon, I'd go around and get the address out of her mother. What kind of mother she was, I didnae know. I thought about what Chrissie said and shuddered. Telling someone was impossible; I'd been sworn to secrecy. And if Chrissie wouldnae tell, who would believe me? Sister caught my eye and frowned. What would she say if I told her? What words could I use? The idea was ludicrous.

She gestured wi her pen, a mock scribble. Oh, the question. 'Explain Hamlet's soliloquy'. I shook my head clear and started to write as fast as I could. Death, life, suicide.

The Prince of Denmark sure had problems.

I ran through the paper, my pen catching up wi the others. Five exams this week. Latin tomorrow. That wasnae my best subject. The bell rang. Scribbling stopped. Sister came down from her lofty height. The noise level of girls chattering rose. I escaped to the hockey field.

I probably should've stayed back to study; Amy would be doing that, like the ace pupil she was. Or I should've gone home to listen to more noise, but it was Monday and

Mum didnae expect me back yet as she hadnae picked up this was exam week. There was no hockey on, but I knew how to get into the hut for a stick and ball. I changed into my sannies and dumped my bag. Took a position near the goal and banged the ball into the net. I ran after it, flipped it up and bounced it off the stick's flat end for a minute or two. I hoped Chrissie's auntie was a decent woman and would look after her. If not, I'd sell my ring and take her cash so she could... so she could what? She wasnae yet sixteen. No one would rent a lone girl a place. Sure, the Council aye wanted a man's name on the rent book. She was stuck. The ball dropped to the ground, I dribbled up the left flank, getting faster and faster, the breeze cooling my face and neck, my muscles loosening. Wham. Into the other goal. Ran after the ball, chased it around, controlled it wi the stick as I whizzed back on the right flank, the field suddenly full of imaginary running girls and entreaties to pass. I skipped ower every defender, skimmed past the goalie and wham.

Stopping for breath, I peered along the empty field, then up at the sky. It was as blue as my blouse, and birds sang in the bushes all around. Up here, far away from the town, I felt safe and unreachable. The convent bell rang out the half hour. I loped ower to the hut, returned the ball and stick, put the key back under the brick and sat down on the grass, leaning against the side of the hut. From here I was invisible, anyone coming around the corner from the school buildings couldnae see me, and ahead was only long grass. Beyond that was the river where boats called out now and then, horns blaring. That was far enough away not to interrupt my thoughts. I needed a clear space to think.

I'd heard of women having terminations. Abortions, they were called, and they werenae legal. But they happened. I'd listened into Mum and Hannah gabbing about that. It was murder they said. A mortal sin. You'd go straight to hell for the murder of an innocent. How did it work? I screwed up my eyes to try to work it out. Backroom abortion meant rusty tools and a kitchen table for an operating bench. Some auld witch poking about your insides to bust the baby's bag and then the baby would burst out dead, to be taken away in a bucket. Maybe Chrissie was only kidding about doing that. Was I an accessory to murder? Who to ask without giving the game away? Without, God forbid, anyone thinking it was me.

Chrissie could have the baby adopted. That might be awright in the end, for the baby and for her. Then she could go to yet another school before getting a job. Or she could keep it. But that didnae seem to be a good idea somehow. She wasnae ready to look after a wee baby. I should know.

My head throbbed. I needed to find out more, but first I needed to do some revision.

I'd be darned if I was going to fail bloody Latin.

I got up and took the quiet lane out of school, skirted the town centre, made my way to the public library and sat at one of the desks they kept for students. Some aulder fellas were already there, university types I guessed, from the swagger and the leather briefcases.

There wasnae ever anybody my age. Most girls had rooms to study in at home or just didnae. That was a waste of brain power. If you could learn, why not? I went ower the Latin text again and again, but Chrissie was on my mind. I'd run up to Shelagh's later and check if a letter had come.

A raft of 'be quiets' came rolling my way. I must've tutted more loudly than intended.

Latin exhausted, I wandered into the reference department to look up Abortion.

*

There wasnae any letter waiting for me at Shelagh's. I'd told her straight that Chrissie was writing to me and I didnae want Mum to open it.

She hadnae turned a hair. 'Righto, Hen, nae bother.'

142

I supposed Mum's reputation sallied before her like a bad smell. She was just too obstinate, never thinking that she might not be right in all things.

Tonight, Shelagh sat at the window wi her beads, and I joined her opposite on the pouffe. The path down the brae was lit by the last of the sun. No sign of the Virgin, but then she only came out in the dark.

When she finished her decade, she crumpled up the beads and slipped them into their box. 'Well, Kathleen, how's those exams coming on?'

'*Hamlet* was awright, Latin tomorrow afternoon.'

'And in the morning?'

'That'll be fine. Maths.'

'Should ye no be studying?'

'No use until the weans are in bed. I'll study later.'

She raised her black pencilled eyebrows. She didnae look at all like Grannie. I peered closer. Maybe some flicker of resemblance under the Panstick.

'Auntie Shelagh?'

'Aye.'

'I'm sore worried about a friend.'

'This'll be Chrissie?'

Lordy she was onto me already.

'Anything ye tell me is in total confidence. In one ear and oot the other.'

I bit my lip. How to do this without giving away a secret.

'It's not about me, nor about Chrissie. Right?'

'I get ye.'

That might suffice. Even if she thought it was about Chrissie, if I didnae say it was, I was covered. 'This pal of a pal, not someone I know directly you understand, only the pal is upset and I told her I'd try to find out a bit more about it, to put her mind at rest, you see?'

'Aye.' She saw well and good. It sparkled in her eyes.

'This friend's friend has gone and got herself pregnant.

143

And she cannae look after the bairn so what should she do?'

'The father?'

'No help there.'

'No surprise.' She pursed her lips in the castigation of all men. 'Family?'

'Aye, her mum and an auntie.'

'Age?'

'Fifteen.' I watched her closely. She was a robust Catholic, but also she had been a woman of the world. And to be honest, when I thought of it, she didnae aye seem enamoured of the chapel.

'Adoption is one way. No a bad decision but ye don't ever get tae see them and that can sore hurt a woman aw her days.'

I hadnae thought of that. What if someone came and took wee Martin? My heart jarred.

'Can she keep it?'

'I don't think so, I don't know, maybe.'

She tapped her fingers on the arm of her chair. 'Was she interfered wi, this friend of a friend?'

'Aye, maybe.'

Shelagh snorted loud as a horse. 'Bastard,' she said. 'Well, Kathleen, my darling, ye know there's only one other way?'

'Aye, I was looking it up in the library and all I could find out was that it's illegal but happens. And you could go to jail if found out. Also, there are some people who think it should be made legal if the woman's life is at risk, or even if she might have a breakdown. I also found out under Scotland's common law some doctors will carry out an abortion if the woman's life is at risk but it wasnae very clear if that was allowed.'

'Willnae help yer friend's pal though.'

'Auntie, if I knew that this person was going to murder her baby, am I sinning?'

'No, Kathleen. This is no yer fault, no yer responsibility. D'ye hear me?' She leaned forward, took my hand and stroked it. I nodded. We both looked down.

She went on, in almost a whisper. 'Sin's a complicated matter. Ye might say I've become an expert in it. Oh, I know what they say aboot me and my rosary beads and how sin is on our heads, and damnation and aw that.' I looked up, startled, and she winked at me. 'I'm no as holy as I might seem.'

For a moment I thought she was as mad as they said. But she smiled, a solid, sane smile.

'But Auntie, you aye tell me to say the rosary and watch for the Virgin.'

'Aye, and I believe wi aw my heart and soul that the Virgin is our protector and that she's someone worth praying tae. But that doesnae mean I believe aw that mumbo-jumbo that comes oot of the mouths of the likes of that Father Murphy doon the road. There's too many rules and most of them designed tae keep us in our place.'

'What place?'

'At the beck and call of men, Kathleen. Sure, if it was men who had the bairns, the world would be a different place.'

I chuckled, she was right, but my mind bent double trying to imagine that one. 'Do you think when a woman is pregnant, and before the baby could be born alive, that the baby has a soul and so is a person?'

'I don't know the answer tae that. But I do know that girls who are forced intae back street abortions are terribly hurt and need our help and sympathy, no our condemnation.'

'So, what should my friend say to her friend?'

'Just say that she'll be there if she needs her and let her make up her ain mind.'

'Auntie, your ring. It might be worth a wee bit of money.'

'Aye, he was a generous soul.' She leant back, her hand

falling away, and closed her eyes, reminiscing.

'But maybe you should have it back, it could be worth, oh, ten pounds.'

She laughed. 'Maybe, pet.'

'What if I were to sell it to help…'

'Kathleen, that was my gift tae ye, tae dae wi what ye saw fit. I'll hear no more aboot it. Now, go fetch me a nice cuppa tea and I'll tell ye aboot my Emile.'

Wi everything that was going on, I'd almost forgot about Auntie's husband, but I needed a distraction and I liked the sound of her voice when she went off on one of her recollections. We settled down, she in her armchair, and me on the floor leaning back on the pouffe. She took a deep breath and sighed, easing her way into the story.

'Ye know I told ye aboot my mother. Well, my father was a baker tae trade, and he taught me how tae bake and cook. We aye had fine breads, cakes, scones and tarts in our house. It'd be apple and blackberry in autumn, rhubarb in summer, aw wi aromatic spicing that got yer lips and tongue zinging. I had a guid childhood; we werenae well off but we were content, had a roof ower our heads, and food aplenty.

'Then the war came. The First World War, the Great War they call it. Nothing great aboot it. By then, Father was in his forties and wasnae called tae arms, and given he was a baker, exempt. But my brother Archie, he volunteered and went off proud tae fight for his country. He was wi the Argyll and Sutherland Highlanders. We lost him at Ypres in France, one of seven hundred killed oot of a thousand, just a few months after arriving in France, in 1917. Ye'll find him in the roll of Honour doon the park on the memorial. Archibald Maclean, aw of eighteen. My mother was never the same after that, but she had the Faith and that took her through.

'So, it was extra hard on her when I joined the WAAC, that's the Women's Army Auxiliary Corps. I was nineteen and desperate tae get oot intae the world. A seamstress and

146

a patternmaker, they had use of my skills, and I was a guid cook too. An unmarried woman, no family tae hold me back. August 1917, after my training, off I went in my khaki uniform, a wee tight hat and a shortish skirt for those days. Had tae be no more than twelve inches from the ground, but I did my hem a bit higher.' She laughed at the memory.

I crossed my legs on the floor waiting for her to continue.

She stared ower my head. 'I was placed at the British Army bakery in Dieppe. Och, it was hard work, but great fun at times, if ye leave oot the bombing raids. That's where I met Emile.' She looked down at me and smiled. 'He'd enlisted in the Canadian Expeditionary Force at the outbreak of the war. Seen a lot of battle, an engineer he was. We met, in passing, at a café after Armistice Day. I was due tae go back home as was he, but we spent a fortnight thegither, before we had tae let each other go. But it was settled, I'd go tae Canada soon as I could arrange it and we'd marry. Within three months I was on my way tae Toronto. We married in 1919. His family were French Canadian, his mother and father auld Quebec stock, wealthy at one time and we lived well, Emile and me. In the early years I was able tae send money back tae Mother and Father.'

'So you were rich, Auntie?'

She shook her head. 'No, but we were comfortable. What a life we had, living in the fashionable side of the city, arty-farty ye might call it. Jazz clubs, dance halls, museums. I got a job as a pattern maker for a big fashion house. Emile worked wi a big engineering company. We werenae blessed wi bairns, my one regret, but that's God's will and nothing could be done aboot it.' She closed her eyes, nodding to herself.

I said, 'What happened to Emile, Auntie?'

She took a deep breath. 'He caught TB. Survived the war only tae die of tuberculosis. We had some money, though, stocks and shares, but that aw went in the Great Depression, his parents' savings too. And of course, the fashion trade dried up. I had tae find my way alone and although no exactly penniless, funds were meagre. October 29th, 1929, Black Tuesday they called it, the day the stock market crashed, and Canada went intae a doonspin.

'There were a lot of Scots families in Toronto, through the centuries they came ower in their droves. I signed on as a nanny, cook, housekeeper, as many young Scots women did then. I wasnae young, oh thirty-one by then. Nor was I naïve but turned oot the wisdom I had of the world wasnae the type I needed.' She sat up straight and leaned forward.

'The man of the house was a tyrant, tae his wife and his children, dear boys and girls they were too. A devil he was in the drink. That poor woman took regular beatings as did the boys. The wee girls were terrified of him. I pleaded wi Agnes, the wife, tae leave him but she was sore weighed down by then, kept making excuses as tae how he was a guid provider and how he'd change. He was too controlling.' She thumped the arm of her chair, peering down at me. 'Never let a man control ye, Kathleen.'

It was hard to fathom. My mum was a bit of a witch herself, yet she'd allowed my dad to shout and bawl when he was drunk. It sounded like he hit her. There werenae any marks. I'd looked for them in the morning and never saw any bruises. Mum was slap happy wi us weans and yet he pushed her about, a strong woman and she had loads of family around who could sort him out. She wasnae stupid and I know for a fact my grannie had never suffered a man like that. Grandpa had been a gentleman. So why would a woman, not offensive looking, wi plenty of backbone, get abused like that? I was determined to never let that happen to me.

'No, Auntie, I'll never let that happen.'

'Guid girl.' Satisfied, she leant back in her chair. 'I was fixing tae leave their employ when the bastard cornered me in an oothouse. It was early evening and I was locking up the chickens when I felt him behind me. I turned fast, but he was aw ower me. A mighty weight, and garrulous wi drink. Smelt like a distillery. But he hadnae reckoned on me. I was strong wi work and I'd learned a few things during the war. Let's just say revenge is sweet and leave it at that, Pet. But know that his poor wife had no trouble from him for a guid while. I left that house the very next day, sold most of what was left of my jewellery and bought a passage tae Liverpool.'

'Oh, Auntie. You've been all around the world. But why Liverpool?'

'That's where the ship sailed. I planned a bus tae Glasgow, but I liked Liverpool and stayed a few days. It was fate. I met my second husband, an aulder man. That's where I got the name. I kept it, in respect. Shelagh Dougherty. He was an Irishman, a fair and loving soul. We lived in Liverpool where he worked as a plumber. The next war got him, and I came home at last. I was forty-five. My parents were long gone. Yer grannie took me in even though she hadnae a penny tae spare. And yer grandpa, no a man like him. A true gentleman and kindly. I got this flat, and I took in sewing again. Still do a bit, by and by, tae augment my pension.' She smiled and nodded. 'I'm content here, what wi my Virgin, and the shenanigans going on in the family. Aye, I'm content enough, but blessed wi you, Kathleen, my darling. Ye've become the daughter I never had.'

I drew in a sharp breath, and a tear rolled down my cheek, but for once I wasnae mortified to show what was in my heart.

I ran down the brae, thinking about married life. If I were ever to have a husband, and that was unlikely given the standard of men and boys I was used to, he'd have to kow-tow. If there could be no equality, then I'd have to be the boss. And it seemed to me, that women, especially married ones, hadnae any rights at all. The nuns looked much more

149

cheerful wi their lot. But then I thought of auld Murphy and wondered if they were forced to obey the likes of him. There was no way out for any of us. It was enough to drive you to drink. But at least we werenae a total loss as a family. Archie Maclean. A hero of our very own. Someone to be proud of.

Chapter 21

Fleas to Finches

It was report card day. Sister called us one at a time to her office. Happy, smiling girls returned; misery rolled its eyes; nonchalance covered faces. We were listed alphabetically, except, when my turn came, I wasnae called. It must've been a mistake. I would be next up, and next up … but after we got to *Margaret Kane,* I realised wi a jolt it was deliberate. Amy went out and came back wreathed in smiles. I gave her a thumbs up. My fate was confirmed when *Theresa Wallace*, aye last for everything, left the classroom.

Finally, *Kathleen Gallagher* was called out and I picked my way along the corridor, glancing out the line of windows to the rotunda where the Virgin stood head bowed, rosary entwined in her clay fingers, surrounded by yellow roses. I should've done more praying.

I knocked the half-open door to the cell.

'Come.'

My nerves jangled. Why did she have to bellow? And *'come'* should be *'come in'*.

I blew out a long breath and entered. Her head was bowed ower the one report card lying open on the desk. It was too dark to see the writing on the card, any light from her wee cubby window dimmed by books. How come they made report cards so wee, the writing in the boxes diminutive, unreadable? How come they were buff coloured? It was all too depressing.

151

'Sit.'

I levered my bum down to the seat. No O-Grades for me. No chink of light in the dark future that was my destiny. The bra factory loomed.

The bell rang, loud and shrill, sending a shudder through my spine, and then there was a flurry of running feet. Doors banged. School was out and so was term. Summer holidays were on us.

'How's your mother now, Kathleen?' She looked up and smiled. I searched her face for clues. How had I done? Why wasnae she telling me? This was nothing to do wi my mother.

'Hmm, better I think.'

'That's grand. I'm pleased to hear that.' She fingered her rosary. 'Well, to business, eh?'

I couldnae speak, just opened my mouth in a grimace. I must've looked ghastly.

'This is a very impressive recovery from before, Kathleen.' The beads dismissed, she turned ower the card and passed it to me.

I ran my eyes ower the numbers and then the comments. Nineties all through, except of course for Latin. That was sixty-five. Comments, though tiny, were enough to make my eyes pop. Even Mrs Ratface had said, '*an unusually gifted pupil*'.

Mortified, I couldnae stop tears falling, unbidden, out of one eye first, and then in a flood ower my cheeks and into my open mouth. I sniffed. A white, gent's hanky appeared. I blew my nose, wiped my face, and to my everlasting shame, handed the hanky back. My mother would've died on the spot. But Sister didnae flinch. She took the soiled cotton and stuffed it in a drawer.

'I'm sorry I left you until last. But I wanted a bit more time to discuss your future. The O-Grade stream starts in August. Two years to study and I want you to do as well as possible. Given the strains you're under at home ...'

I made to protest but she raised her hand. 'Not easy wi young siblings to look after and … everything. I expect your mother might need you to leave this time next year to bring in a wage?'

'Aye.'

'Is that what you want, Kathleen?'

'Oh no, Sister. I want to be a lawyer or a doctor. Or maybe …' I was drooling.

'Well, those might be aiming rather high, given the state of the profession of law in this country and its preference for male applicants, and likewise medicine, but there are other professions, like teaching, or nursing …'

I made a face. This was all pie in the sky anyhow and I figured if a dream wasnae ever to come true it might as well be a good one.

She raised an eyebrow. 'I see you're determined. University, articles … you need to hold on to that Latin.'

Reality was my constant companion and dragged me back. Talk was cheap, dreams even cheaper. 'Och, I'll never get to university. We cannae afford that, Sister.'

She seemed to consider my words, lightly rapping the desk wi a middle finger.

Leaning forward she splayed her fingers in a v shape. 'There are grants, scholarships, ways and means for gifted pupils from less advantaged backgrounds. I can't promise anything, of course. Now, you leave all that with me and I'll expect you to keep up these marvellous grades.' She smiled, right up to those fine eyes. A smile that lifted me from my seat, skywards.

'Sister, I'll get to that university if it takes me the rest of my life.' *Was it even possible?*

I was stepping to the door, report card gripped like a nugget of gold in my hand, when she called, 'Chrissie Hall?'

I turned sharp. 'You've heard from her?'

She hesitated. 'Not directly.' Rapped her fingernails on

the desk. 'I know you know about her misfortune, Kathleen. But the poor child … miscarried.' I caught my breath. How come she knew that? Had Chrissie miscarried? I fell from my fluffy cloud wi a clatter. 'She's returning to school, in Newcastle. She's a smart girl and if she can apply herself will do well.'

'What school?'

'Excuse me?'

'So, I can write.'

She dropped her gaze. Pressed a palm ower her heart. Rummaged in a file. 'Well, Kathleen Gallagher, you warm my soul.' She bent to her desk, wrote out the address, and passed me the piece of paper wi details of Chrissie's new school.

Chapter 22

Morag's Mischief

My eye was off the ball. Mum wasnae any better. I'd thought she'd improved, but she hadnae, I'd been too busy to notice. Being at home the first week of summer meant lots more time wi her and it was a relief the two nights she went out to work. She moaned that she could've worked the whole week if the government wouldnae take the money back, giving no thought to me, her poor put-upon daughter. If she worked full time I'd have to look after the weans full time. A balanced equation. As it was, I had mornings at Rennie's, packing up the papers, taking in and noting deliveries, and balancing Mrs Rennie's books. I got paid eleven shillings a week and gave it all to Mum. I didnae mind, it meant we had some extra cash that the powers that be couldnae touch as I wasnae listed as employed. The Rennies showered me wi their brand of appreciation: smiles, sweeties, and praise for a good job done. Mrs Rennie was kind and motherly. She'd hug me when I arrived and hug me when I left. She said she'd aye wanted a daughter but ended up wi a big clumsy son. But the affection for him was obvious.

It was strange to me, for a parent and a child to be comfortable wi one another, like pals. Never a cross word passed between them.

Tomorrow was Martin's first birthday and I was planning a tea party for him. Morag and Rosie were beside themselves wi excitement. Mum, of course, just gave me a withering look.

'The wean disnae know it's his birthday, so why huv a party?'

'It's not really a party, Mum. And it's so we'll have something to remember.'

'Nonsense.' She stomped into the kitchen, the squeak of the pulley announcing the nappies were dry.

I lifted Martin up from amongst his toys on the floor and set him on my hip. His wee chubby thigh felt warm and sticky under my hand but I didnae care. He twisted his head so to meet my eyes and gurgled. 'Ka, Ka …' He had one word, *Ka*, just *Ka*. It delighted me when he said it.

I laughed and he swung his head back, his back arcing in total trust. That wasnae misplaced. I would've died for my wee brother. He felt like my own child and I resolved he'd want for nothing, even if it meant me leaving school and earning money for the house.

We were trying to get him to walk. 'C'mere, Rosie, and we'll try him again.'

Rosie loved the game. Morag sometimes took a turn, but she lost patience and gave up too soon. She sat on the couch, chin in hands, and watched. I placed Martin on his feet, his back to me, holding his hands up so he couldnae drop. He tried to bend his legs to fall on his bum, but I kept him vertical. Rosie stood in front a few steps away, entreating him to come to her. I stalked him forward, so the left wee foot made a step, then the right, then let him totter on the left foot holding only one of his hands. He swung the right leg around, then fell onto Rosie wi a whoop. We clapped and he opened his mouth in a gurgle of a laugh, showing all four front milk teeth.

It was still warm and light outside although it was nearly seven o'clock. Martin would be down by eight and the girls by nine but there was time for a trip to the play park. Tea was done and Mum was busy ironing.

'We're off to the park, Mum,' I called as I snapped Martin into his pushchair. Rosie fetched his cover from the bag, as it could get chilly in a bit. Morag ran ahead, downstairs.

Mum didnae reply. That wasnae unusual so I bumped Martin downstairs to *Wee Willie Winkie.* He clapped all the way, one hand often missing the other.

We strolled to the play park which wasnae busy. Two wee boys played keepie-uppie at the far end and Morag ran across to join them, soon commandeering their ball and keeping it going for ages. She was good wi a footbaw, that was for sure, but she kept it too long, for as soon as one of them saw the opportunity, he kicked the ball away and the boys ran off, leaving her shouting obscenities after them.

Pouting, she lumbered ower to a swing, jumped up and stood on it, legs splayed. Bending and pushing, pumping her legs, she arced higher and higher, her ponytail swinging behind. I turned away to play wi Rosie and Martin on the chute. Whilst Rosie climbed up the steps, I placed Martin halfway up the slide and let him slip down by himself. Then waited for her to slide and so on. I was absorbed when I heard an almighty clang of metal and a shriek. I swivelled around. Morag was sitting on the ground a few paces away from the swing which clanged as it burled around the high bar. I knew immediately what she'd done. She'd tried to do a jumpy, staying on her running feet underneath, dipping her head, until well clear. But Morag had misjudged the whole thing. The swing had clipped her as she'd run forward; she hadnae dipped far enough underneath. Blood spewed from her head. I told Rosie to stay sitting on the chute and ran, wi Martin on my hip, ower to Morag. I bent down, swivelling Martin onto my chest, careful of the swing's fading momentum. Blood poured out of the gash and her face was so pale I could make out blue capillaries. Her eyes rolled and she slumped backwards to the ground. I looked around, desperate for help, but no one was about.

My heart hammering, I shouted, 'Help, help!' Rosie started to cry on the chute, and Martin joined in. Morag just lay, eyes closed, her skin translucent. I tried to shake her awake. 'Come on, Morag, don't sleep. I'll get someone.'

There was a row of houses at the bottom end of the park. I fetched Martin's pram, dumped him in, sat Rosie on top, and ran to the first door. I banged hard. No one came. I chapped the second door. The key turned. By this time a third door had opened, and two women came out of their respective houses at the same time.

'My wee sister's been hit by a swing. She's bleeding. She's away wi it.' My voice sounded throttled.

'Righto, Hen. I'll come. Minnie, get Mrs Rennie tae call the ambulance. Go tae the house, back of shop.'

The first woman hurried wi me across the green to where Morag lay. She looked fast asleep now, and I swallowed hard, my throat tightening. I must've been whimpering because the woman took my face in both hands.

'It's awright now, she's breathing.' She had a kitchen towel and leant down to press it against the gash. The movement seemed to stir Morag and her eyes fluttered open. I shuddered wi relief. For a terrible moment I thought I'd lost her. It was only then I realised her glasses were gone. 'Your glasses, Morag,' I muttered, scanning the ground. They were lying askew on the concrete, but they bent back into shape wi a squeeze. Thankfully the glass was intact.

I turned to Rosie. She sat big-eyed on the pram sooking her fist. Martin had dozed off.

'It's awright, Hen,' I said and lifted her up. She clung to me, her eyes locked on Morag's face. Everything was quiet for a long time, except for a regular thumping in my ears. The woman kneeling now, staunching the wound, Morag barely conscious, Rosie leaning into my neck, Martin asleep, the park otherwise empty.

Until I heard the approach of running feet.

I turned in their direction. It was Big Jim Rennie and hurrying behind him were his mum and the other neighbour. People came out of the row of houses. Jim stopped and a young boy nodded and ran in the direction of my house. Mum. He'd sent for Mum. Any heat I had left in my body drained away. I felt Rosie being lifted from my arms. Someone took hold of my damp hand and led me to a bench.

'Kathleen.' A pat on my cheek, another. Through the tears I recognised Mrs Rennie's face and that's when I started to bawl.

After warm hugs and more pats, soothing entreaties that it was all going to be fine, that the ambulance was on its way, I calmed down. She gave me a hanky. I blew hard, wiped my eyes and nodded. She had Rosie at her side. I peered into the pram. The wean was still asleep, thank goodness. Jim knelt on the ground beside Morag, speaking softly, and Morag gave a little giggle. Relief flooded through me. Looking up, I saw Mum shuffle ower from the path in her slippers. I got up and stepped forward to meet her. She hunkered down beside Morag, rose up, patted her chest. I moved towards her. 'Mum…'

That's when she bowled into me, almost pushing me off my feet. I stumbled back. She slapped me hard across the face. Was about to repeat that when Jim got hold of her arm and dragged her away. But she was still talking to me. All I could hear was 'Wait tae ye get home. Nae right tae take the weans oot, I didnae say ye could, ye nearly killed Morag…' All I could feel was a sharp sting on my bottom lip. Jim was shushing her, the others standing stony faced. I wrapped both arms around me to stop trembling, my head down, spitting blood.

I didnae want to see the accusation on folk's faces. I knew what they were thinking. I got what I deserved, had let my mother down and nearly got my wee sister killed.

The ambulance came and hoovered Morag and Mum up,

leaving me wi the Rennies, Martin, Rosie and a departing crowd. I dabbed at my lip wi a hanky.

Mrs Rennie and Jim insisted on seeing us home. Jim assured me that after a few stitches, Morag would be right as rain. I saw the glances they exchanged when they mentioned Mum. Big Jim kept shaking his head in disapproval. The penny dropped, they werenae blaming me. But I couldnae have that. It was my fault.

I said, 'I'm sorry, Jim. I should've kept a better eye.'

He looked at me straight. 'No, Kathleen, that's yer mum's job and she shouldnae hit ye like that.'

I was more affronted than hurt. Affronted that folk had seen my mum at her worst.

Sure, this wasnae unusual. It was the situation that was different. I should've expected it. I did. But maybe I thought she'd restrain herself in public. Of course, she was upset, not thinking, worried sick on top of everything else. It was my own fault. I knew what Morag was like. I shouldnae have ignored her, even for a minute.

Chapter 23

Morag the Martyr

The next day, Morag's face was swollen, though only the forehead, just under her hairline, was cut. She had a raggedy line of black stitches and likely would aye have the scar. But I reassured her no one would see that because of her hair. Luckily, her glasses were just a wee bit bent. The kind of bent that meant she had to wrap the leg more tightly around one ear than the other.

Mum smouldered all day, withering me in that way of hers, shoulders sagging wi disappointment, lips pursed, edging by me as if I had the plague. I tried to catch her eye wi a pleading glance a couple of times, but she stared into oblivion. When I went into a room, she'd fidget wi something in her apron pocket and make for the door. I didnae miss her fussing ower Morag, making sure she had orange squash beside her on the wing chair, patting her nape to check her temperature, leaning down to examine her bruises. Morag squirmed under this attention, narrowing her eyes on the approach and rolling them in relief after departure. As for me, it would've been easier if Mum would just slap me. I wasnae sure what was worse: the wronged parent or the fawning nurse wi the personality transplant.

We waited till Mum went to work to have our tea party. Martin's first birthday didnae matter to her. Thank God he was too young to notice. As soon as the front door banged, we rushed into the bedroom and grabbed the goodie bag from under the girls' bed. We had a jam roll wi one blue candle, Kit Kats, fruit gums, and for Martin a big Milky Bar. I laid it all out on the kitchen table, wi a bottle of Irn-Bru donated by Mrs Rennie. Morag smiled at the feast though the effort made her eyes twitch. Rosie had been quiet all day, sucking her thumb and fidgeting wi her buttons, but now she giggled wi anticipation. We agreed that she should blow out the candle for Martin as she was next in line. Morag would've normally butted in, but she graciously let Rosie be. It was a sort of martyrdom. I'd let her have it for a bit. Not for too long or she would be insufferable. Anyway, I suspected the act of blowing was too much for her bruised face. I lit the candle, pulled down the blind and we sang *Happy Birthday* to Martin in the eerie half-dark. Rosie stood ower the cake wi the candle picking out the oval of her face, making her look like a grinning clown. Martin didnae like this altered Rosie and stretched and howled until I picked him up. He pressed his face into my neck only peeking out once at Rosie who jumped from foot to foot waiting for the signal. *Blow* ... she did so and though the flame dimmed and wavered it stood up again and again. Morag finally joined in wi a one-sided blow and the candle sputtered out, plunging us into dusk until I opened the blind.

Martin kicked his chubby legs and strained to get down to the floor. Not for the first time I wished we had a camera. We used to have one and Dad would take pictures at parties and birthdays. I hadnae seen it since he left. We went into the living room and I sorted paper and crayons so that Rosie and Morag could make a birthday card for Martin. Mum hadnae got him one. There wouldnae be a first birthday card from his own mother to keep in the china cabinet wi all the rest. She saved the important ones in a shoebox in the long drawer below the glass shelves. I'd buy a card later, forge her signature and add it to the bundle. He'd never know.

Six cards had come in the post. Five were on the mantel.

One from Auntie Peggy – no doubt there'd been a postal order in it – a glittery one wi stars from Auntie Ina in America – hopefully dollars had come wi that – one from Hannah, one from Shelagh and one from Patsy. I hesitated. Where was the sixth one? I found it in the bin and fished it out. It was blue and had a sailing boat, ducks and a big flashy number one on the front. I wiped off a gravy stain and opened it. *To Martin. Love, Daddy.* I nearly put it back in the bin but had second thoughts. Martin might not know his dad, and maybe he didnae deserve to be his dad, but a wee boy needed a dad around or at least should know he'd sent him this card. Before I could change my mind, I tiptoed through the lobby, past the weans in the living room and put it in my drawer. I'd keep this for him. I was past caring what Mum thought.

When the girls were done, I signed the homemade card for myself and Rosie, and Morag scribbled her name below ours. I stood their card up as best I could on the cabinet. It was floppy and needed leant against the wall, but the girls were pleased wi their creation. We played a game of 'stick the tail on the donkey'. I'd ruled out musical chairs, that was off limits in case Morag fell and bust her stitches. It was good to see wee Rosie play without frowning or sucking her thumb for ten minutes. Martin gurgled along and he even managed, from my arms, to stick the tail six inches near the donkey's rump.

They were exhausted by bedtime and quickly went off to sleep. I tried to read Anya Seton, but couldnae concentrate, so finally gave up, sat back on the chair and closed my eyes.

Wi the silence came memories of yesterday. The clang of metal, the scream, Morag slumped on the gravel. The panic, wee Rosie's white face, the tea towel soaked wi blood, Big Jim rushing forward. Mum. The slap. The intent in her eyes, the wide arc of her hand. Hate coming at me like a truck. The metallic flood of blood in my mouth.

Refusing to be overwhelmed I opened my eyes wide. It was nothing new, why bother?

Mum was just like everyone else's mother, we all got slapped regularly. Sure, the nuns belted you and if you were very unlucky you got a slap-happy dad as well. My book dropped off my knee. But Dad had never hit any one of us, ever. So, why did he hit Mum? Course, she nagged him plenty. But was that reason for him to hit her? Was it self-defence for a man to hit a woman who annoyed or upset him? Was the drink an excuse? It was all too confusing.

Why did people hit out when they were supposed to love each other?

I sniffed away tears. After the sting of the slap came the burning. Falling against Jim. His big hands steadying me. Mrs Rennie approaching, fingers fluttering at her throat. The hot flush stealing ower my neck and face. Jim Rennie stepping towards Mum, his back to me, broad shoulders hunched in a threatening pose. His rearranged stiff features as he turned to me. Mum staring after him, mouth open.

I picked up my book and tried to shake the memories away. But the Rennie's reaction to my mum brought waves of hot shame. It occurred to me that I didnae ever want them to have any contact wi her. They were mine. My friends. They respected me, liked me, and now they knew. Knew my secret. My mother was a nutcase. I wasnae much better.

The book had lost its appeal. I got up and went to the toilet, then took the bin out, just in case Mum noticed the birthday card had gone. Mrs McCann was at her back step cradling a cup. It was still light, a warm summer evening.

'Och, did ye have a nice wee party, Hen? For the bairn?'

'Aye, he loved it. One today.'

'And Morag. How is she?'

'A bit woozy, but she'll be awright.'

'Weans aye have accidents, part of their job.' She giggled as if reminiscing. Then she dipped her head and stared hard at me. 'Listen, Hen. Might no be ma place … But, ye know ye can knock ma door, anytime.'

'Thank you. I'll remember that.'

'Yer Ma, how's she?'

'Busy, run off her feet.'

'She's a proud one that. There's help about her if she'd take it.'

I wondered if she was referring to herself. But she turned and closed the door.

Sounded like she knew more than she was letting on. I sighed. Life was far too complicated. Everyone seemed to know more than I did. I fingered my cheek. Course, it was still a bit swollen, and the cut lip didnae help. My mother's fury was written all ower it.

Chapter 24

TCP

The following Sunday, I met Amy Roberts at church. She usually went wi her parents to the noon mass, but today she was on her tod at the nine o'clock service. I was in the pew wi Mum and the weans. Martin sat beside me sucking his fists and squirming around to see everyone behind. On one of these squirms, I turned to pull him onto my knee and there was Amy, smiling shyly. I nodded and turned back quickly, fingering my lip. It no longer hurt and was all pretty much cleared up now. No need for explanation. I'd hang back and see how she was doing.

Father Murphy was in his element, up on the altar, arms raised to the big Jesus hanging on the cross ower his head. It was a heavy piece of engineering hung by chains from the high domed ceiling. I aye sat far away from it in case one of those chains snapped and the Saviour came hurtling onto my head. Father came down the steps from the altar, floated to the pulpit, and started his rant, hands clutching the brass bar in front of him, swaying back and forth, demented. The Devil was apparently upon us, every one of us, and he managed to sear each attendee to their seat as he expounded, denigrated, destroyed and calculated. Most of it was against Americans. That was what made me listen closely as usually it was a drone I screened out. According to him, they were in cahoots wi the Antichrist wi their owercommercial lifestyles, the sickness of their movies, and the sexual freedoms they allowed themselves. By that I think he meant contraception. A vile practice, against the will of God. I lost track of his argument as I was so busy imagining some of those wonderful, wild things.

Mass must have wound up; I was woken by Mum nudging me to move. Martin had fallen asleep and Rosie played wi her prayer book. She wasnae able to read, but it was the right way up. She particularly liked the pictures of Baby Jesus and the one wi Mary ascending to Heaven. She had good concentration did our Rosie, maybe because she'd learnt to be watchful and quiet. Morag looked punch drunk, both wi boredom and wi the effect of the yellow church lamps on her black and blue forehead. She also still had a stippled cheek where her face had met gravel.

Outside, I weaved my way through the crowds, and located Amy standing on the pavement in a slip of a dress. It came to just above the knee; a swirl of oranges and yellows. I glanced down at my apparel, a blue cotton affair I'd had since last summer that was fashionably short now but wasnae supposed to be. I had grown taller but was still stick thin.

Mum was busy strapping Martin into his pram where it stood along the row of prams and pushchairs against the church wall. I tapped her arm. 'Can I go and talk to Amy?'

She glanced ower her shoulder, nodded, rummaged in her bag and pressed a shilling into my hand. I stared at her. 'Go and get a drink in the café. Ah dinnae need ye today. Take yer time.'

Morag's face nearly dropped to the ground. Then panic shot across it. She gripped my arm. 'Can ah come tae? Please, Kathleen.'

I thought I'd better take her wi me; to refuse might jolt Mum out of what must've been a trance and I was just about to tell her to come on wi me, when Mum said, 'Leave yer big sister be. She needs a bit of time tae herself. Noo, you jist get hold of Rosie and come away hame.'

Guilt made me stand there a moment longer, but freedom was more powerful, and I shot across to Amy. 'Hello, Amy, I'm thinking of getting into the café before the rest of them. Want to come?'

She smiled. 'I was just going to ask you the same thing. Come on quick, there'll be a queue the length of the Clyde in five minutes.'

We took off down Church Street like two colts broken loose from our tethers anticipating a free couple of hours.

I hadnae been in the café since that time wi Chrissie. It wasnae that I'd been avoiding it. More a case of not having the time or money. Still, I avoided the bench we'd sat in and, as there was still some choice, led Amy to the other side of the room, to a table wi only two chairs. Although I'd shaken off the memory of that day and all that had meant, now I could see Chrissie tossing her silver hair and eyeing up the talent. I'd get that letter off to her new school soon as they opened again, but that would be September as in England the school system was different. We'd be back at school here the last week in August. I was looking forward to peace and quiet.

I ordered two cokes and they came quickly, two thick green bottles wi straws. Amy said she'd get the next ones. I was pleased she thought we'd be there that long and sipped my coke to make it last. The café was filling up wi Mass-goers, but few looked our way, just a couple of girls in our year who skimmed past saying hello, but didnae linger.

'How'd your exams go?' Amy asked.

'Much better than I expected. And you?'

'Yeah, Dad was pleased.' She raised her eyes to the roof. 'How's your summer going?'

'Boring.' I raised my eyes to the shiny lamp above.

'Yeah, me too.'

We laughed.

'What have you been up to then?'

'Went to my grandmother's in London for two weeks, got back last week, and been reading or catching up with some schoolwork.'

'London! Wish I could go to London. Did you go to Carnaby Street? What about the theatre? Oh – Buckingham Palace?' I stared into her face as if I could soak up all her adventures.

She sat back. 'Wow, Kathleen. You'd love it. More than me, I expect. You're so much more … enthusiastic, open … than me. I find it all so tedious, to be honest. It's just crowds and noise and I've seen it all before. But Grannie always wants to go up town. Harrods. For goodness sake, on the tube too. I thought I'd collapse with the effort. My grandmother, she's sixty-going-on-twenty-five.' She fluttered her eyes and giggled. I thought she was marvellous.

She reached ower and touched the corner of my lip wi her middle finger. 'You cut yourself?'

'Oh, that. It's nothing.'

She sat back, inclined her head to the side, then seemed to come to a decision. 'I was hoping to meet you today.' She blushed scarlet, and I looked away to save her embarrassment. 'When I heard Chrissie wasn't coming back to school, I wondered if maybe we could spend more time together.'

'I'd like that.'

We both smiled and said at the same time: 'Want another coke?'

We chatted on for another hour until Amy suggested I go home wi her, and she'd make us a bite to eat. Mum said I could stay out all day so I wasnae going home before five. Amy and I walked across the Common arm in arm and I forgot about the weans and Mum and just held on to my friend, laughing and joking about every little thing that came into my head. I was the funniest person I knew, so I was.

When we got to her gate, I thought to ask about her mum

and dad.

'No one's home. Dad's at the hospital visiting Mum,' she said quietly, eyes fixed on me.

'What's happened?' I said, hand on latch.

'Mum's having treatment. She's been in a few weeks. Dad's beside himself all the time.'

'I'm sorry, Amy, and here's me laughing and joking around.'

'No, that's great. I needed some fun. It's been dire around here.'

'Well, in that, you're not alone. Try my house.' I blew my fringe up into the air and we both half-collapsed, laughing, onto the path, clutching each other past the overgrown nettles and up to the front door. Amy took the key from her purse and let us in.

How quiet it was today. The living room was empty, of course, no wayward girls kicking off, no music blaring. I looked up the flight of stairs, imagining Mrs Roberts lying like a princess on her bed. I blushed, and hoped she was awright. What a worry. And what kind of treatment was she having?

We went into the kitchen. It was clean as a new pin; no nappies hung from the pulley, no big pots bubbled on the stove, no grubby hands fumbling in the biscuit tin, no buckets of bleach stinking the place out. I sat on a stool while Amy made some sandwiches wi cheese and tomatoes. She got a bottle of Irn-Bru out of the fridge. Oh, to have a fridge. I went ower and looked inside. It was full of stuff; eggs, cheese, milk and meats.

'Does your dad do the shopping?' I asked.

'No, Mrs Elliot does that.'

'Who's she?'

'The cleaning lady. Dad got her in to help when Mum got ill. She's lovely.'

'Oh.' A cleaning lady? Just like my mum. Except my mum

170

wasnae lovely. She'd take the face off anyone who thought they might be her employer and give her instructions.

I munched on my slab of bread and cheese whilst Amy picked at a corner of hers.

'What hospital is your mum in?'

'Gartcore.' She lowered her head and a tear fell onto the worktop. I was aghast. God, my big mouth. Gartcore was where all the people wi nervous problems went. I'd been there once. Who had I been visiting? I couldnae remember. Someone in a bed. Oh, Grannie Gallagher. She lay in a high bed, or was it that I was so wee? And she gave me a half crown. Then we were ushered out by a nurse and Dad looked back, his eyes watering. I never saw her again. What happened? Why didn't I know? We'd walked down the hill, and I'd looked back at the red-brick mansion, wi its turrets and brass studded doors standing behind red-gold trees. The path was thick wi leaves and I kicked through them wi black patent shoes.

'Amy…' I didnae know what to say so I just got down from that damned stool, went ower, and hugged her tight.

She sniffed and pulled away. 'Sorry, Kathleen, I always seem to be in trouble and you're there to help.'

'Oh, right enough.' I licked at my lip. Hmm, still a bit swollen.

She pointed. 'What happened there?'

'Well, it's a long story. Morag fell off the swing in the park when I was supposed to be watching her, and hey-ho, bust her head open and I got the blame.'

'Your mum?'

I nodded, squirming inside.

'Well, she's been under a lot of strain. No better?'

'Aye and no. Sometimes she seems awright, then out of the blue she can go off the handle. Now, she's not talking to me at all. She willnae hardly look at me.'

'I can understand that.'

'How?'

'Do you think she might be ashamed of herself for hurting you?'

I laughed. Though it sounded more like a groan.

'Really, she hasn't ever left a bruise or a mark like that before, has she?'

'Finger marks when you get a right good slap, but no. Never anything like this. And Jim Rennie was there, in the park, you know, come to help, and he said something to her. I didnae hear, but his face was a picture, and Mum looked … well aye, maybe she was ashamed of herself. No, it was more like rage.' It seemed a bit far-fetched to me. Maybe someone else's mother might be ashamed, but not mine. I changed the subject. 'Listen, never mind me, I can handle her. What about you?'

She slipped off her stool, her piece'n cheese ignored. 'Come on through.'

I stuffed what was left of my lunch into my mouth and followed her into the living room.

It was a nice room, looking out onto their garden, which was a bit overgrown but colourful wi bushes of orange, crimson and yellow roses, blowsy and heavy on the stem. Across the road, big semis were adorned wi ivy and pink flowering clematis growing up two stories across the front walls; their gardens were full of colour. My gran had clematis across her back fence which covered every inch when summer came. I had a photo of us all standing in front of it, Mum wi Rosie in her arms, me and Morag in front and Dad beside us. It was black and white, but I still remember the pink of the flowers adorning the fence. Course, it wasnae her fence any more, some auld man had moved in.

Amy's living room had a wide marble fireplace the colour of old stone and there was a fireguard painted wi red tulips ower the grate. A gilded mirror sat atop. Two big couches sat at right angles and Amy flopped down on one, and I sat on the other. Bookshelves lined the back wall, stuffed full, just like in the library. I twisted round to look at the titles on the stems. Amy got up, went ower, and pulled one out. 'As you know, this is my favourite,' she said, handing it to me, Harper Lee, *To Kill a Mockingbird*.

'Oh wow. Have you seen the film yet, wi Gregory Peck?'

'Yes, loved it, but we could go together sometime.'

'Yeah. I think it's still on at the Odeon. I'll check next time I pass. I'm sure I saw the ad outside.'

'Have you read it?'

'Aye, once. I wanted to read it again and I put a request in at the library, but it's not come my turn yet.'

'Borrow mine.'

'Are you sure?'

'Yes, I've read it. But I'll read it again sometime.'

'Are you rich?'

She laughed, threw back her head, and fell onto the couch. 'No, but I guess we have a good income and Dad got left quite a bit from Gramps.'

'Like real money.'

'Yes, real dough.' She made her eyes large like saucers.

'I'm going to be rich one day,' I said. Though I'd never actually thought of that before. Somehow seeing Amy comfortable in this big house wi a library of her own and a fridge full of food she could afford to waste, made me very sure. 'I think I might be a lawyer like Atticus here.' I tapped the cover. 'That would make me rich.'

'He's not rich.'

'Well, he's rich to me.'

'I suppose he's rich, relatively speaking, like us. Not wealthy but advantaged.'

'Advantaged?'

'In contrast to …'

'You mean as opposed to the likes of me?'

She flushed from her neck up to her hairline. 'God, sorry,

Kathleen, no, well yes, but not in a bad way.'

'No, it's awright. I know what you mean.' I did know. It wasnae any fault of ours we were poor, and poorer still now Dad had gone.

Amy asked, 'Why do you want to be a lawyer?'

'To help people get justice.'

'Bad people?'

'Gosh, no.'

'You'd have to represent them too,' she said.

'Maybe I'd just represent innocent folk.'

She laughed. 'Read the book again, have a think and then see.'

'Och, it's pie in the sky anyhow. No way I'll get to university.'

'Yes, you will, you're the smartest girl in the school.'

'Except for you.'

'You're smarter than me. Think how well you would do if you didn't have the children and the work and all that.'

'Aye, just me and my mum. No thanks. But it might be glorious to have peace and quiet.'

She sighed. 'God, no. I'd love a sister; even a brother would do, but not to be alone.'

I thought about this a moment. No, even Morag was better than nothing and if anyone took wee Rosie or Martin away, I'd just die. 'You're right. They're menaces, but they're my menaces.'

We sat for a few moments; I leafed through the book; Amy twiddled wi the record player. She put on the Beatles.

'Amy, will your mum be home soon?'

'Dad says, after the ECT.'

Chapter 25

Kicking away the Swagger

It was teatime on Friday, and it felt like autumn. Wind slapped your face as you ran, and rain threatened so you could taste it on your tongue, a kind of dampness that hadnae yet solidified into droplets. Luckily, my hood was up, and I had a wool scarf wound around my face; I was in disguise and had to blend into the tenements behind me. I'd planned to do this next Friday, but once the notion got hold I couldnae shake it. Anyway, I was only checking him out, to see if he still worked at the Yards. Next time I'd see where he was living. One thing at a time. Mum thought I was at the library for a certain maths book, an emergency as I'd only three weeks to study for an exam on the first day back at school. A lie, and though my mother wasnae a fan of education, she loved nuns and they could do no wrong, so whatever they demanded she'd supply.

She was keeping my tea warm on a plate ower a pot of hot water, so it'd be a bit frizzled around the edges and that would annoy her. So I didnae have much time and would have to pretend the book in my pocket was the one newly borrowed from the library. It was the thinnest one I had so didnae take up much room.

When the sirens went off, I stepped back against the wall and peeked around the corner. The street was packed wi women, weans, prams, and dogs on leads, waiting for men to come out wi the wage packets. I hoped I wouldnae lose him in the rush. Course he was taller than most and stood out amongst most of the ugly mugs around here. I wasnae anywhere near the old spot where we used to meet, just in case he looked that way. I chastised myself. Why would he do that?

The big gates opened wi a loud screech followed by a wave of gruff voices, whistles, stomping feet. Sounds of men freed from their labours and excited about the coming chance to let off steam in the town's pubs. Was every welder, plumber and electrician the same? Did some not just go home, for Gawd's sake? Not every wife was like my mother, and it corresponded that not every man was like my father. For instance, what about Big Jim? A decent sort, hard worker and devoted son, who didnae go off drinking his wages away. Mind, maybe he should get out a bit more himself. It occurred to me, I didnae know anything about Jim's life, other than in the shop. He might have a girlfriend or be interested in fishing, or football, or motor car racing. Something to find out. Then there was Amy's dad. I'd been a bit cautious of him at first, not being used to English voices, and that talk about him being in the Knights of Columba disturbed me. They were even holier than the Saint Vincent crowd, but higher on the social ladder. I hadnae been able to find out what they actually did. Good works. But who for? We hadnae seen any sign of them around our place. But Mr Roberts had been nothing but kind and helpful to me. I'd met him several times now at their house, and he loved Amy to bits. No, he wasnae what was called a drinking man. The liquor in his crystal decanter just stayed at the same level. Then, I remembered Mrs Roberts on Amy's birthday, out for the count on her bed, the whisky bottle upended on the carpet. But she was mentally ill and, by definition, not responsible for her actions.

A dark thought came to me, Chrissie's stepfather. I shrugged it off.

I nearly missed Dad, catching the tail end of him as he laughed his way out of the gates. He slowed, glanced in the direction of our usual spot, shrugged, and strode up George Street. Maybe he did wonder … Men were being waylaid all the way up, rummaging in their pockets, deals being made on the spot wi their women. But not him, a free agent. The cheek of him, when he had a family at home, a wife to keep, a baby son he knew nothing about. My face flushed, my chest burned, I blew out several times to calm down.

Awright, I'd established he was still working at the Yards. No point following him to the Cutty Sark. But my nose got the better of me. I wanted a closer glimpse of his face. I hurried through the crowd, keeping my head down. I didnae want anyone to recognise me and tell Mum. Or Dad, for that matter. I turned after him on Main Road, keeping my eyes glued to his bouncing curls. He was indeed taller and broader than the men around him, and his swagger was easy to keep track of. Hadnae a care in the world. We were barely holding on and he was jesting wi his pals, now and then stopping to take one or the other in a head lock, like wee boys. No wonder Mum didnae want him back. He was useless. An eejit. My head burst wi the exertion of anger. It gripped my throat and I lost my wits. I raced forward and tugged him by the back of his jacket. 'Stop,' I yelled.

He stopped and turned. The other men halted wi him a moment, but backed off shamefaced when they recognised me, moving on when he nodded it was awright. 'Kathleen, darling …' He opened his arms in greeting, a wide grin on his face.

I kicked him.

My shoe met his thigh wi a satisfying thump. Even more rewarding was the way his leg gave way and how he staggered back.

But he was quick; he steadied and gripped me round the trunk, swinging me forward so that I couldnae kick him again. I was enraged. *How dare he?* Struggling, I kicked into air, and squirmed, but he held fast. My breathing knocked in my ears; I was vaguely aware of his hushing me, a rhythmic toll of sound.

A group of men approached. 'Awright, Hen?' One of them stopped, squaring his barrel chest.

I spat out, 'No, no …'

Dad's grip weakened, he let go and as I bolted, the man swung at him. I heard a cry, a groan and then, 'She's ma fuckin daughter, eejit.' But I didnae stick around. I was halfway through the play park when I stopped for breath.

Realisation hit in waves. I'd crossed a very clear line, one written in blood. Mum could never know about this. It was sedition, the worst act I could've done. No matter that I hadnae planned to speak to him – that had been a sort of accident – I'd contacted the Devil himself. She'd throw me out on my ear. Where would I go? But worse, I'd be the cause of her suicide. I'd come home one day to find her slumped in front of the gas oven, head on the enamel, tongue poking out, apron askew, Martin roaring in terror on his highchair. Gawd, how could I have been so stupid?

The rain was coming down in a torrent by the time I got to our gate. But at least my face was clean, rain clearing the tears away.

All these lies. It was doing my head in. A raft of *what-ifs* hit me. What if he came to the house? He hadnae tried to see us before. Would this make a difference? Mum would go backwards, even if she didnae end it all, everything would go to rot again, just when things were looking up. Sort of.

What if someone saw me, one of his pals or the other men and told Mum? I'd just deny it, swear on my life. Reason began to dribble through the panic. That wasnae likely.

Mum had few friends who gave her the time of day. Hannah might hear but she wouldnae tell Mum. My mum wasnae someone folk confided in or would dare approach wi an issue like this. The town might talk about her behind her back, but no one had the guts to confront her.

What if he came to the school when we started back, tried to see me? I'd die of shame. That wouldnae be missed. A parent walking through the gates, this parent wi his swagger and grin. Sure, he never did anything discreetly. Anyway, Sister Philomena would know by osmosis, the way she knew everything.

I trudged upstairs, took off my soaked coat and hung it in the press. Morag and Rosie nosed out the living room.

Morag said, 'Where ye been? Yer tea's wasted.'

I slid the book from my pocket and Morag pointed. 'Ye took that one wi ye. How come?'

Mum came to the kitchen door. 'Yer tea's on the pot, Kathleen. Did ye get that book?'

'Aye, Mum. Just in time.' I threw Morag a warning. She zipped her lips wi her finger and thumb.

Guilt rushed through me like fire, but Mum didnae notice. Of course, she didnae, she wouldnae notice if my hair went up in flames. That was one blessing, at least.

Chapter 26

The Closure

Word flew round Havoc like pennies at a scramble. But it wasnae a celebration, it was 'The Last Day'. Women flocked into the street, aghast, as if warding off the banshee. Men allowed themselves to be swallowed into the pubs.

The Yard had closed. In a thousand homes, a thousand tragedies. And it wasnae even Friday.

Mum was po-faced. 'Makes nae difference tae us.' She pushed the pram through the throngs in the High Street. The noise level there was aye high on a Saturday morning but today it was fuelled wi panic. Men paid off, and no other jobs to be had. People worked from one pay packet to the next, there wasnae any surplus. I knew how hard it was to get by on Assistance. What was the matter wi my mother? She knew families who would be affected.

Some of our own kin too. Not the sisters, thank goodness, and not Peggy or Shelagh, but Dad.

What about him?

Morag looked up at me and winked. 'Looks like Da's gonna be as skint as us. Whit'll he dae fer the drink?' She meandered along beside me, each of us holding Rosie by the hand. Rosie noticed and tried to wink too, but couldnae manage one eye at a time, so it was more a series of blinks.

Already folk were talking about jobs in England, of men going to London where there was work for skilled and unskilled labour building roads. Of course, this was the only yard closing, there'd still be work further up the Clyde. Didnae necessarily mean Dad would be moving away.

It was of no concern to me, where he went, or how he lived. Would be good for him to get a taste of his own medicine.

We threaded through clumps of gossiping women, some stony faced, others tearful.

Mum ignored it all, set as she was on the haberdasher's where she bought her knitting patterns and wool. School uniforms needed to be made for the August return and the state of the world would not be getting in her way. As usual, she showed no interest in anything outside her own concerns. At the very least this was fodder for gossip or, if operating at a higher level, pity and compassion. My mother was hardening, determination stiffening her bearing, tightening her lips, and frosting her ice blue eyes.

Maybe I was a bit dighted myself, but I couldnae help but watch and listen. It was fascinating, exciting even. I was shot through wi adrenaline and couldnae get enough of it all: the problem wi the orders, the big loan the company had taken on to update their equipment, the secrecy of it and how no one on the lower echelons had got wind of any of this, and in the end how precarious the world of work was, particularly when you had no qualifications. We were all pawns of big business. Not knowing what was going on left you powerless. Maybe that was why I was aye so nosey. Yes, being curious was an essential survival skill, so I watched and listened. Asked questions. What about folk's rights? Did they not have any recompense? What about the union, what had it done? No one had answers.

First chance I got, I asked Big Jim in the shop. Foolishly, I started wi, 'Good job you're not affected, Jim.'

He clumped down his ladder, wiped his hands together, staring at them as though they were foreign bodies, then looked at me as though I were a big puzzle needing solving.

I was quite put out. I stepped back. 'What is it? Have I said something wrong?'

I had. He gave me a lesson in commerce.

'Kathleen. Where dae ye think yer wages come from?'

'Out the till,' I said pointing to the big metal box on the counter.

'And where does the money come from, that's in the till?' He arched his hairy eyebrows.

'The customers.'

'And where dae they get their money?'

The penny clanged.

'Sorry, Jim. I see what you mean. But not all the customers work in the Yard.'

'Thank the guid Lord for that or we would be out of business.' He grinned and I was relieved I hadnae offended him.

The possibility of Rennie's closing struck me as the most tragic of all. What about my job? Panic took hold and he must have seen it in my face.

'Don't worry, Kathleen, we've got a bit of rope, business folk like us have tae make sure they can buck the tides when they come. We still need ye. And if the worst comes tae the worst, we'll make sure ye're awright.'

I loved Big Jim for that. He was solid, through and through, but he also had access to resources that helped him buck those tides. My mother hadnae any of that. Her disinterest in the town's calamity was becoming understandable. You could hardly give what you hadnae got. Her crises had already happened.

I left Big Jim stacking his shelves and wandered ower to the empty play park, sat on a swing and eased myself into a steady rhythm, measuring my chances of avoiding penury and destitution in life. If nothing changed, I would follow in my mother's shadow. Dependent on a man for security. Dependent on work that paid pennies to live. I dragged the swing to a stop wi my feet and stood up. Steely eyed, I made a promise. The long view needed to be taken. Education was my way out and I wasnae going to let anyone, including my dighted parents, take it away from me.

The effects of the shut-down played out across the town, in those waves Jim mentioned. There were at least five suicides spoken of in hushed voices, a couple of murders in the pubs and at least one poor woman who got a doing at home. Of course, murder was public, but bashing your wife was a private matter. Excuses were made for the men. Being made unemployed, having a bit too much drink, being nagged to death by the woman. I listened to all this wi a sense of incredulity. But then I was still only a hapless soon-to-be fourteen-year-old wi no sense at all.

Chapter 27

Even Fleas Can Fly

School started in the morning and Mum was up to her eyes in navy blue wool, finishing off the last garment. We had new jumpers, even Rosie, who was starting Primary 1 at Saint Aloysius. Mum had tried to make Morag wear another knitted skirt, but she howled her protest so loudly, Mum gave in and my clever wee sister had a shop-bought one laid out on the bed beside mine. Poor Rosie had the elasticated waist and the ribbed panelling of Mum's primary school skirts. The waistline left a scarlet ridge around your belly for hours after the skirt came off. It was cleverly done, and they lasted forever, more's the pity. But Rosie didnae seem to mind that, so anxious was she about going to school and being left there alone. Mum was to take her to school wi Morag, and Morag promised she'd seek her out at playtime and no tae worry, naebody would batter her wee sister. At that, Rosie howled and had to be comforted all morning. I reassured her no one was going to batter anyone. The nuns would never allow it. Morag hummed and hawed at that till I threw her a warning look.

'Rosie,' I said, 'you'll love it, just like me. You'll have lots of pals; it's Sister Mary in infants and she's lovely.'

I was looking forward to school. Amy and I had spent the rest of the summer together. Or, mostly she spent the rest of the summer wi us. Me, Morag, Rosie and Martin. Her mum came home and was much better. The ECT worked and she seemed to have settled down again. I couldnae see how that kind of treatment could work. It sure had to be a bad thing to electrocute somebody, but I kept that to myself. Amy was happy and that was all that mattered.

We'd gone as planned to the pictures and watched Gregory Peck in *To Kill a Mockingbird*. I'd read the book twice more as I knew it had to go back on Amy's shelf and I might not have the chance again. I dreamed of living in America and being a hotshot smart lawyer. When actually I lived in boring auld Scotland and would probably be a hotshot smart factory worker. Amy was fired up to go to university and go into … well this week it was medicine, last week it was law and earlier in the summer, journalism. She could do anything she liked. I wasnae jealous, she worked hard, and had her share of pain at home. I also realised how much she missed having a sister or a brother when I watched her play wi Rosie and cuddle Martin. She even won ower Morag by playing keepie-uppie. At first, Amy let Morag win, but soon realised that Morag was good at it and Amy couldnae keep up wi her. Amy said I was lucky to have such a wonderful family. I scowled and said she wouldnae say that if she caught their bloody head fleas.

Morag's scar was a red thread under her hairline. She was far from worried about it now and regularly raised her fringe to show her badge of honour. It irritated me to hear her tell how she'd done the swing run but just failed to dip at the right moment, something she'd got the hang of now, would anyone like tae see her acrobatics jist up there at the play park? And she had got the hang of it. My stomach lurched when I went to fetch her one teatime and saw her from a distance leaping off a swing and running like the wind underneath. I said Mum would tan her arse, but she just laughed and called me *'scaredy-cat'*. Privately, I began to think it was marvellous. She was fearless, my wee sister.

My birthday had come and gone. I got lots of cards, and

dollars came from Auntie Ina. Shelagh had given me ten bob and Hannah had bought me three pairs of stockings. Amy gave me a new copy of *To Kill a Mockingbird,* inside a message: '*To my best friend Kathleen, even fleas can fly! Love Amy'.*

I was really touched when Mrs Rennie had taken me aside and presented me wi a parcel and a card. In the card it said, '*to my favourite girl, love, Tilda'.* I hadnae considered she had a first name before. The present was a lovely purse wi two half-crowns inside. Dad sent me a card too. It didnae reach the bin because I got to the post before Mum. It was a picture of a pink princess and in it he'd written, '*To Kathleen, happy fourteenth, love, Dad'.*

A pink princess? He'd no idea. But I checked the postmark to see where he might be. Glasgow. Somehow, I felt a sense of relief, then shrugged it off.

The problem wi being fourteen was that I could leave school next summer, just short of my fifteenth birthday and if things went on as they were, I would need to get a full-time job. Dad hadnae come up wi any help to keep the house and Mum's Assistance didnae stretch far. Her measly wages helped as did my few shillings from Mrs Rennie, and the Saint Vincent de Paul chap came religiously every Wednesday wi ten bob. Although Mum thanked him and saw him out civil-like, she put that ten-bob note on the kitchen windowsill every time and looked at it wi scorn. Well, we couldnae afford to be fussy so she just had to bite down her shame.

She was less moody now. A few weeks before, she'd taken Morag to the doctor to get the stitches out and Morag said she'd been sent outside to wait a few minutes while Mum chatted to him. Morag was sure they were going to be talking about her, so for that reason it was okay to listen at the door. But it wasnae about her. She told me that Mum had said she was feeling down and vile-tempered.

'What?' I said. 'She admitted that?'

Morag bowed her head and opened her arms wide in supplication, as if she was the deliverer of the Ten Commandments. The doctor had said something about depression and said Mum needed a prescription. They'd gone to the chemist and Mum got two bottles of pills. I'd looked for them in the cupboards just to see if I could find out what they were called, but didnae find them. She must have had them on her person or in her bag, which wouldnae be worth searching because if caught the risk would be death. I was no longer *persona non grata* so it wasnae worth risking that elevated position either.

I'd talked to Amy about the pills instead. 'What might they be?'

'Mum's on a cocktail of stuff,' she said, 'but her condition's severe. Your mum's just a bit stressed.'

'What might he have given her that calmed her down?'

'Might be Diazepam. It's new. Mum has that as well.'

'What's it for?'

'It calms your nerves, I think.'

'Righto.'

'Maybe she has a sleeping pill as well.'

'Aye, maybe. She's better in the mornings than she was.'

'Could've been postnatal depression, except Martin's a year now. Plays buggery with your hormones apparently.'

Whatever it was, Mum was almost back to her auld crabbit self, as opposed to the Devil in an Apron she'd been since the night Grannie died. Course, then there was the trouble wi money. She'd been fine after Dad left, I thought. Or maybe I hadnae noticed. Or maybe she'd never been fine at all. Or maybe it was the dental operation and the false teeth.

It was all a bit of a mystery, but the good thing was the house felt lighter, less forbidding when you opened the door and put a first foot on the stair, and I was being lent a lot of rope. I could go out when I liked so long as I was back for her work at night and I could get time away from the weans. At first, I didnae go too far, worried as I was that Mum would unravel and there'd be trouble. As things calmed, I began to think more about Dad and how he was to blame. I hated him wi a vengeance.

We didnae ever talk about him. It was as if he'd been erased from history. Despite nursing my hatred there was stuff I wanted to know. Like where was he living exactly, and was he working? And did he still have that woman friend? I'd have liked that camera back too. I could ask Peggy. But she might tell Mum, and that idea made me shiver.

But tomorrow was school, and I had my bag to pack, three shirts to iron and wee Rosie to keep cheerful until bedtime. I sat her down beside me on the wing chair and read her stories from the *Blue Fairy Tale* book she'd got from the library. Morag lay on her belly on the floor reading the *Green Fairy Tale* book. Martin was walking and into everything. At that very moment, he pushed his doggy on wheels up and down the lobby. There was the occasional crash when he hit the wall. I didnae know how Mrs McCann put up wi us. Maybe she was deaf. Mum was in the kitchen making soup. I'd made sure the salt was by her elbow at the cooker so there couldnae be a repeat of the earlier mix up.

She was a bit stressed today as she'd had to find the money for three school meals. We had to apply when we got back each year and there would be a week of worry till it came through.

That was something else that irritated me. Why didn't some official work out how stupid that was? If you needed free school meals in the first place, you couldnae wait a week to eat. It was self-evident. At least Mum was handling it. I'd offered to pawn my ring, but she pooh-poohed that idea. 'Ower ma deid body,' she said. 'We've no got tae the stage of havin tae cross the threshold of that dirty pawn shop in the High Street.' I flushed from head to toe.

God help me if she ever found out about that.

The girls went to bed at eight, the usual school bedtime. I tiptoed in at nine, wishing I still had the light in my cabinet bed to read by. There was still a bit of light outside, so I opened the curtains and sat at the window wi my library book, *Little Women,* wishing I was as brave and clever as Jo March.

Chapter 28

Chrissie's Letter

I climbed the twisting metal stairs to the secretary's office, clutching the cool handrail, trying not to look down the stairwell. This was the highest point in the building, above Sister's office and way above the first, second and third floors of the old school building. Miss D. had another cubbyhole at Refectory where she handed out the free meal tickets and first aid but up here was her bolthole where she typed and answered the phone. No one was supposed to be up here. Only she and Sister, so I was breaking more rules.

Miss D. liked me, had made allowances before on my behalf, and this was something I sensed she wouldnae want anyone earwigging about as I was asking her to break rules of confidentiality and that was a tall order. But it was worth the risk. I hoped she'd agree wi my right to ask, even if she disagreed wi the act itself and said no.

It had to be her. Amy offered the use of her phone, and I could've asked Mrs Rennie, but it was unlikely I'd have made headway at the other end. It needed to be an adult, someone in authority. Sister had given me the name of the school. I'd taken it that meant she expected me to contact Chrissie there somehow, go visit, waylay her at the gates. Or write a letter to be passed on. Aye, that might've been it. But I couldnae risk that. Schools were too big, too institutionalised. How would I know that the head teacher wouldnae open the letter? Or that Chrissie might get in trouble or was trying to keep the head down and boom … attention fired her way by yours truly. No, this was more discreet. Secretary to secretary, low key. Just right.

Taking a deep breath, I knocked on the wood-slatted door firmly closed against me. There wasnae a name on it or a function mentioned, just a keyhole and a doorknob at waist height. I swallowed hard. Maybe she wasnae in. But I was a supersleuth and had darn well followed her up here, and unless she had wings, she was in that room. I knocked again. A cough wi a touch of indignation. Silence. Then a voice said, 'Enter.' This was laden wi a huge sigh. I wasnae welcome.

No bother to me, I was never welcome.

As I opened the door, it came out at me forcing me to shimmy through the gap.

The room surprised me, not a den like Sister's, but large and airy wi a big rectangular window under the eaves which framed sky. Blue today, cloudless but wi that icy aqua of a chilly autumn around the corner. Oh, to work in an office like this, all on your lonesome. How come some folk got all the good jobs? The shelves on one wall were tidy wi books and papers, all filed in groups according to size. In order too was the desk, a typewriter sitting square in the middle. My fingers ached to dance ower those robust shining keys. Everything was spotless.

'Cat got your tongue, Kathleen?' She stepped from behind the desk, bringing me back to attention.

'Sorry, Miss.' I chewed my lip. That was deliberate to show humility, that I knew this wasnae in the rules.

She didnae react so I tried hopping from foot to foot.

'Do you need the lavatory?'

'Oh no, Miss.'

I attempted a wan smile; she wasnae going to make this easy.

She sat back down behind the desk. Drew her glasses up

to her face, the chain shimmering ower her pink fluffy cardi. She was nice looking for an auld lady. Good dress sense too. She wore a tight black skirt that hugged her hips and a sharp white blouse. Pearls glinted at her ears and around her neck. Were they real? Who'd given them to her? Some auld geezer, a boyfriend in her youth, maybe…

'Kathleen Gallagher. How can I help you?'

I passed her the crushed note from my sweaty palm.

'Yes?' She dropped it on the desk and pinched her nostrils.

'I wondered, Miss, if you might help me get a letter to Chrissie Hall. I'm fair worried about her. She promised to write to me but hasnae and she's had a hard time.' I wanted to lay on more catastrophe, but Miss raised her hand.

'You might write to her via her head teacher.' She pressed the note out on the table. It spoiled the ordered effect of her workplace. She tapped the paper wi long pearl fingernails.

I said, 'Hmm, aye. But I cannae be sure if they might open it first.'

She considered this, nodding her head in slow motion. 'So, what is it you'd like me to do?' She stared hard at me, but a smile danced behind her eyes, and I knew I had her. I needed to play this out carefully and not rock my chances.

'Well Miss, I thought if I had her home address, I could write directly, you see. It occurred to me that you might have it on record as a former pupil moved on, like.' I didnae really expect that, but it was an opening gambit.

'No, Kathleen. Sometimes, if a pupil moves locally … but in this case, no, it's England you see.'

I knew that, of course, but I let my face fall in despair, even managing to squeeze out a tear.

Her face crumpled in sympathy whilst her nails rat-tatted on the desk. After a moment she picked up the telephone. Before dialling, she waved me to a seat against the far wall. I sat down and watched, listening wi fascination as she worked her way through, ower, and under regulations, put the handset back, wrote something down and handed me a piece of A4 wi Chrissie's new address written clearly in capitals.

'You never got that from me. Alright?'

'Yes, Miss … no, Miss. Thank you, Miss.'

*

Before resorting to Miss D, I'd already been round to Chrissie's house. The first time I walked right up to the door and knocked. Lights were on inside and I hoped Mrs Hall would answer but it was him. He stood behind the door peering out, his blond greasy hair sitting on a collar that had seen better days. His shirt flopped unbuttoned as though it'd been rushed on. He gave me a slimy smirk. In earlier days I might have called it friendly, but I knew him better now. I could taste the sourness of my disgust.

'Is Mrs Hall in?'

'No, away to the shop.' He looked me up and down and the smirk widened into a mouthful of yellow teeth.

'Is there any news of Chrissie?' As the door widened, I stepped back from a hit of body odour.

'She's fine. At her Aunt's.' He watched me closely through narrowed eyes.

I kept a deadpan face. 'Would you have the address please?' This came out in a higher octave than I intended, blast it.

'No, not me, her mother'll have it.'

'I'll come back another day.'

'Suit yourself.' He laughed, and spat out onto the path, to the side of where I stood. There was a loose brick lying there next to his green spew, and I had the urge to pick it up and crack his skull. I imagined the crack, a red wavery line on grey bone wi soft bluish matter seeping out. It'd be a pleasure, and a service to all women.

Instead I turned and walked stiffly to the gate and past the hedge. The door didnae close behind me, and I glanced back.

He stood in the doorway watching me. My spine tingled as I broke intae a run.

Despite being a coward, I did go back. Several times. But I didnae knock. I walked past in my usual disguise at dusk and peered ower the hedge into the living room hoping to see Mrs Hall. But I never did.

The woman had slipped off the face of the earth and in my wildest flights of fancy I imagined her broken body, knees to chin, beneath the soil in their backyard.

I made no mention of this in my letter to Chrissie and made sure to put Shelagh's address on the top right-hand side. I still didnae trust Mum enough not to open any reply that came. I trusted Shelagh wi my life. She might be a mad auld pseudo-catholic, but her values were on straight. Every week we'd do the praying, before having a great gab. She'd have her gin, or a sherry and mine was a shandy. Wi real beer. She treated me like an adult. I asked her advice about the letter.

'Auntie? Should I mention trouble in the letter, or should I just concentrate on cheerful things?'

'I'd say a bit about how yersel is getting along. Good and no so good, but no the worst.'

'Aye?'

'And then go intae how ye've been missing her and hope she's doing awright.'

'Aye?'

'And wind it up wi how ye see this going.'

'How d'you mean?'

'Well, are ye going tae see her again?'

This brought me up short. I imagined I'd see Chrissie in the future when she came back. But now I wondered, what if she never came back? A deep chasm welled in me and my eyes watered. I took a slug of shandy. 'Maybe I could go to Newcastle on the train sometime.'

'Aye, ye could do that.' She nodded sagely.

'I'm nearly fifteen.'

'Jist turned fourteen.'

'Well, aye. But I've two good legs on me and I could save up the fare.'

'Righto. Say that then.'

On Friday, I posted the letter at the Post Office and got a reply the next Wednesday.

Shelagh came to Mum's looking for me. Mum was surprised to see her come up the stairs, but didnae see the letter pass hands. Shelagh had brought a tray of home-made tablet that had drawn attention the way a loaf spilled from a bin attracted a squall of seagulls from the heavens.

Shelagh left after tea, winking at me as she went out. 'Need a bit of the clear stuff now, Kathleen. Yer mammy cannae cook for peanuts, how d'ye stand it?'

I thought back to the soapy soup. That was my standard and everything else wasnae as bad in comparison.

The letter was under my mattress and I waited until lights-out to read it. The only place you could get the light on after that was the toilet, so I sat on the pan and opened the white envelope marked wi Chrissie's handwriting. My fingers shook as I took out a filled page.

Dear Kathleen,

Thank you for writing to me. It was lovely to read your letter. And all your news. I'm glad you have a new friend. Amy is a nice girl. And I'm sorry to hear about Morag's accident.

You'll need to watch her like a hawk, she's a tough one, she is. Don't worry about me. I'm fine now. The problem I had is gone and I'm at a new school. Another new school! Did I ever tell you how many schools I've been to since I was five? Well, I've been to seven so it's water off a duck's back to start again. Anyway, this will be my last term. I'll leave at Christmas and get a job.

Auntie Reenie is nice. She's not really my auntie, she's Mum's friend who she was brought up with in the home. It's just her and me in her two-bedroom flat. I have a nice view out to fields and there are ponies, a lovely white one I've called Harvey. It's a bit boring though! I wish you were just around the corner. It would be great to see you if you could get the train here, we could spend the holidays next summer together. But your mum will need you. Maybe a few days, then.

I wondered if you might do me a favour. Mum was supposed to come after me, to get away from that you-know-who. I can't write his name down. But she hasn't been in touch for ages. Reenie says six weeks now. Could you knock and ask her to write to Reenie, or even phone her at work? She has the number. I don't know who else to ask.

Well, honey, I'll close now and look forward to your next letter.

Let me know how school is going. You'll skate exams as usual, you clever thing.

Love,
Chrissie x

Chapter 29

A Hero to the Rescue

I couldnae sleep for images of Mrs Hall keeping my eyes wide open. I saw her trying to fight off Pete, until he bashed her ower the head, first wi a vase, then a whisky bottle and finally a spade. At that, she fell in a heap at his feet and was dragged by the arms through the back door, her dress riding up. In the dark he bundled her into the shed, where her eyes stared lifelessly at me in accusation.

What if she really was buried round their backyard? He was a violent son of a bitch. A level of violence of a different order to Mum's. I shivered. But what if Mrs Hall had finally woken up to his treatment of Chrissie and threatened him wi the polis? I got up and sat on the side of my bed rocking wi fright. What was I to do? Eventually I must have fell ower, for I woke up wi Morag's face in mine. She was shaking my shoulder. 'Kathleen, it's late. Get up. We're aw ready fer school.'

I jumped up, confused, until it came flooding back.

Morag's eyes widened. 'Whit's up? Ye seen a ghost or somethin?'

I shook my head and stumbled to the toilet. As I washed, I tried to work it out. Was I overreacting? The woman had probably just forgotten to write, or maybe if she'd been brought up in a home, she couldnae write. But Chrissie would know that. Maybe Mrs Hall felt guilty and couldnae speak to Chrissie because she was to blame for some of it.

197

But they'd spoken at least once since Chrissie left. Maybe the letter had just got lost in the post. For Heaven's sake that had to be it. I threw cold water ower my face and took a long breath. I was over-imagining things.

All day I kept turning possibilities in my head. There was only one thing for it. I'd have to go round there. But I couldnae go on my tod, that might be too chancy if indeed this man was a desperate killer. He was a rapist of young women which was bad enough. At times I heard myself moaning in despair. This was too much for me. I had to tell someone. Maybe I should go to the polis? But if there wasnae a problem, that might backfire on Chrissie. And I couldnae tell what he'd done to her.

Shelagh might know what to do, but I knew she'd say, 'Go tae the polis, tell them ye're worried, show them the letter, they'll check and if she's okay, well and guid.' Sister Philomena? She'd want more information. Amy Roberts? I hadnae told Amy about Chrissie's trouble and I didnae want to do that. Mum would slap me one and tell me to mind my own business. Big Jim? Aye, maybe I'd ask Big Jim. He had form wi confronting violence. And he was big. And he didnae ask a lot of questions. I could say that Chrissie had asked me to contact her mother, she was worried, but that I was feart of the stepdad and didnae want to go round myself. He didnae need to know anything else. It occurred to me that this was a job for my dad.

How good it would be not to have to worry about how to get a man's help, just to be able to go into the living room and tell your dad your worries and him to get up onto his feet, get his jacket and take the matter ower. But Marty wouldnae have reacted that way, he'd have told me to mind my own business and resumed his scan of the *Daily Record*. Because he was a bastardin coward, and a wife-beater.

There it was.

After school, I made a detour round to Rennie's. Big Jim

was emptying out a sack of totties into separate bins. His sleeves were rolled up ower forearms that were enormous hunks of mutton. He smiled when he spotted me. 'Hello, Kathleen. Mum's in the shop.'

'Well, actually, Jim' — I smiled back wi what I hoped, despite my shame, was a little girl lost look — 'it's yourself I need.'

He put down the sack and gave me his full attention. 'Everything awright at home?'

'Och aye, Mum's much better. The doctor gave her tablets.'

He nodded, unconvinced.

'Jim, it's my pal, Chrissie.'

'Aye?'

'Well, see, the thing is she's in Newcastle at her auntie's and she's not heard from her mum in weeks and she's fair worried. She asked me in a letter if I'd go round and ask Mrs Hall if she's awright. But I'm feart …'

'How come?' His features crunched up and his fists balled, already ready to batter anybody that frightened me. What a great dad he'd have been.

'You see, the stepfather's a bit sleazy …' I bit my lip.

He took off his overalls, went ower to the sink, washed up his hands wi carbolic, the water running brown, and said, 'Awright, Kathleen show me where this eejit is.'

I hadnae really expected to go there right off but might as well, now I'd the support I needed.

We turned down the path and he asked, 'Chrissie … now … that'll be the wee blonde lass wi the big smile and rosy cheeks.'

'Aye …'

'And her mam, that'll be the woman who does the catalogue.'

That stopped me in my tracks, but I caught up fast. 'How do you know them?'

'She comes intae the shop. Like everyone else round here.'

I hadnae considered that. I had them isolated without any neighbours. Dunce!

He looked at me sideways. I'd underestimated his guile; it was seeping out of his eyes. 'Ye're right tae be worried. There's been talk. I'd like tae see for masel what's going on. And ye've gied me a reason tae go round there. Ye don't need tae come. Awright?'

'But I must. I have to tell Chrissie.'

'Let me handle things.'

'Definitely.'

We walked on a couple of streets. He didnae say anything else. This was a man who didnae need to fill silence. A couple of times I opened my mouth to speak but thought better of it. There was nothing else to say. It was yet to be found out.

We turned the corner of Chrissie's street. It was dusk now and through their windows we saw people moving around. Maybe we'd see Mrs Hall and that would be that. But I had the notion that wouldnae be enough for Jim. I'd lost the management of the whole thing, and I couldnae decide if that was welcome or not. Jim's determined chin was set, his gaze steely ahead, and I knew he'd sort it out and look after me at the same time.

'What house?'

'The fourth gate up.'

We walked by the hedge, looking in. The curtains were open and the lights on but there was no sign of life. Then, Pete walked out of the kitchen and passed into the hall. I shuddered, images of a murdered Mrs Hall threatening to floor me.

Big Jim walked right up to the door and knocked hard. I slunk behind him.

The door opened a crack. Pete peeked out. 'Aye?'

'Want a word wi Mrs Hall.' Jim sounded like a man in

200

charge.

'She's no in.' Huh, this was a different Pete from the big man who answered the door when I came around on my own.

'We'll come in and wait.' Jim thudded the door and it flew open, Pete jumping back in shock.

'Hey, wait a minute.'

Jim charged past and I hurried behind, keeping close to his back. Pete looked at me in enquiry. I looked away. He shut the door and followed us.

Jim commandeered the middle of the living room, me hiding behind him. Pete stood at the door, his face white, fingers fidgeting wi his chin.

'Kathleen here has a letter from Chrissie. She wants us to gie her mum a message.'

'Aye, leave it wi me.'

'No.' Jim said this slowly but surely.

Pete stepped back. He was shivering now and it wasnae cold in here.

'Where is she?' Jim took a step closer to Pete. I held back.

'Out to work.'

'Naw, she's no.'

'How do you know?'

I thought the same thing, was he just trying his hand?

'She's no been intae the shop for a guid few weeks.'

'She goes someplace else.'

'There isnae someplace else.' Jim moved fast for a big man. He was ower the room in one step and had Pete by the neck. I swear he lifted the smaller man off his feet.

'Awright,' Pete squeaked.

Jim let go but didnae move away.

'She's up the stairs.'

Jim shoved the shaking fool ahead. 'You first.' He turned to me. 'Kathleen, wait here.'

I nodded, frantic now. Why was Mrs Hall upstairs? Why had she not come down?

Oh my God, oh my God; I breathed out the prayer in a litany as I listened to the creaks on the steps. I heard a door open above my head. And then total silence.

I froze, my ears trained to the ceiling. A shuffle, a door banging, a woman's moan, footsteps hurtling on the stairs. Pete swung round the door, slithered across the kitchen linoleum and out the back door, letting it swing on its hinges. There was a crunch on gravel and then a gate squeaked. He'd gone. I ran upstairs. Stopped at the bedroom door. Mrs Hall sat on the bed in her dressing gown, Big Jim beside her hushing her sobs.

He looked up. 'Kathleen, I want ye now tae sit here while I go get some help. Can ye dae that, Hen?'

'Aye.'

'The bastard'll no come back the night, but just in case, I'll get a neighbour tae stand at the door.'

'He went out the back, ower the meadow.'

'I'll lock the back door before I go. I'll bring some water up first.'

As he got up, the bed half collapsed. Mrs Hall fell sideways onto a pillow and made no attempt to right herself. I stood, my mind whirring. Jim came back upstairs wi a glass of water and handed it to me. 'Feed her a sip at a time.'

He thudded downstairs, the back door slammed, the key turned in the lock and then he paced down the path and out the gate. His steps faded away, and then there was a sharp chap at a door. Voices, a woman and a man. More footsteps coming closer, the front door opened.

A voice calling from downstairs. 'Mrs Hall, Kathleen, it's Millie Boyle from ower the road. Ma man'll keep guard at the front door. Ma eldest boy is round back. Ye're safe noo. I'll bide here. Call me if ye need anything.'

Mrs Hall lay back on the bed. Her wrists were black and blue and there were lengths of rope curled on the carpet at her feet. Her skin was pasty white, and she had a cut lip and a helluva old yellowing bruise across her forehead. There were other marks on her … ones I couldnae identify, all ower her legs and arms. She looked as if she was in a faint. I stroked her arm. 'A wee drink. It's Kathleen, Mrs Hall. Chrissie's pal.'

At this she rallied. 'Chrissie,' she said between thick lips. 'Where's my Chrissie?' And she started to sob again.

Chapter 30

Mortal Sin

Amy's bedroom had become our bolt-hole now winter was almost on us. Her mum and dad welcomed me into their home wi open arms, and I'd grown fond of them both. Ginty was bright, lively and fun, not to mention gorgeous, and Eddie was the opposite: dry, witty, considered in his actions and words, and pot ugly if I was being honest. He'd the look of a sad, apologetic bloodhound in his checked shirt, tie and blazer. He often walked about patting the air ahead as if to calm it. Maybe that was what came of being married to his wife, the tornado.

They were in love, that much was obvious. Outside of the cinema, I'd never seen two people so affectionate towards each other. They held hands, played footsie under the table, and he brought her flowers every Saturday when they went out dancing and to dinner.

Which was lucky for us, as we could have the house to ourselves. At least when I could escape from the madhouse. Like tonight.

We sat on Amy's bed sharing a crossword when an ice cream van's horn blared outside. I nearly jumped out of my skin.

'Kathleen, it's alright, it's only outside.' She stroked my back.

'Phew, I'm sorry, I keep doing things like that. I nearly dropped Martin and his stinky nappy when the ice cream van

204

came last night.'

'It hasn't been that long since poor Mrs Hall. You're bound to be nervy still.'

'At least she's awright now, that's the main thing.'

'It was good of Jim Rennie to drive her to Newcastle in his van.'

'Big Jim is … I don't know … he's just great. You should've seen him grab that turd by the throat and lift him off his feet.'

She smiled and nodded even though I'd told her all this before.

'Then he was so lovely when he found Mrs Hall tied up in that bed.'

'Poor thing.'

'And those marks on her. I can't believe he was burning her like that, how could anyone do that?' Tears stung again. I hadnae realised what the marks were until Mrs Hall told Jim while we waited for the ambulance.

'A prisoner in her own house and just because she was leaving him.'

It wasnae just because of that. I'd kept Chrissie's secret. It was up to her to tell. Mrs Hall had indeed woken up, threatened to go to the polis and charge him about Chrissie, and that's when he'd battered her, then tied her up and fed her pills to keep her quiet. She thought he'd kill her eventually. I got to know this as I waited wi her in that room for the ambulance to come. So did Big Jim. I'd never seen him so angry. Rage seeped from his eyes, his fists and the veins in his neck when the penny dropped that Chrissie had been assaulted. But he kept his counsel and never spoke of that to me again. Pete Hall had been caught and charged wi Mrs Hall's assault, at least that's what it said in the paper. There was nothing about his abuse of Chrissie, but I supposed that couldnae be reported, or maybe Mrs Hall hadnae told the polis. Chrissie had her mum back. I told myself that's what counted.

I said, 'Your mum and dad, despite everything, they're so in love.'

'Yes, they are. It's such a pain sometimes.'

'How come?'

'Well, it's like they only have room for themselves. I'm not part of that relationship.'

'But they love you to bits.'

'I know, and that's okay. It's just that they have a special bond I'll never be part of, but I'm still glad they're my parents, even when Mum goes … you know …'

'Yeah.'

We sat in silence for a bit, hip to hip, occasionally filling in the crossword. I thought my mum and dad were wanting in comparison wi Mr and Mrs Roberts, but a lot better than the Halls. That was an extreme comparison. Mum was hard to live wi, but Dad was just as bad. Worse, his dereliction of responsibility hadnae helped. And there was no justification for battering anybody. But this tied me up in strings. Surely you could defend yourself, stand up for yourself or your family. Course, the Roberts were well off. That must make a difference, not having to worry about money every day. And educated too. Well, at least he was. Did that make any difference to family life? I didnae know, but it must help people if they can talk out their problems, put stuff into words. I'd never heard my mum and dad have an actual conversation that wasnae an argy-bargy.

'Amy?'

'Yes?'

'I saw my dad a while ago. Before Mrs Hall.'

She sat up straight. 'Does your mum know?'

'Nope. Well, not as far as I'm aware. I followed him after work to see if he was still at the yards and he was, but then I got mad, ran up to him and ended up kicking him and running off.' I turned and grimaced. It sounded so pathetic when said aloud.

She didnae look shocked or embarrassed. She looked straight at me, accepting like.

'Quite right. He deserved that. But what now?'

'How d'you mean?'

'Do you want to see him again, Kathleen?'

'I don't know. It's just I was thinking he's not as bad as some.'

'Maybe your mum and him just can't get on. That doesn't mean you shouldn't see him, you know.'

'I don't love him, Amy. I know I'm supposed to, but he scares me. It's the drink and the unpredictability. To be honest, I think he's been battering my mum for years and she's just put up wi it. As everybody does round here.'

'Not everyone, Kathleen. Well, it should be your decision, not your mum's.'

'She'd go apeshit.' I widened my eyes and we laughed. 'Anyway, the Yard's closed. I don't know where he is now, working, or whatever. And I don't want to rock the boat. Mum's doing awright and she's been specially nice to me after Mrs Hall.'

'So she should be. You were very brave, Kathleen. You are the spunkiest person I know.'

'I'm just nosey. Cannae ever seem to keep out of other folk's troubles.'

'Well, I'm glad you didn't keep out of mine.'

'Amy?'

'Yes?'

'Have you thought about what it would be like wi a boy?'

'Sex?'

'Aye, sex.'

'Course, you dimwit.'

'I was thinking it would be best to try them out before making a firm commitment. But the church says you must wait till married. That's risky, because how do you know they will suit?'

'My dad's very clear that God finds the right partner for you.' She rolled her eyes.

I copied her. God must've been on his holidays the day my mum and dad married.

'He's in the Knights. He's gotta say that. What's your mum say?'

'She says to keep safe and to make sure you get respect.'

'What's that mean?'

'I think she means you get to know each other well and trust each other before you make any commitments.'

'Sounds good.'

'You got anyone in mind, Kathleen Gallagher?'

'Not at all.'

She shoved me off the bed and as I clambered back up, I remembered that time when I was so hung up about sex, a time when the ramblings of the Church had me in total panic. It wasnae that long ago but it felt like a lifetime, so much had changed, so many questions.

Amy was staring at me. 'Kathleen, where are you? You must have someone in mind, you're dreaming, girl.'

I caught up. 'No, I havenae the time, what wi rescuing abused women and assaulting errant fathers, not to mention changing dirty nappies. Oh, then there's schoolwork, exams, my job at the shop etc, etc … Who has time for sex?' And I was thinking, *who has time for guilt and mortification?*

Later, as I walked home from Amy's my mind took me back to the major embarrassment of my life. Thank God the confessional was private and no one would ever know my shame. It was a Saturday morning and I had piled up the Carmel Hill against a bully of a wind to say my Confession. Such a trek, but I was desperate to wipe the stain of sin from my soul, sure that if I died that day, I'd be wheeched out my coffin straight to Hell. I couldnae risk going to St Ali's in case I got Father Murphy, so it had to be the new parish, St.

Luke's. The backs of my legs were loupin wi the effort but I didnae want to miss the Confessions after Mass. Asking Mum for thruppence for the bus was out of the question because she'd have cottoned on something was up. It was rough that end of town, so it was, and I was worried I might run into the boys from the borstal. I pedalled my legs faster as I approached the borstal gates.

Of course I didnae know if this was classed as a mortal sin but I didnae like to take the risk. There were too many stories of Hell and Damnation for any sin that was mortal. You couldnae scratch a toe, you had boils all ower your bum, and as you were buck naked that was fair humiliating, not to mention the fact you were on fire and roasting in the pit. But, there's the thing. How did you know when a sin was mortal or venial? I'd checked my missal.

'A sin is mortal when the act is gravely wrong and committed with full knowledge and clear consent.'

But that wasnae much help. I qualified wi the full knowledge and consent but was flummoxed wi the gravely wrong category.

At the library I examined books on the Catholic Church and sin, pouring ower them as if studying for exams. That librarian fella kept strolling by my seat and nodding like he knew what I was up to. Anyhow, it said in there that this was a grave sin but nowhere was the damn word *'mortal'*. It had plenty about *'ejaculation'*.

At the borstal gates my heart decided to sprint, and I flushed up to my hairline. Two lads were hanging about having a fag. They werenae looking my way, I could get by unnoticed. I rushed past, but they whistled after me, and shouted unmentionable words. Well, bugger that. I did a Morag and screamed back a retort that would certainly land me in purgatory. That fair shut the twits up.

The wind bowled me out of range, before the inevitable revenge, and round the corner into the church lane. It wasnae as grand a parish as St Ali's, being modern. I pricked my ears to *Sweet Sacrament Divine*, went in and sat through the interminable Mass. Afterwards, I hung about at the back, after all the parishioners had scattered, and looked around for the queue. None. Maybe there wasnae any Confessions on. Maybe I'd come back another time.

Then I saw the priest, angling into the lavatory. As he came out, I nabbed him, an auld fella, a bit shaky on his feet. He'd got big thick glasses on him; maybe he wouldnae ever recognise me again.

'Can I help you?'

'Can you hear my confession, Father?'

His eyes batted for Scotland behind the jeely jars. 'It's not the time. Come back at four o'clock.'

'I cannae do that, Father. I might die by then.'

He shrugged. 'Come on then. I hope you've murdered someone.' He peered into my face. 'You're no one o mine.'

'No, Father, Saint Ali's.'

'Another escapee.' He shook his head.

I tiptoed up the aisle behind his crow-like figure, a crow wi a limp. In the box at last, the cross of Jesus at my head, the lattice grille between me and salvation. Specks of dust pranced in a ray of sunshine falling ower my trembling hands, but Father was a murky shadow.

'Bless me, Father, for I have sinned …'

'Have you robbed a bank?' A tight, weary voice.

'No Father, I've been disobedient ten times. I've …'

'What is your mortal sin, my child?'

I couldnae believe I was going to say this to a man. The word was cotton-balling in my mouth but, elevating myself to a higher plane, I said, 'I masturbated one time …'

Chapter 31

Fireworks

We were in the living room on Sunday after Mass. Mum was knitting a jumper for Martin. She'd been at it for no time and it seemed almost done. Knitting seemed to soothe her, and we were quiet while those needles clicked their calming rhythm. Morag lay on her belly at the fire, reading *The Beano*, only occasionally snorting out a laugh, or tutting, or whispering bits aloud. Rosie sat beside me on the couch, thumb in mouth, the other arm around her teddy. I was reading a Latin text. Martin was fast asleep in his pram behind the couch.

A loud bang interrupted the peace. We all started up. Mum hesitated, listening for the source. Puzzled, she put the needles and wool into the basket beside the chair. I got up wi her.

Morag was already opening the door when Mum pulled her back.

We smelt burning, heard crackling. Mum stepped into the lobby, I followed close behind. Morag and Rosie pushed in behind me; I batted them back. It smelled like the bonfire at Guy Fawkes. Smoke hugged the kitchen ceiling in blowsy grey clouds. Mum moved towards it, just enough to peer in. I kept close to her. The pulley hung precariously from one strut, the clothes aflame, two pegged nappies all but eaten black, orange embers at the edges. Fire raced up the ropes on the pulley, they were already black strings where flames had consumed them. Wooden struts crackled and spat. The

211

blue flame was still on, under a blackened pot. Mum made to cross the room, I jerked her back from the wall of heat.

'We need to get out. Now.' I coughed, the smoke irritating my throat. She backed out, breathing heavily, closing the door fast behind her, dulling the sound.

I turned to the weans. Morag and Rosie stood stock-still, eyes bulging. Everything seemed to happen in slow motion, and I had to push myself to step to the press, snatch their boots and coats, shove them at them and shout to wait in the street, pushing them along the lobby. Morag grabbed Rosie's arm and pulled her away. By this time, Mum was at the living room door wi Martin clasped to her chest, wrapped in his blanket. I followed her downstairs to the street, only looking back once to see smoke belching under the kitchen door. Outside, Mum passed Martin to me, paced around the building and battered downstairs door. A minute later, she came round the corner wi a white-faced Mrs McCann clutching her coat and hat.

The commotion brought several neighbours out and, despite warnings from others, two of the men rushed into the flat. Someone called, 'Phone the Fire Brigade,' and two teenage boys ran down the street. The men came back out of the house, their faces soot black, saying they'd managed to douse the flames wi blankets from the beds, but the kitchen was a mess. By the time the Fire Brigade came the fire was out, but the house was smoke filled, the walls blackened. We werenae allowed back in.

It was a cold October day and the sky was darkening. The trees had turned, leaves cracking underfoot. I only wore a cardi but someone brought me a coat. Mum stood stonyfaced gazing up at the windows. She hadnae said a word, but her hands shook. All at once, steady hands took Martin from me. It was Big Jim, his mum right beside him.

She said, 'Kathleen, pet, you get the wee ones and your mum, and come up to ours for the night and we'll see how things look tomorrow.'

*

We stayed at the Rennie's that night, and in the morning, Mum went wi the Council Officer and the fireman to view the damage. The verdict was it'd be weeks before we could return home. The flame under the soup pot had spurted and caught the pulley rope. Although there was no structural damage, the kitchen needed renewed and the place cleaned and repainted. The council would be responsible for that, but we had no house insurance. Anything damaged that wasnae council property was ours to replace. Nor would the council accommodate us.

Or, rather, they'd accommodate us weans in the local home, but Mum said she nearly took the man's eye out when he said that. Mrs Rennie offered two spare rooms for as long as we liked, but Mum was too proud to accept that offer and anyway, Big Jim hadnae thawed any as far as she was concerned. I was relieved. It was an odd and uncomfortable arrangement. Two distinct parts of my life together in one place.

Also strange was crossing the threshold between the shop and the Rennie's home.

Other than the downstairs toilet I'd never been beyond the shop and had only glimpsed the hall area behind the beaded door screen. It was like entering another world. It wasnae posh like Amy's, nor elegant or modern. It reminded me of the jumble sales round at the Salvation Army hut at the Common. Every surface held figurines, or photos in frames, brass plates, china dolls. Magazines were stacked in piles against walls and in the lounge there were at least ten Spanish doll dancers, each wearing a fabulous lace dress of jewelled colours.

Morag's jaw dropped to the floor as she surveyed it all, but she recovered quick enough when she saw the framed photograph ower the fireplace.

213

'Jim, Jim, is that you?' She pointed, eyes wide.

I took in a sharp breath.

Before Jim could answer, Mrs Rennie drew up her four-foot-eleven. 'That's Jim in his heyday. The gentle giant he was known as.'

Morag and I stood staring at the image. Wee Rosie kept looking from Jim to the picture, her head like one of those nodding dogs.

Jim wasnae interested in fishing. Or motor racing. He was a heavy-weight boxer.

There he was, wi his huge gloved fists at his square jaw, posing for the camera.

Turned out in his youth he'd won lots of fights, made a bit of money, bought the shop, got started up. Now he trained other boxers. I never knew ... though you only had to look at him.

Morag had the cheek to ask him to train her up. He said to wait till she was twelve and he'd sort that out down at his club. Poor Jim didnae know what he was letting himself in for.

*

There was a family confab that afternoon at Patsy's between Mum, Patsy, Hannah, and Auntie Shelagh. Patsy's three, Morag and Rosie were taken out by Uncle Joe to give us space. I was there to look after Martin while the so-called grown-ups drank tea and considered what to do. It was funny how we'd been in private crisis for months wi no help to be had, and now, in a public crisis it was all grist to the mill. Great what nearly burning to death can do to bring out the best in your relatives. Course, I didnae have a say about anything. It was as if I was invisible, which was my normal state of being. I sat at the window wi Martin on my knee playing wi a toy car on the windowsill, pretending I wasnae listening.

Hannah started wi her big gob. 'Nellie, ye gied us such a

214

fright. Whit wur ye thinking aboot, leaving a pot on the gas like that and nappies on the pulley?' At this, she blew smoke out in a whorl, like a dragon might. Then pursed her lips in pain.

Mum said, 'Well, it wasnae as if ah meant it. And ah huv got four weans tae keep clean.' She threw darts at Hannah.

Shelagh intervened wi, 'Right yous lassies, it's time tae work oot what tae do aboot it aw, no argy-bargy.'

Patsy added, 'Aye, Ma wid huv a fit tae hear yous two at each other.'

Mum said, 'The council say it'll be three weeks anyhow. And they offered the weans Langside.'

Hannah made a decision. 'Whit, the care place? No way.'

Mum said, 'Ah said naw, silly. Course we'll aw stay thegither.' She looked up wi that sly look of hers, the one where she's going after you. 'We could aye come tae yours. The weans can bunk up and ah can sleep on the couch.'

Hannah stubbed out her fag, crossed her legs. 'Ah've no the room. It's a wee hoose. We're tight as it is. Whit aboot Patsy's?'

Patsy said, 'Aye, ye could aw come here. It's fine. Though ah've only got three bedrooms, ah don't know where ye'd aw go. Yous could bunk up wi ma weans. But ah don't keep well, as ye aw know, so the weans wid need tae be awfy quiet.'

Hannah said, 'Ah don't suppose that waste of space da of theirs has come roon tae help?'

Mum replied, 'Huvnae seen him in months. Ah dinnae need his help, thanks. He's oot the yards wi the rest of them.'

Hannah offered some gossip. 'Bastard landed on his feet but, got taken on at Lithgows.'

Mum looked surprised. Nodded her head. 'Aye, ah should've known, charmed his way in when a thousand men cannae get work.'

Shelagh said, raising her hands, 'Right. Enough! Ye

cannae go tae Patsy's and yer wee sister willnae have ye. So, there's only one thing for it. Ye'll aw come tae mine.'

Confusion set on everyone's faces as they stared at Shelagh. She only had one spare bedroom. And this was mad-hatter Shelagh.

Shelagh confirmed it. 'No, don't worry. Come tae me.'

Mum's face was a picture of incredulity, but it cleared; she got up and hugged Shelagh. I almost burst wi pride, Mum hugging someone in gratitude. It was a great day.

Shelagh caught my eye and I winked at her.

*

Earlier, before the meeting, I'd taken the opportunity to leave the weans wi Mrs Rennie after Mum had gone out. I raced up the hill to Shelagh's.

She hugged me. 'Are ye awright, Hen? I was that worried. I went doon tae the house when my neighbour told me what happened but Mrs McCann doon the stair said ye'd aw gone tae Mrs Rennie's place, so I knew she'd look after ye.'

'Aye, but it was scary. The fire was dancing across the ceiling. You should've seen it ...'

She interrupted my fascination for drama. 'Well, put that behind ye. What's the verdict?'

'Three weeks, anyway. We'll need a new table, chairs and cabinet. And a cooker. But the National Assistance people might give us a grant for that. The rest of the hoose is awright, maybe just new bedding, the chairs in the living room recovered and the carpet replaced.'

'Cost a wee bit, aw that?'

'Aye. But Auntie? I thought I'd sell my – your – ring to pay for it.'

She nodded slowly. 'No, pet, keep that. It might be more use tae ye later, when ye're aulder, rather than pull yer mother oot of this.'

'Mum doesnae have the money, but.'

'What aboot yer Da?'

'She's not going to ask him.'

'I've a few bob away. I'll help her oot. What aboot Hannah, she's no short.'

I shook my head.

'I'll sort her.' The emphasis was on *her*. She pursed her lips. 'But, meantime, where yous aw going?'

'Mrs Rennie offered but Mum willnae accept.'

'No, should be family, they're guid people, but that wouldnae do.'

'I wondered …' I looked around.

She tittered. 'Here?'

'Aye, how not?'

'Stay wi a mad auld bat like me?'

'It's all an act. You're the most sensible relative I have.'

'Why, thank you, Kathleen Gallagher. And you? Ye're the slyest of us aw.'

Chapter 32

Anniversary Blues

I heaved my schoolbag through the tiny hall and slung it in the bedroom. It slapped against the headboard of the bed I now shared wi Morag and Rosie. Ready to storm into the living room to protest to Shelagh about the wickedness of that damn Mrs Richards, I stopped short and clamped my mouth shut at the door. The sight was both mortifying and mesmerising. The living room was dark except for the firelight and a small lamp in a corner throwing an amber glow ower my mum who was on her knees peering down the brae. Morag and Rosie crouched in front of her, noses at the window. Shelagh's beads tinkled as she said the rosary. Morag turned to plead wi me to get her out of this. I raised my eyes to Heaven, it was a done deal, she'd need to stick it out. She scowled and turned back to the view, no doubt the same one I'd endured until I got the measure of Shelagh. Martin played in front of the fire wi a toy bus, rolling it up and down the carpet. 'Brrr, Brrr,' he said as he went. I glanced at the fire to make sure the guard was on, and it was, but I still didnae trust Mum, and Shelagh was inexperienced wi bairns. When he noticed me backing away, he got up wi the car and toddled out after me. I picked him up and gave him a kiss on his cheek and he giggled, dropping the car to the floor. Cuddling him, I stole another glance at the supplicants. Mum was grim faced, fingering her pearl beads; wee Rosie looked baffled, her forehead creased wi perplexity. Morag stabbed venom at me, but Mum slapped her head back into a forward position. I narrowed my eyes at Shelagh who shook her head in warning. What was up?

Things had been going well the last two weeks. Mum was bordering on cheerful, on her best behaviour. She and Martin had Shelagh's bedroom. Shelagh slept on the couch.

We'd protested until she showed us the mechanics of it. You lifted up the seat, which was one piece, like on the bus, and pulled it out and up, and hey presto, something clicked, the back went down, and you had a bed wi a join in the middle like your notebook. In the compartment underneath were sheets, a pillow and blankets. She said she often slept in the living room when the weather was cold as it was warm by the fire, so not to worry. She was a good cook too. Even now, a delicious, meaty smell lingered in the flat; beef stew I guessed, already salivating.

But she'd given up this practice of praying in public to the imaginary Virgin. She told me that it was a ruse to entertain the troops when they came to see her. It was devilment, in fact, I told her, as had I not been scared silly last year when I first had to do that? I pressed Martin to my neck as we both watched the little group at the window. It must've been almost a year since I started coming here to visit Shelagh. A cold sensation ran down my spine. What was today's date? I hurried into the room and wi one hand took out my English school jotter and dropped it on the dresser. I rifled through it. We aye had to write the date of class. Martin balanced tightly on my hip, I leant down. Today was the date Grannie died, her first anniversary.

A ripple of alarm sped through me again. Martin must've picked it up as he kicked and punched his way down my front. He scrambled out to his bus and began to play again, getting louder and louder wi his brrrs. I followed him into the hall, watching him, hoping this wasnae going to send Mum backwards.

The decade of the rosary was ending, the murmurs of the *Glory Be* finishing it off.

Mum got up. 'Thank you, Shelagh, it was guid tae say a wee prayer fer her today. And ye're so right, how marvellous tae see the Virgin's image there.' She looked pointedly at Morag and Rosie. 'Just as if she was real. But she's no, girls, awright?'

Morag nodded vigorously and Rosie smiled and blinked. Released from their labours they ran towards me. 'Kathleen, Kathleen. A letter's come fer ye,' they yelled in unison.

Shelagh slipped it out of her cardi pocket and passed it to me. Mum humphed, possibly displeased that Shelagh had usurped her authority, but I was pleased that she had. Mum still wasnae past opening anything addressed to me, even though I was fourteen. How come it was okay for me to be an adult, look after the weans and leave school for work, yet be too young to open my own correspondence? I took the letter into the bedroom, shutting the door fast on Morag who was at my heels. She moaned at the door but didnae try to open it.

'Aw, Kathleen, can ah no come in? Honest, ah'll jist sit there and no bother ye.'

'In a minute, right?'

'Awright.' I heard her slump to the floor and sit against the door. Almost immediately there was another thump. That would be Rosie. God Almighty, there was no peace to be had anywhere. This house was far too wee for us.

Chrissie's handwriting was on the envelope and I peeled it open and took out the blue sheets she aye used. I read through the page quickly, turning it ower to finish. Turned it back, read again in dismay. They wouldnae be coming to Glasgow as expected. The case had been dropped. The sleazebag had made charges against Mrs Hall to say he was protecting himself by tying her up as she was a madwoman and had been assaulting him for months. All lies, Chrissie said, and of course they were. What about the burn marks? He was saying she inflicted them upon herself. Chrissie said her mother had been advised to withdraw the charges because her own history wasnae faultless. They had evidence that she was a bit wild when she was a teenager and she'd a stay in a psychiatric facility at one time too, after an earlier difficult relationship had broken down. Chrissie finished by saying it was a relief, anyway, for them both and not to worry. He'd gone off on the ships as a merchant seaman and wouldnae be anywhere near either of them. She hoped to see me again in the summer if I could find the time to visit and signed off as '*your good friend, Chrissie*'.

Morag wheedled at the door. 'Kathleen, aw, come on, let me in.'

I got up, letter still in hand, opened the door and flopped back down onto the bed. She fell in scrambling on the floor, got up, and sat on the bed beside me. Rosie sat where she was at the door wi her teddy. I smiled at her and she grinned back.

'Is it Chrissie?' Morag asked.

'Aye.'

'Is it the bad man?'

I narrowed my eyes. How did she know about this? 'How d'you mean?'

'Ah heard Mum and Shelagh talking aboot it aw, and Hannah and Patsy. Ah knows aw aboot it.' She pursed her lips like Mum.

Not wanting to risk Rosie's ears, I got up, helped the wee soul to her feet and deposited her in the living room.

I came back and sat down on the bed. 'So, what did they say?'

'That Mrs Hall got battered and burned by that sod and the polis took him away, and that Big Jim wis a hero and chased the bastard.'

'Morag!'

'That's whit they said, ye said tae say whit they said.'

'Well, he's got off wi it.'

'Oh, naw, how come?'

'He's a man, that's how come.' I was fuming. This wasnae fair. It shouldnae count what Mrs Hall's history was. I thumped the bedcover. Morag copied me. I got up and put the letter in my folder. I'd write to Chrissie again when I had some space.

Mum stuck her head around the door. Nodded to Morag to go. My nosey sister opened her mouth to protest, thought better of it and slipped off the bed and out the room.

'Ah'm guessing that's from Chrissie. Is she awright?' Mum sat down beside me.

'Aye, I think so, just they've dropped the charges.'

She nodded.

'You're not surprised?'

'It's hard tae get a conviction when ye've been living wi the man. The court'll ask why she didnae jist leave. But ye live in hope, every day, that things'll get better.' She smiled ruefully. 'It's hard tae leave when ye've nae money and weans and … But at least the poor soul got away from him. Ye did well, Hen.' She leaned ower and patted my leg.

I looked down at her ringless left hand. It had been hurting my brain too long, and this seemed like a good moment. 'Mum, where did your rings go?'

She drew in a breath. 'Hannah took them tae the pawn shop in the High Street and sold them fer me. She said they were only any use tae buy messages, and she was right.'

That was a turn up for the books.

I said, 'I've just realised it's a year since Grannie died.'

'Aye, a long year.' She smiled. 'It's a sad day, but …' She giggled.

I caught my breath in wonder. 'Mum?'

'Och, it's auld Shelagh, she had us aw look oot that windae fer the Virgin. Ah nearly wet masel.'

222

'Aye, I had to do it last year, before …'

'Before whit?'

'Never mind, let's just say she's not as daft as she looks.'

'Aye, ah'm beginning tae think she's ahead of us aw.'

She put her arm around me and hugged me tight for a long moment. I was feart to breathe in case I spoiled it. Then she got up and said, 'We'll get hame soon, Kathleen, and things will work oot, ye'll see.'

Shelagh had prepared a beef and sausage stew that melted in your mouth and we sat in the living room wi big bowls of it and chunky bread to dip in. Martin sat in his new, second-hand highchair being fed by Mum in-between her own spoonfuls. After that we had a homemade apple pie wi thick yellow custard.

'Tae celebrate,' Shelagh said. 'A first anniversary of a wonderful sister, mother, and grandmother, never tae be forgotten.' She raised her glass and Mum and I toasted wi shandies. Morag had lemonade wi a spoonful of beer in, and Rosie just the lemonade.

After tea, Mum and Shelagh sat sipping from their glasses whilst Morag and I did the dishes. Rosie played cars wi Martin. I did the work, and Morag stood behind the door listening attentively to the conversation, sharing titbits as she caught them.

Morag whispered loudly, 'Mum says she's got the Cooncil in the morning at the hoose – she says she hopes it'll be ready tae go back tae soon. Shelagh says … we can stay as long as we need tae … Mum says it's been great, she's been a tonic, but the weans need stability and a bit mare space … Shelagh says … Aye.' Silence for a while.

'Mum says she needs tae see the lawyer as well soon. Shelagh says best get on wi it. Noo they're talking aboot Mrs Hall. Oooh.'

'What is it?'

'Shelagh called the man a very bad name …'

'Don't say it.'
'Effin…'
I slapped her wi the dishcloth.

Chapter 33

Splitting Hairs

He sat down on Shelagh's best chair, the one nearest the fireplace, relaxed, cross-legged, his right shoe swinging at ease. It was shoe-shop clean, the heel sharp and unworn. I was fit to spit.

Auntie Peggy held Martin tightly as he tried to wriggle free. Rosie clutched my hand, leaning heavily on my leg, her left heel pressed on my toes. I lifted her up, partly to hide my face which wouldnae stop scowling. It was too naked and if he noticed he'd have the upper hand.

Auntie Peggy sat down on the couch and let Martin climb down her nylons onto the floor. The fire was unlit, and Peggy asked Dad to light the stacked coals, which he did, but neither of them made to move Martin away. I rushed forward, levering Rosie down as I went, and caught Martin up around the belly. I sat him on the couch. 'Stay.' I pointed at him, went ower to the fireguard, opened it out and placed it securely in front of the fire, then sat beside Martin. Rosie plopped herself on my other side, sticking to my hip like a limpet. Martin wriggled, watching me for approval, but seeing none, stayed put. I took a packet of milky buttons out of my pocket, hoicked the slabbery thumb from his mouth, fed one to him and passed another to Rosie, a ruse while I got my features in check.

Shelagh and Mum had gone out by prior arrangement. I'd asked Shelagh to stay but she'd said, 'It's no my business,

Kathleen, and anyhow I'd be hard pressed no tac skite the bastard.'

Peggy tapped the arm of her seat, wrinkling her forehead. She looked uncomfortable, as well she might. Her brother was a piece of work, so he was, and here she was passing him off as a responsible parent, here to see his offspring as though it was his right. I flushed as I met her eye. She indicated wi a slight nod of her head towards him that I should say something.

Instead, I addressed her. 'So, Auntie, how was the journey down?'

'Aye, it was busy today, with the match on.' I fed Martin and Rosie another button each.

Peggy managed a shaky smile, turning to her self-righteous brother. 'Marty, isn't wee Martin getting big? And look at Rosie. Such a sweetie with those big blue eyes.'

Marty nodded, not in the least bit interested in the weans. He was too busy peering at me. 'Where's yer sister?' he said.

That was a good question. Morag had been seething for two whole days since Mum had dropped the bombshell in her usual sensitive way. We'd been shovelling in our breakfast before she could tidy away the table.

'Righto, lassies. Ye've tae see yer da on Saturday. Here at Shelagh's. Aunt Peggy will bring him, and she'll stay wi yous.'

My eyes had darted ower to Morag. Paralysed, she twisted her spoon, and porridge dribbled down her school tie. Her freckles were pinpricks of orange in her paling face. Mum was at the sink cleaning the pot, broaching no questions. Wee Rosie watched me as I watched Morag. Martin gabbled in his highchair. I came to, reached ower, took Morag's spoon away, leant back for a tea towel off the rack and sponged the porridge off her tie. Luckily it had missed her cardi, the damage would be invisible.

I wasnae surprised by Mum's announcement, having been

forewarned by Shelagh on Wednesday. Although I regretted not being able to tell Morag, my reasoning was she couldnae keep her mouth shut and I'd be in the soup. At the table, she pushed her bowl away and bucked up, enquiry sharp in her eyes. I shook my head for her to keep shtum.

When Mum lifted Martin out of his chair and went into the living room I whispered, 'It's so we can get back in the house.'

Two deep channels solidified in Morag's forehead. 'How come?'

'Dad's name's on the rent book. The council willnae let us back in unless he signs.'

'He's no paying, but.'

'Disnae matter, he's the man.'

'Right. Like he disnae live there, disnae pay nothin, but can throw us oot?'

'Aye.'

'But, Kathleen, how come he didnae throw us oot before the fire?'

'I know, but the council need his signature now before we can get back in.'

She stood up, pushed the table forward a foot, nearly toppling Martin's chair. 'Ah'm no goin.'

'Ah'm no goin as well.' Rosie slapped the table wi both hands.

I nearly fell off my chair. Rosie never broke the rules.

*

Dad was waiting for an answer. I gave it to him wi both barrels. 'Morag's mad at you. She thinks you're going to throw us out of our flat and we'll end up in the poor house.'

Peggy interjected. 'There's no poor house anymore, Kathleen.'

'Or in a children's home. There's one of them down the road.'

'None of ma weans are goin anywhere near there,' Dad

227

said. He looked confused, as though he hadnae thought of outcomes like that. Confusion turned to his usual wheedling.

'Listen, Kathleen, ah'm no wantin the house. Ah'm staying wi Peggy now.'

'What about your work?'

'Ah get the Havoc train down.'

I hadnae heard about this. Mum couldnae know or Shelagh or Hannah would know, and then I would know. Where was the fancy woman? I stopped short of asking that.

Morag had done a runner. We'd all been kitted out in our Sunday best even though it was Saturday so that Dad could see how well we were doing without him. She'd sat at lunch wi a hanky tucked into the neck of her blouse nibbling at her roll n' sausage, glowering every time Mum turned her back. I knew she was up to something but she hadnae shared what exactly, so I waited and watched. It'd be me that would get the slap if she didnae present her angelic self to our waste of space father. I didnae know what it was like to go on strike but during that hour I was hard pressed not to down tools and join her. But I kept thinking of how good it would be to get back home, so I warned her. 'Morag, no nonsense, awright. Just stay five minutes, then I'll send you out a wee message and you can forget to come back.'

She dipped her curls to the side and said, 'Mibbe aye and mibbe naw.'

I reckoned she'd turn up awright, she wasnae altogether daft, and if nothing else she was nosey. As soon as Mum and Shelagh had passed the Virgin tree, she'd made for the lobby.

I went after her. 'He'll be here soon, don't you dare …' But the door slammed.

*

Peggy strapped Martin into his pram while Dad struggled wi pushing Rosie's arms intae her coat sleeves. She resisted; arms stiff as sticks.

228

'It's awright, Rosie. Just a wee walk wi Auntie Peggy.' I took the coat, sat her on my knee, and fed her arms through. She narrowed her eyes at Dad as she slid to her feet and went to Auntie Peggy. He shrugged. What did he expect? When I glared at him, he dropped his gaze, and followed the others out. I passed Shelagh's mirror on my way back to the living room. A sour face wi blistering eyes stared back at me.

I tried to concentrate on a book for half an hour but couldnae settle so fetched my coat, made sure the cooker was off and the windows closed, and opened the door to go out to look for Morag but got a fright when I found her skulking on the landing.

It was her, but a different her.

The same cheeky mug and the knowing eyes under the thick glasses, but oh her head.

A nice, round pert head and a swan-like neck. I'd never noticed that under the riot of red curls. Even caught up in the tortuous ribbon her hair was aye bountiful. I noticed it now because the curls had gone. They'd been sheared off, hair sticking out at odd angles. Her fringe had only an inch left, was too short to lie down, and stuck out like a roof tile. Self inflicted unless she'd gone to a blind hairdresser.

She slipped by me. A mucky fist shoved the living room door open. 'Where is he, then?'

I followed her in. 'Away out to the swings wi the weans.' I was fascinated by this new crazed look. 'What have you done?' This came out as a moan as I realized how much trouble she was in. Trouble I wouldnae be able, under any circumstances, short of intervention from Shelagh's Virgin, to fix. 'Mum'll go ape shite.' I grasped my head and sank into the couch. Gawd, the endless curling tongs, the curlers, the shampoos, the brushing out. Even when we had nits, Mum refused to have our hair cut.

Morag stomped to the window and peered through the nets. 'Nae sign of them, when they comin back?'

It was worse at the back. Course it was. Hard to do a salon job on yourself. Looked like a knife had been the instrument of destruction, but how …? I had to sort this. Hair lacquer might stick it all down, maybe I could even it out a bit. 'Scissors,' I muttered.

She stepped away from the window, looked at me for a long moment, as if deciding.

'Aye, here ye go,' she said, digging into her pocket. Out came Shelagh's scullery scissors, blunt, thick bladed and rusty.

Before I could reach for them, there was a scramble at the front door. The pram wheels caught as they were pushed ower the step. A tinkle of laughter from Rosie. Peggy's voice. 'Shh, don't wake Martin.' The brake set. Dad in the living room door.

'What the fuck?'

And Morag. Feet splayed square, her chin set. 'Hello Fether. How's you?'

Peggy was already past Dad, Rosie clinging to her hand. I shrugged at Peggy's look of enquiry. She pulled her hand from Rosie's and took off Rosie's jacket and her own coat and hat. 'There you go, poppet, sit up nice and Dad'll get you a wee juice and a biscuit.'

Peggy turned to Dad. 'Marty, go fetch the juice and biscuits out of the kitchen.' I moved to help him, but she said, 'You stay here, Kathleen. Take off your coat. Morag, honey, give me those scissors and your jacket.' She smiled, ruffled Morag's short hair, eased the scissors from her hand as though they were a loaded gun, placed them on the mantlepiece, gathered up the coats and took them into the lobby. I heard her talk to Dad in the kitchen, his voice rising.

'Awright ah heard ye, if ye think that's for the best.'

She returned wi a tray of cups and a plate of biscuits. 'Well, what are you all standing there like statues for, come, sit down and we can have a wee blether.'

The wee blether consisted of Peggy persuading Morag of the wisdom of a professional remodelling of her crowning glory before our mother had a screaming fit. Marty kept well out of the road and didnae reappear until the door clicked shut behind Morag and Auntie who had Rosie's hand firmly clutched.

He came in and sat down. 'She did that to spite me, didn't she?'

'Aye.'

'Must hate ma guts.'

'What did you expect?'

'Ah'll no come back, ah see the way of it.'

Whilst that option lifted my spirits, I knew he was letting himself off the hook, and so he'd win again. 'You bloody well will come back. You'll take the crap, all of it. And you can start by changing Martin's nappy, he's stinking.'

Chapter 34

Honeysuckle Close

Mum was hanging out the window, waving at me to hurry it up. Her jaw cranked at a hundred miles an hour. I couldnae hear her but I knew what she was saying awright. Move it, so's I could take ower the tea, the nappies and the tidying up. I dawdled, just for spite. It gave me a lift to know I could get the better of her, now that she was in much better spirits.

At last she shut the window. I knew fine and well I had to be in for half past four so she wouldnae be late for her shift. It would be 'Kathleen, get yer head oot of they books and dae something useful' or 'Kathleen Gallagher, look at the state of this ironing'. Everything was my fault. You still couldnae answer her back for fear of a slap across the legs and that sure stung for ages. It just wasnae worth it. I'd been giving her a wide berth since we got back home to the flat. At first, she was in a good mood, and then she started to lose her restraint and became slap-happy again wi the weans. And me. I'd suffered a few crackers on the legs. She wasnae in a bad mood, no, she hadnae gone back there. It was as if nothing had happened and we were all back to normal. Her normal.

I hung my duffle coat in the press and dumped my schoolbag in the lobby. Mum was shouting at the weans ower the drone of the wireless. 'Morag, pick Martin up.'

He strained at the reins, jumping up and down, making the pram squeak loud enough to jab a pin in your skull.

Mum turned to me as I sauntered into the living room. 'He'll need changing.' I looked at Martin kicking his way out of Morag's arms, and I must've looked scunnered because Mum added, 'Wipe that cheek off yer face.'

I don't know what came ower me. 'How'm I supposed to wipe my cheek off my face?' I said it in that singsong manner that often goes wi a smirk. Might as well have added 'stupid bloody woman' because she slapped me hard across the chops.

My head snapped back, and I stumbled into the fireplace. I had to push against the wall to roll away from the heat. It could've been shock, or maybe the glare behind those jars of glasses. Maybe it was the tightness of her mouth, or the stink of Martin's nappy. Or that I was supposed to break down and say, 'I'm sorry, Mum.' Or maybe it was being whiplashed back to that night in the play park and all the shame of that. Whatever it was, it started a bolt of energy that sizzled through my chest into my arm.

I slapped her back.

Anaglypta walls swooped sideways. Her line of country cottages tilted on the sideboard.

I blinked the room steady and framed the weans, wide-eyed in the doorway. Martin was standing beside Morag, nappy rolling down his Buddha belly, the pin at his knees. Mum hadnae moved an inch, her palm stuck to her cheek, glasses slipping down her nose. The back of my leg toasted. Martin started to whine. Rosie's thumb was stuck in her gob and her eyes were discs of fear. Morag swung on the doorknob, knickers skimming the floor, wi that '*whit hiv ye done noo*' look on her mug.

Mum stepped back. I flinched, but she looked right through me, muttering, 'Ah'm no feart of you, girl,' and made her way past the weans. Martin tugged her skirt, but she pulled away down the lobby. I took the chance to save my throbbing leg and swept him up by the oxters, cupping his nappy. He tangled my hair in his fist, flattened my nose wi his forehead and gabbled, 'Ka, Ka, Ka.'

Mum got her coat and bag out the press and tapped down the stairs. The door clicked shut. I carried Martin ower to the window and peeled away the net. I could just make out the shape of her in the dark, brolly taut against the wind.

Wi my free hand I turned down the wireless. Rosie was holding her breath. I thumped her on the back, and when she coughed, sent her for the tray. I got out the towel, sank Martin to the floor, undid the pin and tried no to gag as I caught up each morsel in the muslin and plonked it on the tray for Morag to take to the lavi. She bit her lip, weighing up the damage.

'It's awright,' I said, trying to still my hand.

'Ah cannae believe ye hit Mum.'

'I can stand up for myself.'

She shook her head. 'Ye've had it. Ah've had it. Rosie's had it.' Nose scraping the ceiling, she marched the nappy away.

Martin chattered nonsense, forcing me to pretend a smile as I knelt ower him. The toilet flushed and I shouted, louder than I meant, 'Mind and plop the nappy in the bleach bucket till it's covered.' She wavered back wi warm water in the basin. 'Good girl.' I stroked her arm before I noticed the brown crust on her blouse. Och well, I'd get the stain out and put it on the pulley for the morning.

After washing Martin's bum, I heated my hands at the fire, then poured a puddle of olive oil onto my palm and rubbed it into his skin before the new muslin and nappy went on, nice and fresh.

I hefted him to my hip and dropped him into the pram, clicking him in, so's I could get on wi the girls' tea and bed. It wasnae their fault I was in this pickle. I hoped I'd be able to concentrate on my homework.

That very day Mr Abernethy had taken off his glasses,

let them hang ower his chest, the chain glinting under the lights, and said in front of the whole class, 'Now, Kathleen, you have an excellent prospect of attaining ten O-Grades. You're the best all-rounder in this class … considering.' An excellent prospect. I was soaring again. That was me, Kathleen Gallagher.

The gas flared wi a whoosh under the mince pot and I carried the totties to the sink, drained them and rattled the masher out of the drawer. I wished I could get out more nights at Amy's. Wished I could be going for O-Grades like her, and Mum would stop saying I was trying to be something I wasnae.

Her, whose only ambition in life was to collect cottages. Ornamental English country cottages wi summer gardens and picket fences.

Her that lived in a council flat in boring auld Havoc.

Her that expected me to leave school in the summer, and work in the bra factory or the distillery and earn money for the house, like she and Auntie Hannah did at my age. But Sister Philomena had said I could go to University; there were grants for students like me. I could even get a bursary for fifth year to do my Highers. Mr Abernethy said today, 'No reason you won't be a credit to this establishment.'

The genius that was me, Kathleen Gallagher, lording it in a courtroom or teaching medical students in my crisp white coat.

Mind, it was hard to get into those jobs if your mum worked on the Playtex line and your dad had run off wi some bit of stuff. After that first visit, he had come back every Saturday and had been on his best behaviour, until it was agreed he could come without Peggy. Last time there was a whiff of beer and an expansive mood. His darlin girl, he called me. And Morag? She'd given in, been fooled by his jokes and his compliments, the pocket searches for treats. He'd tried to give me a hug when he left, and I nearly fell for it, but the stink of beer brought a crash of memories of drunken nights and I stepped back. In that moment I knew that too much had happened for me to ever trust him again.

Course, no one told me anything. As usual, I had to earwig from the lobby to hear Hannah and Mum gabbing, so I knew what was going on.

Hannah saying between draws, 'He'll no be that long at Peggy's. Aw they rules and regulations. There'll be another bit o stuff soon.'

And Mum. 'She's welcome tae him. Dae ye know he'd the cheek tae tell the lawyer ah wouldnae let him in the bed, he slept on the couch. Four weans tae.'

'Aye, but Nellie, ye only had four weans in fourteen years. How'd ye manage that?'

'Huv ye no heard of abstention?'

I clapped my palms to my ears and nearly boaked.

The totties mashed, I bucked up and refused to give in to fate. I could work more hours at the shop. Mum might let me work getting the shop ready for the week on Sundays. I could work all summer too and then I could give her the money. Then I could go back to school. I stopped for a moment. When I thought aboot it, she actually hadnae mentioned recently that I couldnae stay on at school. Things had been a lot better around here. Yes, I had to admit Mum had been much more relaxed since we'd moved back home. And now I'd lost the head and spoiled it all.

Miserable and out of all hope, I put out the tea, and afterwards the girls walked Martin into the living room while I did the dishes. I turned up the wireless. There was some commotion going on, some geezer saying President Kennedy'd been shot. Maybe it was a wind-up or a play or something.

As if that could happen.

I was nearly done wi the drying up when there was a tug at my back. Rosie was fair stretching my jumper. I twisted round. 'Whit is it?'

'Mum's good cottage got broke.'

'Not the end one in Honeysuckle Close?'

'Aye.' She chewed her lip. Morag squirmed behind her. She really was a tough cookie. Only yesterday, she'd been hauled in front of the Head for beating up a big boy in the playground. But she knew this was bad.

I moaned, 'Who did it?'

Morag yelped, 'It wisnae me, no this time. It wis her. Ah tellt her no tae play wi it, but she jist stuck her tongue oot at me.'

Rosie nodded, squirming.

I dashed to the sideboard and there it was, a chunk bitten out of the rim of the roof, now a row of slates on the carpet.

When Rosie saw my face break up in horror, she wailed, and Martin joined in. It was bedlam. Mum'd be home at quarter past ten and this needed sorting, or we were dead.

Course, I'd be more dead as I was in charge. Rosie would get her bum skelped and I'd get a slap on the cheek and a litany on my uselessness. Mum's favourite ornament. Paid ower months from Auntie Hannah's catalogue. Morag was puffing red, fit to burst wi the weight of the night's calamities and her total innocence. Rosie was losing her breath.

I clapped her on the back. 'Wheesht, it's awright. I'll say it was me. I'm in her bad books anyway.'

'Will ye?'

'Come on, Hen. Calm down. I'll get the glue out. She'll never notice.'

Her lips trembled before she stuck the thumb back in. Morag wagged her finger at me behind Rosie's back. Gawd, she looked just like Mum. Her hair was growing back, bright ginger curls wisping on her forehead, but wi the glasses and the fierce expressions she was Mum's double. A shiver ran down my back. Two of them, and now Rosie was starting…

The girls got into their jammies and I tucked them in,

changed Martin, fed him, settled him in his cot. I rummaged under the sink for glue to fix Weymouth Cottage.

The ornament was in two clean pieces. I opened the tube. It was good stuff, and I lined the rim wi it, placed the broken piece back in and pressed it there for ages. I wiped it clean and noticed a mark on the underside. Something was written there, in blue ink.

Rose Meikle. Grannie? And a date. November. Gawd, the day she died. What? I didnae understand.

I put it back and said a super-quick 'Hail Mary' for Grannie. Decided to check on the weans, instead picked up the next-door cottage. Turned it upside down. *Morag Mary* 11.3.53.

Her birthday.

Then Bluebell Cottage. Oh, that was mine. *Kathleen Rachel* 9.8.49.

I moved down the whole street. Every single one was dedicated by Mum. Mum who slaved at the factory, working the back shift, and I'd gone and hit her. My own mother.

Grannie'd be sore disappointed in me, so she would. I replaced the last cottage, slumped to my knees, rubbed my eyes, and took a great shuddering breath.

What did Mum mean she wasnae feart of me?

Everything sunk inside. Aye, Dad and his right handy fists. Gawd, I was turning into my dad. I deserved to be beat up well and good for making my mum feart of me. Just when things were looking up. Nothing was ever going to be the same again.

Everything was broke.

I made myself go into the weans' room and kissed our Morag and Rosie and told them never ever to say a word about the cottage on pain of death and they hugged me so tight I could feel their ribs under the winceyette jammies. The sweep of Rosie's pony tickled my hand and I wondered, if Mum threw me out, how the wee soul would get on without me. Oh Gawd. Who'd slap the wee mite on the back when she choked? Who'd fix all her forthcoming breakages?

I was about to put out the light when she turned around in the bed, her eyes big as pennies, and stretched out her arms for another cuddle. I fell ower Morag and into the middle of them. We tickled and giggled ourselves silly till I hauled myself up, rubbed the silk of their heads and put out the light.

After I finished the dishes, it was equations. That helped to keep the gloom away. It was like winning the pools when all those puzzles came right. I waited for the Beach Boys to come on the wireless. But there was only one thing all ower the stations that night.

President Kennedy was dead in Dallas.

Mum's cameos of Jack and Jackie Kennedy smiled down on me from the living room wall. This wasnae gonna help Mum get back in a good mood. Just my luck.

Chapter 35

Philomena's Heartbreak

In the morning, Mum was up at seven as usual and the weans were all fine and dandy, but she didnae look at me once. The whole weekend went past as if there'd been a death in the family. Even Martin didnae dare greet and Morag sloped about nodding her head sagely. I hadnae dared ask if I could go round to Amy's.

On Monday the nuns were skittering about like bluebottles because we had an extra assembly to pray for President Kennedy's soul. I couldnae concentrate on a thing.

A plan was rolling about my head. I'd say, 'Mum, I'm right sorry for last Friday night, I don't know what came ower me.' Sometimes she put her arm around me, like she used to, and said, 'That's awright, pet. I shouldnae've slapped ye either. Ye're ma special girl.' But most times it ran something like, 'Bloody right. And ye can get yer bags packed and get oot of ma house. Go and live wi yer da. See how ye like that.'

After school, I went straight home, making sure I wasnae late. I took a deep breath before climbing the stairs and I was sure surprised to see Auntie Hannah wi Martin on her psychedelic hip, the dress halfway up her bum, you could see her suspenders. I was struck again by how pretty she was, for an aunt.

Something was up.

'Where's my mum?'

'At the school.'

'What school?'

'Oor Lady's, ye dunderheid.'

Could've been the wee school, so it wasnae me was the dunderheid. But there were some things not worth pointing out. 'What for?'

'Tae see Sister Philomena.'

Oh Gawd. I could hardly bear it. To see the headmistress. My mum who wouldnae know an equation from a pot-to-pish-in. She'd have her work clothes on too. Sure, and she wouldnae tell Sister what I did? I'd die of shame. Sister would see me for what I was, a bully and a cheat. An undeserving case. There'd be no bursary for me. But Mum wouldnae say anything, would she? She aye said that whatever went on inside our walls stayed there.

Hannah stubbed out her ciggy, and said, 'Hear ye slapped her?'

Gawd. So much for keeping things secret. Mind, this was Hannah, her sister and lifelong best pal. I decided it was best not to answer.

Hannah raised her pencilled eyebrows.

The place was too quiet. I said, 'Where're the girls?'

'Away wi ma Diane fer chips.'

Jings, what was going on here? Chips on a Monday.

Mum's footsteps clicked upstairs. She put her coat in the press, came in and stood by the fire, her soaked stockings foosty in the heat. She smiled at Hannah and Martin, ignoring me flat.

I glanced ower at The Close. The cottage hadnae moved.

Hannah put Martin down and he tottered away to play wi his cars. She said, 'Well, Nellie, are ye no going tae tell us how ye got on?' She lit up again and passed Mum the ciggy.

'Fine.' Mum took a draw, and passed the cigarette back.

'How fine?'

'Quite fine.'

'Whit did auld Philomena say?'

Auld Philomena! I crossed my legs tight. Oh, my Gawd, I'd never be able to go back to school. Maybe Mrs Rennie would give me a job full-time. Maybe I'd go and jump off the Elvern bridge, though I'd probably break my feet as the water was only three inches deep. Or I could put my head in the gas oven. A woman round the corner had done just that, only the other week. I imagined kneeling there, head resting on the hard enamel, waiting for death.

'She's heartbroken, Hannah.'

Oh, my Gawd.

'She cannae believe anybody could dae such a thing. The hatred there is in the world.'

I was expelled.

She turned to me. I bit my lip. 'Kathleen?'

'Uh-huh?' I jerked my gaze ower to Hannah. She ignored me. Martin was squealing wi delight, his mouth a pocket of slobbers, oblivious to what was going on. I wished I was him.

'Kathleen.' Mum sat on the couch, pulled her skirt down – it was her good skirt – ower her knees, all prim like. 'As ye've heard, ah've jist had a meeting wi Sister up at the school.'

A meeting? My jaw could catch flies.

'She said ye're the brightest pupil in yer year and she expects great things from ye.'

Hannah piped up, 'Sure, and tell us something new.'

'What did you go for, Mum?'

'Shelagh said ah should.'

'Aye, bout time.' Hannah was never short of an opinion.

Mum looked me straight in the eye, which she hadnae done for ages. I had to screw my face tight and peek back. A tear fell from under the rim of her glasses. Maybe it was sweat. No, she sniffed and wiped her nose.

'Kathleen?'

242

'Uh-huh.'

'Ah've decided …'

Oh, Gawd.

'Ah've decided ye're going tae the University and ah'm takin up Shelagh's offer tae watch the weans when ah'm at ma work.'

Hannah nodded and flicked a pod of ash into the fire. 'Glad tae hear it. Jist tae that waste of space man of yours pays up, an ye can stop working so hard.'

Mum said, 'It's too much fer ye wi yer study and there'll be nae mare, er … carry-on aroon here. Sister says that ye …' Her voice kind of bent. 'Says ye could be a science teacher. She's even scientific, Hannah. Jist like ah was at school.' I was gobsmacked. My mum scientific? 'Or a nurse even, or an English teacher, she's a great all-rounder. Whit dae ye think of that? Eh?'

I nearly intervened. Nurse, my arse. But thought better of it, I needed to know what else had been discussed.

Hannah rolled her eyes and took another draw, letting out a fine snake of smoke.

Mum said, 'We never got the chance, but now there's grants been brought in and she can get one of them. And a bursary fer next year tae.'

'My, my …' Hannah offered.

Mum nodded, then glanced at the cameos on the wall. 'Poor Jackie Kennedy, losing her man like that. Ye never know the minute …'

Hannah made a rough sign of the cross wi her fag.

The weans clambered up the stairs, giggling. Morag peered at me from around the door, her face smeared wi tomato sauce. She ditched the giggles and carved her mug into *huv ye fixed it yet*? Rosie's face appeared from underneath. Her round eyes scanned the room. I grinned and they aped me back like two wee clowns.

Mum came ower, put an arm around my shoulder and

leant into me. 'Ah'm sorry, Kathleen. Ah've been stupid …' Her voice cracked. She sniffed. 'Ah'm that proud of ye.' She hugged me closer and whispered, 'Oh by the way, ye did a guid job wi that glue, Hen.'

Chapter 36

Ring a Ring o'Roses

August 1966

My whole future depended on the sale of the ring. We'd come up to Glasgow on the train. *'A day oot,'* Great Aunt Shelagh said. She was dressed for it too, in a thirties style long velvet black coat wi fur collar, sheer black stockings and high heels. Her face was made up like a doll, wi round patches of rose blusher on her cheeks, and heavily mascaraed eyes. Black hair was combed up into a roll showing off long silver earrings shaped like the crescent moon, and her lips were ruby red. Now and then I caught a whiff of her perfume, powdery and sweet like rose petals when they begin to wither.

After the initial shock when we met on the station platform, I'd become fascinated by the effect Auntie had on other people. Some stopped in their tracks and stared. One fella fell ower his own feet, and I watched ower my shoulder, as he was helped onto a bench to recover. Shelagh noticed none of this, she merely sallied forth in total abandon. My great aunt was a most interesting woman and I was thrilled to be her companion for the day. But even more heart-stopping was the task in front of us.

We sat in front of a shiny wooden desk, the likes of which

I'd only seen at the pictures. One of those so highly polished you could see the rings of the tree it had been centuries ago. The thin man sitting opposite looked just as auld wi his long wispy strands of white hair and hooked nose. I fashioned him as an elf, an other-worldly creature. He was intently peering through a glass portal which presumably gave him advanced insight, wisdom beyond us mere mortals. In reality, he was a jeweller, and this was his workshop, perched above the Argyll Arcade, wi a wee bevelled window looking down on the glitter and sparkle displayed in rows of windows beneath. I imagined this room as the centre of the jewellery business, the rest of the galleries growing magically brick by brick, window by window, tray by tray of shimmering gems around it. I tasted tin, silver and money.

We awaited valuation of the ring. Shelagh's ring, though she insisted it was mine. 'Money for the University,' she kept on repeating, and once or twice a tear fell. She even remarked to an elderly woman sitting opposite on the train that her niece, Kathleen, turning and leaning her head on my shoulder, was starting Glasgow University in the autumn, as if I were the only student in the city.

Sure, I was the only member of my family who'd ever got into a university, so it was a great privilege. I'd even got into the last course I'd picked, first and second preferences in several universities having escaped me.

Today was to celebrate and sell the ring. That might give me just enough cash to see me through on top of the grant and the money from Auntie Peggy, who'd been saving in an insurance policy at the bank for my further education all my life. And I still had my job at the Rennie's corner shop so I could bring cash home.

Morag had been most put out. 'So, how come you get tae go tae the university and ah don't?'

'I'll go first and when I'm done, I'll pay for you, so work hard, Morag.'

Rosie bowled in wi, 'Ye'll never get there then, Morag,' and ran out the room, Morag chasing behind.

Auntie Peggy came every Saturday to see us, generous as always, her shopper laden wi treats. Lollies for the girls and Martin, stockings for me, and a few groceries for Mum. Dad came now and then, when he could be bothered, or maybe when he wasnae too drunk, but Peggy had taken up the baton and passed on any messages. She'd also managed to get him to pay up every week and so we were doing much better all round. Marty was a puzzle.

Was he a villain or an imbecile or just the product of our town? Did he love us but didnae know how to show it? Or was he just too selfish to see further than his own nose?

When Morag gave up chasing Rosie, Peggy had sat her down. 'I've an insurance for every one of you so if you don't work, Morag, yours will go on down the line to Rosie and so on.'

'Whit if ah don't want tae go?'

'It's for education, so whatever course you want to do, even if not university, will qualify.'

'Righto.' Morag got up and backed towards the doorway, leant back against the door frame, reached up wi one arm, stuck out her pigeon chest – all this in slow motion, at least in my head – and said wi a moue, 'I wannae be a film star.' The final action was a cock of the head and a slink of one shoulder.

'Drama school, then?' Peggy kept her face deadpan.

Morag came to. 'Where's that at?'

'We'll find out, don't worry.'

And Morag went spinning round the room only to collapse and bang her head against Mum's china cabinet. 'Bloody hell,' I spouted as the cups and saucers trembled. But I forgave her. Her sparkling eyes aye saved her from condemnation. And she wasnae as clumsy as she used to be. Big Jim's boxing lessons had paid off; she was far more disciplined about who she battered.

I blinked the memory of Morag's eyes away and concentrated on the elf who was still at work. Shelagh had told me to be quiet and let her negotiate. She was able to keep shtum for long periods of time in apparent comfort, whilst I fidgeted wi my gloves and bag. The occasional hum and haw came from our jeweller, but Shelagh merely stared ower his head wi an expression of total confidence and entitlement.

But this wasnae just any pawn shop and he was hard to read. I was told on good authority that this was the best place to come for a fair deal. Although Shelagh had given me the ring years ago, she astonished me today by providing a receipt, a guarantee of ownership. That made the item more saleable for the purveyor. It really was a lovely ring, catching wee explosions of light as the elf twisted it around, its blue centre deepening as it turned. I'd never worn it, it was too showy for me, and it had languished in my sock drawer waiting for better days. I'd held on to it, a miserable selfish bitch in the face of family calamity, doomed by my stone of a heart for all eternity. Och well, I was never any good at Confessions. And Shelagh had colluded wi me; her own brand of the Virgin was a stoical gal. Also a stoical gal was my mum. How she got us through those years I'll never know. Even today, before I left the house, she winked and said, 'Ah hope that ring turns oot tae be a belter, Hen.' A change of tune from her, who'd aye said it was worth nought.

It hadnae all been plain sailing. I passed my exams wi A's. Every time I thought about my certificate, now in pride of place in a frame at the front of Mum's china cabinet, my heart leapt wi joy. Ended up wi six Highers, top of the school, even bested Amy. I had aye figured money would be the problem, and maybe at the back of my mind, I knew the powers that be wouldnae let a girl like me in, but I hadnae expected the obstacles in my way.

Sister had tried to warn me, suggesting nursing or teacher

training. But I dreamed big, my first pick was Law. After I got my results, I told everyone that I was going to the university to be a lawyer. I had these daft ideas of saving the country from injustice and discrimination. What I didnae realise was that not only did you have to have a lot more dosh than I had, a legal firm had to take you on, and there was only one in our town, up back stairs behind the bank, wi tarnished lettering on the windows, a dark and dingy place. This didnae add up to my dreams of the kind of lawyer I wanted to be; a female Atticus Finch. It seemed I'd be holed up there every day and besides I didnae know the proprietor and wasnae likely to get an introduction anytime soon. The alternative was to go to Edinburgh or London as a trainee barrister. Sister nailed that on its head. There were ways and means, I could be financed, but it would mean living away, and it would take a long time for me to be able to earn any useful money. I didnae want to be rich, not really, that was a childhood dream, but I would need to help at home.

Then came the nail in the coffin. 'It pains me greatly, Kathleen, but it's not just a matter of funding, it's a matter of privilege. It's an occupation for the elite. By the elite I mean men. Even if you qualify you need to be admitted to chambers and although there's no employment barrier to that, most practices have a no-woman policy.'

It struck me that this was a disgrace. The very people who upheld the law were discriminating against the poor, keeping their profession unsullied by the masses. And now I learned I wasnae the right gender. Women made up only six percent of applicants. And those women were mostly rich, or at least, didnae have kin to support.

We discussed medicine. Though I didnae like dissecting frogs in biology class, I guessed I could grow some tolerance for blood. After all, I'd dealt wi accidents and bruises all my life. But Sister soon dissuaded me when I learned about the equipment I'd need, the books, and that it would take ten years before I'd get any wages.

Amy also had problems getting into medicine. The eejit in the striped suit, centre of the row of academic men who interviewed her, suggested she might be interested in nursing, a worthy profession and one that might suit her er … home life. She persisted and was accepted. Could hardly reject her, given her grades, but she suspected she had a token female place. Poor girl was mortified for me, not even getting to the starting line, and was about to withdraw, but I assured her there was more she could do to change things from within the profession than from outside. Especially as a psychiatrist.

I'd gone down the list of courses wi Amy's mum and dad. They helped me pick out one that might suit my '*temperament*', as Mr Roberts put it, and one that wouldnae take too long or need equipment other than a pen and paper. One I could do whilst still working and living at home. One that would use my brand of skills. I asked what they might be, and he said, 'Tenacity, quick wits and ambition.'

Of course, I didnae make a decision until I'd spoken wi Big Jim and Aunt Shelagh.

Jim said, 'Can be a tough gig, that, Kathleen. Yer mouth'll get ye intae trouble and when it does ye know where I am.'

Shelagh'd raised her glass. 'Here's tae temperance, Hen.'

So, I was going to be the first woman Prime Minister one day. I chose to study politics. I was excited about it as, after all, I had been fighting social injustice all my life.

I'd written to Chrissie to tell her my news and she was ower the moon for me. She'd done well too, having stayed on at school to do her A levels. Her mum had been adamant that there was no reason for her to leave and get a job as she was doing well wi her catalogue selling and had moved into the Tupperware business. Chrissie was going to study as a social worker. We'd worked that out last summer when I'd visited Newcastle. It was the first time I'd seen her in two years but the girl waiting on the platform was unmistakable. Her silver hair shone in the sunlight and a grin split her gorgeous face as she ran into me, nearly bowling me ower. She was dressed in a shockingly short miniskirt but wi her long legs and perfect figure she pulled it off. Gone was the troubled girl I'd seen after that night at the pictures. This was the Chrissie I'd first met, but even more glamorous and animated, as if she'd been set free.

The elf coughed. I bolted forward in rapt attention. Shelagh dipped her eyes and crossed a black stockinged leg.

He laid the ring on the gold velvet cloth between us, sat back, and crossed his hands on the desk. 'It's a very nice piece indeed. Art Deco, Ceylon sapphire, halo of sixteen old cut diamonds, set in eighteen-carat gold.' He looked at me directly, narrowing his eyes. I was mortified; he must've seen the desperation in my face and the poverty in my coat, my gloves, and because of these I'd given the game away and lowered the price, just by being me. My shiny new kitten heels hadnae made any difference. Hurdles everywhere.

He looked ower at Shelagh. I followed his gaze. She had that pursed moue on her face, the knowing one she used when she got you on your knees to say the rosary at the window. It said your total redemption was in her hands and refusal impossible. The elf coughed, poor miserable sod that he was.

After that the settlement of the ring didnae take long.

The figures being bandied about astounded me. I stared, open-mouthed as Shelagh kept raising the stakes, cool and determined. It was as if she'd known all along what the ring was worth. She didnae turn a hair when she stood up, took the elf's outstretched hand, and said '*done*' to an enormous nine hundred and fifty-five pounds.

The End

Acknowledgements

Thanks to my writing friends who have diligently read and digested every short story and poem I have fed them over the last ten years. Special thanks goes to Patricia M. Osborne, who has been a brilliant editor and proofreader. Also thanks to Maggie Mackay, Trish McGrath, Corinne Lawrence, and Sheena Bradley for their support and encouragement.

Thank you to Sally and Brian Johnston. Sally for starting me off on my writing journey, and her late husband Brian, for noting that I should write as I speak in Scots language. I am forever grateful for their enduring love and friendship over forty-five years.

I don't know how these things happen, but Ringwood Publishing drew me out of my hiding place, set me on the road to publishing my novel and have helped me every step of the way, with astonishing patience and skill, through a year of life-changing loss. In particular, I am thankful to Sandy Jamieson; Isobel Freeman; my editors, Eleni Koumentakou, Keira Ovens and Kayla Orr who also guided the book through the proofreading and copyediting stage; and to my support workers, Bea Crawford and Anna Salomo. *Kitten Heels* was originally a short story, one of four about the same family. All of these short stories have been published as follows:

Honeysuckle Close, Ink Tears 2017

Ailsa's Red Patent Bag, Creative Writing Ink 2018

Buttoning Ailsa's Coat, The Bournemouth Writing Prize, Imprint, 2022

Kitten Heels, Ringwood Publishing, 2022

Thank you to my family and friends for their support over the years when I'm sure they were puzzled by my new career as a writer. To my late sister, Bernie, who never failed to ask me about my writing life before I poured her a gin and lemonade.

Finally, thanks to my darling late husband Frank, who, although he never read a book in his life, was my biggest fan.

About the Author

Maureen Cullen is a retired social worker living in Argyll & Bute. After thirty years' commitment to social work, she turned to writing poetry and short fiction, completing a Master's Degree in Creative Writing from Lancaster University in 2015 and achieving a distinction.

Maureen has had poetry published in multiple magazines and online webzines, and had a poetry conversation written with Patricia M. Osborne, *Sherry and Sparkly,* published by the Hedgehog Press in 2021.

She has been shortlisted in numerous short story competitions, including the V.S. Pritchett Prize, the Fish Prize, and the Bristol Prize. She also won the Labello Prize for short fiction in 2014, and the Ringwood Short Story competition in 2022.

More to read:

If you enjoyed *Kitten Heels*, you might like these other Ringwood books:

Bodysnatcher
Carol Margaret Davidson

In the late 1820s, two Irish Immigrants, William Burke and William Hare, murdered 16 individuals and sold their corpses for use in anatomical dissections at the University of Edinburgh. Their killings ended when Hare turned King's Evidence, and Burke was hanged.

However, the question of whether their female accomplices, Nelly McDougal and Margaret Hare, were involved, has never been determined. Told by way of alternating confessions, *Bodysnatcher* is both a graphic depiction of one of Edinburgh's most notorious crimes, and a domestic story of a relationship unravelled by secrecy and violence.

ISBN: 978-1-901514-83-4
£12.99

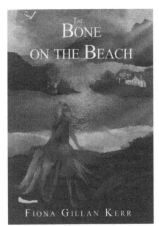

The Bone on the Beach
Fiona Gillian Kerr

In 2002, in a tight-knit Highland community, a young woman named Deirdre mysteriously loses her life.

When a bone suddenly washes up on the beach, Meghan, a lawyer in a city law practice, finds herself embroiled in a dark and twisted mystery.

Meghan wonders what took place in this village all those years ago. What are the terrible secrets they have buried? Who was Deirdre and what really happened to her?

ISBN: 978-1-901514-91-9
£9.99

What You Call Free

Flora Johnston

Scotland, 1687. An unforgiving place for women who won't conform.

Pregnant and betrayed, eighteen-year-old Jonet believes nothing could be worse than her weekly public humiliation in sackcloth. But soon she discovers that a far darker fate awaits her. Desperate to escape, she takes refuge among an outlawed group of religious dissidents. Here, Widow Helen offers friendship and understanding, but Helen's own beliefs have already seen her imprisoned once. Can she escape the authorities a second time?

ISBN: 978-1-901514-96-4

£9.99

The Carnelian Tree

Anne Pettigrew

A dead body, a disappearance, and an epic lost in time. Unrelated incidents on the surface. Judith Fraser's Oxford sabbatical quickly takes a sharp turn when she gets tangled in the mysterious murder of a colleague. With threads leading nowhere, conflicting impressions about people around her, and concern for increasing risk to her loved ones, whom can she trust? Her eccentric housemates? The CIA? Or, herself?

A uniquely amusing and page-turning mystery novel set in 2003 on the eve of the Iraqi War, *The Carnelian Tree* follows the journey of Judith Fraser as she probes into people, power, politics, and sex, only to discover that some things remain unchanged.

ISBN: 978-1-901514-81-0

£9.99

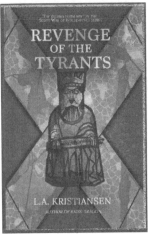

Revenge of the Tyrants
L. A. Kristiansen

Scotland, 1306. While the King of Scots wages a desperate, bloody war for Scotland's independence, four intrepid Scottish knights flee from cunning Templar Knight Geoffrey De Charney's labyrinth on a treasure barge. What follows is a journey directly to the heart of the conflict, and a vivid depiction of the scheming, treachery and violence it entailed. Meanwhile, Kings Edward the first of England, Philip the fourth of France, and Haakon the fifth of Norway each plot to destabilise each other and become the dominant force in Europe. They each have their own reasons to thwart the Scots, and each will stop at nothing to gain their victory.

ISBN:978-1-901514-76-6

£12.99

Song of the Stag
R. M. Brown

Cait and her childhood sweetheart, Kenzie, are from Storran's borders: idyllic, traditional and completely opposed to separatism.

When Kenzie is called up to the ranks of the Queen's Watch to hunt down Storrian Separatists, they move together to the city of Thorterknock, where Cait quickly realises that her charming countryside life is not the reality for every citizen of Storran. Struggle abounds on the cobbled streets, as does the battle for Storran's liberation from the Five Realms.

Cait finds herself swept into a struggle for freedom, with Kenzie and the Queen's Watch on one side, and the Fox and the Separatists on the other.

ISBN: 978-1-901514-70-4

£12.99